Mavis Cheek was born and educated in Wimbledon. She is the author of eleven novels including *Janice Gentle Gets Sexy*, *Mrs Fytton's Country Life* and *The Sex Life of my Aunt*. She lives in the English countryside.

For James, who once asked me to write a book.
For Fran, who once showed it to someone when I did.
For Agent Anthony, who filed down the antlers.

Under the arch of life, where love and death,
Terror and mystery, guard her shrine, I saw
Beauty enthroned; and though her gaze struck awe
I drew it in as simply as my breath.
Hers are the eyes which over and beneath
The sky and sea bend on thee, — which can draw
By sea or sky or woman, to one law,
The allotted bondman of her palm and wreath.

Mr Rossetti

I deck myself with silks and jewelry,
I plume myself like any mated dove:
They praise my rustling show and never see
My heart is breaking for a little love.

Ms Rossetti

The sun, though weak, was warm. The beginnings of Beauty Parlour weather. The signal for women with the whey faces of winter to come creeping from their centrally-heated hibernations and begin to think about pink cheeks, bright eyes and the hope that springs eternal after a good rubdown with exfoliating cream.

Tabitha, nose up, scenting the first delicious hints of post-Easter spring underlying the morning exhaust fumes, contemplated the months ahead like a pointer after prey: the Christmas turkeys, the Shrove Tuesday fry-up, the gluttony for protein where only an apple was required, all brought to a head (in many cases quite literally) by Easter and its chocolate. It was a busy time from now on.

Tabitha, whose life was her Beauty Parlour, felt her heart lift as she turned the corner into the High Street. Not that the High Street itself presented a heart-lifting aspect but there, at the end of it, past the building societies, the Woolworths, the Victoria Wine and the banks, was the little cream-painted sign, swinging gently in the breeze, its elegant strawberry-pink lettering proclaiming the legend 'Tabitha's Beauty Parlour – an appointment not always necessary'.

She screwed up her eyes to focus on it and thought that it seemed further away than usual. She refocused, relaxed her face and patted the skin of her temples as if to rearrange any temporary creases. Nonsense, she thought briskly, and hurried along. When she looked again she could make out the lettering perfectly well. All the same, the lift in her heart seemed to die a little, despite her attempt to revive it.

The spring air, with its promise of burgeoning summer, is also a warning. Well might Sage Grandmother state that Beauty comes from within … raising her trembling old finger to stab the air as she insists that you will never find a Beautiful woman who is ugly inside, shaking her grizzled locks to emphasize that Beauty feeds on a sap of kindness …

Well indeed might her quavering voice offer up all these ancient wisdoms, but Tabitha smiles – Hot Wax to that! She turns the key smoothly in the lock. Beauty feeds on the opportunity that Nature has bestowed, and which Nature, fickle mother, then spends all her time trying to take away again. It is Tabitha's job to intercede, and redress this capricious clawing-back as best she can.

She removes the key and pushes down on the doorhandle which is shining and golden and delicately chased with cupids: fitting for a door which opens on to a little piece of Paradise.

It is a nice idea, she thinks, that Beauty radiates from within, but – she places her hand on the rose-painted door plate and gently pushes – my best friend at school, Brenda, was the sweetest-natured girl in the world. Utterly well-meaning, utterly lovely of character, utterly beautiful inside and utterly devoid of Nature's Opportunity. She had everything against her – small piggy eyes, florid full lips, plump cheeks on a face shaped like a fat pear, and a body like a tube. Open her up and she was enchanting. Look her over at a dance and you'd pass by on the other side. She could stand there all night exuding Beauty from Within and thinking Nice Thoughts, but she still had to buy her own lager-and-lime and pay her single bus fare home.

Whereas Wendy Woods, who had a toad for a soul and a desert where the milk of beautiful kindness should flow, had only to cross her legs, open her china blues and pout a bit and she was positively drowning in Babycham. Fights broke out on the bus over who should be allowed to pay her fare, be the lucky swain to take her home and have his adolescent balls crushed by her cruel and knowing ways.

It was in contemplation of this phenomenon that Tabitha's first interest in the World of Beauty began. An interest much deepened by giving her youthful heart to a chap with hair like an angel's, face like a god's, body willowy as aspen, skin soft as down and a heart as black and hard as granite – now referred to, in her most private considerations, as the Arsehole. The cream-coloured door opens noiselessly upon the salon's eau-de-Nil carpet, soothing as a secluded pool. She smiles a little grimly at the fleeting reminder of one to whom she applies such an uncharacteristically crude name. Never again, she thinks, never, never again.

She steps silently upon the velvety carpet and her nostrils take in the rich, gratifying smell of geranium oil, still hanging in the air from Saturday's broken capillaries. What Tabitha enjoys most is giving her ladies faces that fit, the confidence to get what they want and to keep it. Which is what she tells her little trainee beautician, the sparkling Chloe. Tabitha looks at her watch. The girl will be here soon. Better get the post sorted. Once she arrives there is work to be done, lessons to be learned! As she herself once learned at Bettina's Boudoir, many years ago.

Tabitha sighs for poor schoolfriend Bren. How she could have helped her now. And *that* was what those very plain women, who painted signs across the windows of Bettina's Boudoir, did not understand. Malicious signs suggesting all manner of unpleasantness, in very nasty letters of dribbling white paint. Words implying that the concept of society requiring your face to fit had its ultimate expression in Nazi Germany.

Well, it was a long time ago, as Bettina remarked, and should be viewed on the Great Plain of History as a blip, much as Victorian phrenology is now viewed as no more than fairy dust. So said Bettina, a wise woman, currently working on a history of cosmetics. Tabitha still sees her old teacher, now plain Betty, from time to time. Especially when Tabitha feels a little concerned about Chloe's progress and needs advice – which, oddly, has been a little more necessary of late.

She crosses to the window, stooping to retrieve a small trimming from a false eyelash, shaking her head over it. If only she could persuade that particular client how much more pleasingly natural an eyelash *tint* might be. But poor Miss Potter, one of Tabitha's first-ever regular clients, would not be told. Azure blue lids and a wink like a nest of spiders. No wonder she had never achieved her desire to be married.

Mostly what her ladies want is a mate, though the delicate concept is never openly discussed. On the Beautician's Couch the brash and explicit have no place. She tells Chloe this, often. It is something Chloe finds quite hard to take on board.

A good girl, though, and so lovely, thinks Tabitha as she pulls up the hint-of-a-tint-pink blind with its satin ruffles and observes the world beyond.

Out there are countless women all striving to be beautiful, to get what they want. Or at least to get the chance to belong. What Betty

3

told those slogan-women, very crisply, was that we are all equals in the boudoir. Even Hitler found his Eva and had his moustache trimmed to oblige. Betty, a mere commoner from Hampton Wick, had done the make-up for the Coronation Ladies-in-Waiting so she knew about equality all right.

Tabitha pulls down the opulent blind with a snap, for the sunlight is too strong for the faces of her ladies. The simple truth, and one not to be muddled up with politics, was that if you grin like a vacant baboon and flutter bald eyelashes you will wait a lifetime to belong. Toss a head of scented curls, smile curvaceously and …

She smiles.

She knows.

Political indeed!

She opens the post.

Almost every piece of advertising matter confirms the simple truth: even Dynarod, where the woman in soft pink clasps her hands in rapture as she watches her Schwarzenegger ramming it up. Nothing is without a picture of a couple, or a male and female who are potentially a couple, and they are beautiful. 'Exactly so,' thinks Tabitha, and she slips her arms into an eau-de-Nil overall and tidies away her outdoor garments into a pink and cream cupboard with a motif of shells and cornucopias *en bras*.

She remembers the sudden enlightenment during English, where she and Brenda sat side by side at school and wanted to be Wendy Woods: Beauty Ruled. In the sudden clarity of understanding Tabitha went on to write a very passionate piece on the subject, which she told Chloe about the other day. She quite often tried to lift Chloe's sights a bit. And not without success, she fancied.

Tabitha recited 'On His Blindness' and explained that when the poet Milton wrote of ten thousand flocking to do God's bidding, it was on the basic assumption that God was very Beautiful. God, as we know, positively shines with Beauty. God does not have a squint and a pimple on his/her/its nose. Or dewlaps. God is firm, bright-eyed and, like all beauties, given to jealousy. Hence that fist-smiting rage at the Golden Calf; hence lying around in Heaven frothing at the mouth and kicking the Divine Walls over all those subsequent attempts to set up other Beautiful rivals; hence giving everyone boils and whatnot. Look on my glory only, said the Lord/Lady/Thing, or I will punish you by going away for ever.

4

It is as well to know about these things, Chloe, she told her.

Chloe nodded and said *'Quite.'*

Which was considerably better than saying fuck a duck, which is what she used to say rather a lot. The modern way, Tabitha supposed.

Male God, she thinks, squirting the air with bergamot freshener, but we girls do what we can. Squirt, squirt.

Mother Theresa, Golda Meir – admirable, fearsome women, but they – Tabitha switches on the gentle lighting – forgot to cleanse and moisturize. She returns to the reception desk and leans against its pearly quilting.

Let us not, observes Tabitha to the tenderly curled rosebuds in their pink and white display, fall into the Reality Gap. Let us not, she dots each one with rose oil, get carried away on a notion of the way we would like it to be. Let us accept it as it is and Get On With It. Those silly women with their hairy legs. She shivers again at the thought.

'You only have to use your eyes,' she tells the frieze of Three Dainty Graces which adorns the walls. 'See a beautiful woman dining with her chap in a restaurant, and see the chap's eyes stray to stare at another impressive female, and if he survives without the Châteauneuf-du-Pape being wrapped around his ears, he is doing well.'

Ah, but – 'See another table in the same restaurant, at which sit a chap and his plain female companion, and then watch what happens if his eyes stray. Plain Female Companion will appear not to notice, go on sipping the Chardonnay and become riveted by the fishbones on her plate, rather than show the slightest hint of a miff.'

The Three Graces dance on. They, being plaster, have nothing to fear from time, she thinks. But even born-in Beauty is a holding position. A brief gift. No wonder Sage Grandmother says it comes from within. Sage Grandmother would, wouldn't she? But did she say that when she was wearing white dresses and tripping through the cornfields with a beau? Tabitha shakes her head. 'Not unless she was lying through her still attached teeth.'

Tabitha looks at her watch. Chloe – unless she gets a real move on – will be late again. Tabitha begins her hand exercises: flex, flex, flex.

Even the delicate rose – she touches one again – will droop and die. But pop an aspirin in its water and you can keep it going for quite a while.

Tabitha sees herself as a large white aspirin for her ladies. But not an artificer, as Chloe would have it, more a decorator. As if there were a plain plaster ceiling which mouldings and a fine carved rose would beautify. She looks up at her own, all fruit and flowers, with its central dropping chandelier of Venetian glass lilies.

Lovely.

Where *is* that girl?

If she is not here soon, she will arrive just as the first ten o'clock appointment arrives – disturbing the calm, swirling the air, her youth forgetting to hold its tongue as it marches across the threshold, rustling and fiddling as she puts on her overall and settles herself in.

Tabitha smoothes cream into her hands. Calm must always prevail. What happens when her creations go forth is none of her business, nor is it her business to engage in controversy, no matter how her ladies try to encourage it. It would hardly be appropriate to add to their insecurity by telling them that in her opinion they are making a grave error by agreeing to their lovers' demands for bondage, or letting their mothers-in-law stay for a month.

If her opinion is sought on anything more than a shade of lipstick, or whether to have overhanging lids corrected, she simply smiles, keeps the response safely locked within the confines of her skull, and the soft, pink pads of her fingers never falter. She can sigh and shake her head, or smile knowingly in a hundred different ways – full of meaning, saying nothing. A woman's art, soothing, the kind of art that no man could fathom, nor should. Tabitha has perfected this art of saying nothing very well.

She could wish, she sighs, that Chloe had grasped the notion completely. Tabitha's assistant will *still* venture an opinion of a controversial nature, for she is but young. Such a thought brings a creeping warmth to Tabitha's neck and cheeks. A new phenomenon. She touches her face with her hands. Best not think about that, she decides. Very probably all it requires is a little less heating now that spring has arrived. Nevertheless, the pads of her soft pink fingertips are cool by comparison. She sighs. Time. Time moving on.

With those same cool fingers she re-attends the post, throwing away extraneous matter as she would exfoliate the dead cells from tired skin. Improved salon design? She does not need that. The salon is perfect. Though Chloe's description of it, like walking into a warm ice-cream, does not *exactly* express what Tabitha had in mind.

It had certainly been something of a tussle, sending back the bright red handset when a new telephone system was installed. Chloe had been quite sulky. She even painted her nails to match, so that when Tabitha first walked in and discovered Chloe using the equipment it had looked, in that beautiful, pale setting, like a spattering of bloodspots on a ballerina's tutu. That was the first occasion on which Tabitha felt the rising flush.

'Red as the phone,' Chloe had giggled.

Not a very nice thing to say in the circumstances.

Where is the girl?

The last envelope contains an offer of financial help to expand the business. Tabitha throws it away. She must now consider retirement. Already daylight has become a little too cruel and the subdued glow of the salon no longer disguises the march of age, Beauty's Doom …

And anyway, her finances are rosy, if her cheeks are fading, and she will retire to comfort somewhere in south-west Spain: Andalucia, Granada – where the Moorish connection with the perfumed, softened, tantalizing delights of the female body is in the very air of the lemon groves; where the ancient Arab memory of harem whisperings stirs the almond-blossomed boughs, and the bees weave their way drowsily through hot loops of scarlet chillis to where the fat pink flowerheads await their pleasure. Tabitha will retire there, for she has, she feels, done her bit.

I, Tabitha, she thinks.

I, Tabitha, who knows.

Training Chloe is her enduring gift. For *what* she knows is that, despite the lobbying of short-haired feminists in army boots, the service she gives is one as old as time. Older, even, than the Oldest Profession. Of course it is. Before selling your wares you need to make them as desirable as possible. Marks and Spencers irradiates food for a longer shelf-life; Tabitha irradiates women. The more peachy they look, the higher the price.

Older than the selling of favours is the manner of enhancing them. A little berry juice on a nipple here, a little ash beneath the eyes there, and, with the flames thrown high against the walls of the cave, you can charge an extra goatskin *easy*.

She switches on sweet music so that the gentling sounds of rain in a forest and the charmed song of birds susurrate soothingly around the room. Idly she rearranges the lipstick display. A shocking palette of brightness in the cool scene, but not as shocking as it might be. For Tabitha the post-punk tendency is not pleasing, and she will not accommodate it – purple lids and vampish lips are too strident in her opinion. It may be what some women feel they want but, very gently, Tabitha will dissuade them. But only gently, for the boudoir denies them nothing, unlike the angry world outside.

She opens her appointments book and listens to the Ansaphone. A new day.

Looking up, she sees Chloe hurrying down the High Street – beautiful even in her speed – good posture despite her clutching to her bosom a pile of books. Tabitha sighs again, for the books have pulled up her skirt a fraction at the front to reveal her only physical fault – her knock-knees. A small imperfection in one so otherwise perfect, muses Tabitha. And then she stares, startled.

Books?

She thinks.

Books?

She sighs.

Whatever is the girl up to now?

2

To relax, Tabitha does more hand mobility exercises. But they no longer soothe. She is aware of a little stiffness – her supple fingers are not what they were. In the old days she prided herself on her delicacy with effleurage, her confidence with petrissage and her accuracy with tapotement; now she is no longer so adroit. Not losing her touch, exactly, but a shadow is coming, very definitely. She can feel it, quite literally, in her bones.

Chloe arrives, delightful in her breathlessness, sweeping away Tabitha's doubts with the radiance of her smile, a nymph with pink cheeks and sparkling eyes – hair, fair as corn, dancing around her face, lips curved and pink as a cupid's bow above a pile of books clasped to her sweetly rounded breasts. She smiles above the weighty tomes. Gives a little apologetic *moue*, and plonks them down on the reception desk.

'Blimey,' she says, 'talk about heavy … Should've used Mum's shopper.' She rubs her shoulder. 'This arm's giving me real gyp. Now *I'll* need the doings. Ha Ha.'

It sometimes takes Chloe a while, especially after a weekend, to resume The Boudoir Mode.

She stops. She notices Tabitha's expression. She puts her perfect hand to her mouth and says, 'Oops, sorry,' and gives a sweet smile. She straightens her beautiful neck and looks down her nose as Tabitha has taught her to do. She rearranges herself and says 'Not doings, *massage*.' Her voice is strangely different, with all the vowels rounded.

'Good morning. So sorry if I am late. I called at the library on my way.' It would not have been surprising if she had added 'Look Peter, see the dog,' or 'Run, dog, run … ' in the manner of an infant reading book.

'So I see,' says Tabitha, mollified, but eyeing the books in some puzzlement. Up till now books have not been a great feature in her assistant's life. 'Why?'

'Because,' says Chloe proudly, 'I am going to improve myself. And improve my conversation with the clients. Like you said I should. Poems – Milton – that sort of thing.'

Tabitha closes her eyes, momentarily.

Chloe reaches for a book which has a small piece of paper marking a place. She opens the book at the place and reads from it, finger raised.

'Helen of Troy was considered so perfect that when – ' she pauses, checks that Tabitha is listening, continues ' – that when the potters of Greece learned their art, they moulded the first bowls upon her breasts … '

Thoughtfully she gives her own a squeeze, looking pleased, before closing the book. 'Now *there's* something to tell the customers. And it's – ' she checks the title again – 'Ancient History. Nothing controversial in that – now is there?' She folds her arms a shade defiantly.

Tabitha has no time to debate. Her ten o'clock appointment is nearly here and she has yet to complete her own toilette. She thinks, fleetingly, of Spain, before entering her massage cubicle to cosmeticize. Chloe will deal with the client until she is ready.

But something clutches at Tabitha's heart. She turns, looks upon the lovely face of her assistant and she, too, raises a finger. Her voice is as neutral as she can manage. 'Chloe dear,' she says, '*not* the bit about the potters, I think … ' She speaks with feeling. 'Just try the weather: warm for the time of year … possibility of April showers … That sort of thing?'

Chloe nods, those golden curls belying the blackness of her thoughts. Tabitha, in her opinion, is bland. She resumes reading, safe in doing so until the client arrives. By now Chloe's beautiful eyes are like saucers.

When the ten o'clock appointment, a shade early as Tabitha always advises, enters the salon, usually a profoundly calming experience, she is somewhat confused to be greeted by Chloe with the information that in her humble opinion they'd got this thing about Helen and Paris all wrong.

'Ah,' says the ten o'clock appointment, stumped.

'As in Troy?' says Chloe, checking her book. 'Homer?'

The ten o'clock appointment nods.

Chloe takes it as encouragement.

'Well it's all wrong. Written by two blokes – can't get my tongue around the other one – Uripiditis or some such – sounds like something you scratch, anyway. Well – naturally they've got No Idea.'

Chloe winks.

The ten o'clock appointment widens her eyes.

Chloe stabs at the the book for emphasis. 'Because *they* don't know what it takes – never been in a beauty salon in their lives, have they?'

Considering Homer and Euripides, the ten o'clock appointment is bound to admit this is unlikely.

'Anyway – this Helen is said to be the most beautiful woman in the world. Father a bleeding swan,' Chloe tuts, 'mother raped.' She tuts again. She shrugs. 'Tell me about it … ' She looks heavenwards with her eyes.

As does the ten o'clock appointment, upon whom it seems to be incumbent.

'The thing is,' says Chloe, now prodding the air for emphasis, 'Paris never *saw* her. Just kept writing to her saying he'd heard how beautiful she was, and was coming to get her. Sometime. She hadn't a clue when. All he said was he'd be there when he'd got a boat. Well – you know men.'

Chloe shrugs. So does the ten o'clock appointment, who is longing for a cup of weak tea with a slice of lemon. It was all she expected as she came through the door, just weak tea with lemon – not a walk down the annals of time. 'Ah,' she says again.

'See,' says Chloe, 'he didn't write and say that he'd heard she was a good lay or fun at a party or anything like that. Just,' she checks the text:

'You fill my vision by day and it is you
My soul sees by night when my eyes are asleep.
What can it be when I see your face,
You who have conquered without my seeing you?
No woman of beauty is like you,
Not Phrygia nor anywhere under the sun … '

Chloe closes the book.

'Phrygia,' she says kindly, 'doesn't mean she's gone off sex. It's just a bloody great chunk of the world apparently. And Paris is *nothing* to do with France at all.'

She looks confused for a moment but brightens. 'So there she is, Helen, not sure when he's going to arrive, all done by letter and never seen a photograph, and wanting to be at her best. After all, she's a Babe. So she stops going out so she gets enough beauty sleep, drives her husband nuts with her wanting new clothes and make-up, makes him shave every night he wants a bit of nooky in case he roughs her up, and goes demented when she gets her period because of the spots ... Well, we've all done it, haven't we?' says Chloe expansively.

The ten o'clock appointment chooses to concur.

'And then, of course, *late* – he gets there. And what's happened? Helen's got fed up waiting. Her hair's a bloody mess, she's been out with the girls the night before and come in fancying a bit – hubby hasn't shaved but what the hell – she gets up in the morning hungover and spotty because its that time of the month again, she's all roughed up on her supposedly milk-white and rose-petal cheeks, hair like a nest for nags, and her maid nips in and says, "Paris will be here in ten minutes, he's just going through customs now."

'*Ten minutes!*

'So she has a cry, then a scream, chews her frock, smacks her hubby one for duffing her up — and Paris comes in to find her looking like the back end of a chariot and throwing a wobbly.

'Her husband, King Menewotsit, has had enough and says "Take my wife."

'Paris says, like blokes do, that he's got sudden urgent business elsewhere in Phrygia and backs off. Helen ping-pongs between them for a bit and the Greeks feel a bit insulted. After all, he wrote and *ordered* her so to speak. So they go to war, which is just about the only *other* thing blokes can think of to do.

'And that, I reckon, is more than likely the truth.'

She puts down the book and smooths her overall. 'Now,' she says, 'how about a nice cup of weak tea? With lemon, isn't it?'

And the ten o'clock appointment, still reeling, sinks on to the soft leather couch gratefully.

Tabitha is ready. Recovered from her history lesson, the short woman in T-shirt and leggings is also ready. Very ready. She rises from the couch and wrests herself from the tantalizing promises of

Beauty Today. Before discovering Tabitha's Beauty Parlour, Mrs Baker could never bring herself to study such magazines; now, triumph within her grasp, she can look – appraise – *dare*.

*

Mrs Baker was undergoing treatment for cellulite, among other things. She had already enjoyed several sessions of Slimatone wherein her buttocks and thighs had been plugged into an impressive series of rubber discs which vibrated and tingled away her years of exuberant eating and several childbirths. She could definitely see an improvement in her shape, and with Tabitha's strenuous, knowing fingers doing follow-up massage, she felt well on the way to a full recovery.

All she wanted was to be able to tuck her T-shirt *in* one day – not much to ask in these days of greed and avarice. And perhaps to have a builder or two wolf-whistle at her …

Mrs Baker found her domestic life rather boring on the whole. She was given to musing out loud, as she lay on the couch, about its iniquities and Tabitha was aware that Mrs Baker needed watching on this. She sought diverse opinions and could be outspoken.

Tabitha ducked and wove skilfully, maintaining the Golden Rule of the Beautician's Art: all conversation to be kept to uncontroversial matters; no politics, no religion, no children's upbringing. Outside these pale and pretty walls wars may rage, mosques may burn, children show no mercy – but here, at Tabitha's, the world becomes small, quiet and cosy. A world of women flowering for their menfolk, be they employers, husbands, lovers or sons.

And if some client should begin upon a topic destined to raise the level of vascular activity, or lead to erythema, Tabitha stays silent and keeps the rhythm of her fingertips unhurried, regular, unimpressed. It is an art: passed on to her by Bettina, passed on by her to Chloe. Along with the textbook guidance for Beauty Parlour Employees: personal appearance must be immaculate and indicate the nature of the work.

Chloe's appearance *is* now immaculate. But it has taken effort.

She arrived with perfect features – an ideally proportioned face is one which has equal measurements from the tip of the nose to the lowest part of the chin, and from the outer corner of the eye to the tip of the nose – blonde hair, blue eyes, generous lips, compact hips, small waist, full though not disproportionate bust, a good height of five foot six (being tall enough to see over the reception desk without craning her medium stretch-unlined neck).

She also arrived with grubby fingernails, bitten cuticles, ill-cut hair, eyes like a panda's from black mascara, and an ambition to become a super-model. And she smoked. Fortunately for Tabitha she had one defect: knock-knees. It was this misalignment that saved her from stardom and saved her for Tabitha's Parlour. They dealt with it positively – by lowering the hem of Chloe's overall and saying no more about it.

After the knees there was another problem, for she came with a predilection for curry (cheap night out with the boyfriend) but Tabitha put a stop to that. Only the scents of nature's perfection, or man's bottled emulations of such, were allowed: flowers, blossoms, herbs and roots, or their laboratory equivalent – woodland, pasture and garden. No more birianis then, or chicken korma – vulgar, smelly stuff. Tabitha's assistant must set her diet above such things.

Now the obedient Chloe glows in Tabitha's textbook image.

She is young. She has neither comedone nor milia, line or furrow, seborrhoea or pustule – her skin is alive and taut and her eyes gaze forth with the milky white purity of a breast-fed babe's. She is fresh as woodland flowers even if, occasionally, there may also be a whiff of woodland smoke about her, a hint of the woodland bonfire. For the curries she has abandoned, the filter tips she has not. With the flaming joy of youth that knows it will live for ever, Chloe smokes secretly; her one rebellion.

In all other respects she is as willing to become what Tabitha requires as Tabitha is to create her. For Chloe is ambitious. She came to learn the Beautician's Art, first as handmaiden, later as equal, and finally – the last great powder-puff of achievement – as successor. Something which Tabitha looks kindly upon. It was the same with Bettina.

But though the girl has charm, though the girl has poise, though she has ambition, Tabitha knows that she will never – quite – succeed to her cloud. Tabitha sits at the very peak of Salon Cirrus, dispensing beauty as Athena showered stars. At best, Chloe will attain the puffy edge of Stratus, to go no further, always remaining there, looking up. Chloe will remain there, ambitious as she is, because Chloe has never had, and never will have, a broken heart.

It is this dimension of compassion, born out of lost love, which took Tabitha to her Cirrusian heights. She gives her All to this most ancient of arts. Into Beauty and Beauty's Ways Tabitha has plunged her fallen hopes, thrown her bruised grief, hurled her salt-stained tears.

Chloe sees it largely as a business.

And the world beyond the salon walls seems ready for such a departure. Chloe sees no point in giving a depth that extends further than the skin's Stratum Corneum. Whereas Tabitha's giving reaches beyond, down and deep, to the very living Stratum Malpighii itself.

She returns all concentration to her client.

'Interesting girl, your assistant,' says Mrs Baker cautiously.

'Interesting?' says Tabitha, equally cautiously.

'Well – she was telling me all about Helen of Troy ...'

'Not the Greek potters?' says Tabitha a trifle sharply.

'No –' says Mrs Baker, perplexed. 'No – nothing about them ... '

Tabitha's heart lifts. 'Well *that's* all right then ... '

'Well –' Mrs Baker says, even more perplexed. 'I suppose it is ... '

Today her client is even more chatty, more nervous, than usual. Less inclined to lie back and enjoy the quiet pinkness of her cell. She requires a manicure. Something in the outside world has made her nibble her nails. Tabitha gives her a deep cleanse, then sets and checks the Slimatone pads before calling Chloe.

Chloe needs to be called a second time because she is immersed in another of her books. Also, she sometimes forgets to answer to her name. This is because it is not her real name. Her real name is Maureen (dew of the sea) and though Chloe (green shoots on the bough) becomes her, out of hours her friends and family alike refer to her as Mor – thus may she be forgiven. But as Tabitha pointed out, Maureen hardly sets the right poetic tone for a Beauty Parlour.

She is called again, and responds.

Her mind is suddenly back on the job. She looks at her hands. One of her nails is broken because she went bowling last night and, strictly speaking, she should have spent time on fixing it this morning. Now she is to give a manicure and it is hardly an advertisement if one of her own nails is duff. She had better keep it hidden from Tabitha.

She enters the cubicle.

What she needs is a boyfriend who does not take her to bowling alleys.

15

What she needs is a boyfriend with class. Or at least with *brass*.

What she needs is a boyfriend who has money, which Wayne hasn't.

And a boyfriend without brains. For which Wayne *does* qualify.

And *you* try getting a condom on someone after they've had six pints and a vindaloo.

That's what broke the nail – not the bowls, which were easy to hold on to by comparison.

Thus does Chloe's mind wander.

Tabitha, meanwhile, keeps her cupid's lips firmly closed as she tucks up Mrs Baker and switches on the machine. For Mrs Baker is talking about Sonny, her four-year-old son, and his birthday party yesterday. An event to make Helen of Troy and her tantrums pale into insignificance. Tabitha nods and coos from the back of her throat, turning away and pretending to look for a wire at the point where Mrs Baker mentions thirteen small boys' behaviour with the ice-cream. What Tabitha would like to say, of course, is that small boys who repaint sofas in strawberry and vanilla should have their bottoms smacked.

She does not say this

She must thank such small boys really.

Several mothers of small boys are her most regular clients.

Frazzled, and afraid of what the frazzlement might do to their looks and therefore their marriages, they come as frequent suppliants to Tabitha's haven. So Tabitha listens to Sonny's birthday antics silently. Having seen the results of family life, Tabitha is quite glad that she avoided it.

Chloe pulls the trolley, all the while concentrating on keeping her broken nail hidden, only half listening to Mrs Baker's birthday party tales and what a *naughty* boy Sonny really was. She negotiates the couch, concentrating on keeping the flaw from Tabitha's sharp eye, and perches on a white leather stool at Mrs Baker's side. Made it, she thinks, and gives Mrs Baker a bright smile.

Mrs Baker, it seems, is still banging on about the naughtiness of Sonny. Tabitha listens imperviously, nodding and agreeing, and showing a light darkening of the eyes in sympathy of the tale which continues to unfold. Chloe emulates her, while she places the client's nearside hand on her towelled lap.

'Yes,' says Mrs Baker, with grim satisfaction. 'After he licked up the ice-cream he poohed on the carpet *again*, so I threw away the book and put him in the garden for the night. To hell with it, I thought, I *must* teach him a lesson somehow, and it was quite warm. I might keep him out there for one more night – just to be sure he's got the message about toilet training. What do you think?'

Tabitha continues to nod with a semi-smile, and there is a hint of approval in her eyes. 'You may well be right,' she says.

Chloe is astonished. This seems rather Draconian to her. After all, on the whole Sonny is a sweet little boy. She picks up Mrs Baker's hand and begins cleaning it a shade too fiercely.

'And then, if he still doesn't respond, I shall just have to put him in the cellar ... '

Chloe, who has been adding more nail-varnish remover to fresh cotton wool, drops the bottle and looks pleadingly at Tabitha. Tabitha is unwavering.

'You know best,' she says lightly.

Mrs Baker is satisfied.

Chloe is aghast. Anglo-Saxon forms upon her lips, though she does not speak.

The Slimatone pads in place, the fluffy warm towelling tucked all around, Tabitha switches on the machine and departs, saying 'Chloe will take care of you now.'

Not half, thinks Chloe, and she retrieves the bottle.

She grabs Mrs Baker's hand anew, in a strong and aggressive grip. Mrs Baker yelps. Chloe glares. Tabitha is out of earshot preparing fruit extract masks, a pleasing task which scents the salon with sweet seduction – from which Mrs Baker, at this point, is very far removed. Instead she is on her own with this virago from Childline and there is nothing seductive about it. In fact, she would quite like to go home.

Impossible. She is, after all, naked, and attached to rubber with electrodes.

Chloe finishes cleaning the nails and begins trimming the cuticles. She cannot get the image of Sonny cowering in a cellar out of her mind, and becomes careless and vicious with the sharp end of the cuticle clippers. 'Ooh,' says Mrs Baker, non-committally.

'Hurts, does it?' says Chloe with satisfaction.

Something in her voice suggests to Mrs Baker that she must bear up.

'Only in parts,' she says weakly.

Chloe digs in harder.

Mrs Baker jumps around so much that the Slimatone pads are wrenched from their moorings. She has a sense of being in hell, but does not like to mention it since she has never had a manicure before – perhaps they are meant to hurt in this way. Tabitha may have been economical with the truth in saying it was a soothing business. After all, her pre-natal teacher said labour was Just A Bit Uncomfortable ...

Chloe, meanwhile, feels vindicated. Cruel woman, she thinks, and finishes off the manicure in disdainful silence. And she refuses to offer more lemon tea. Contempt wrinkles her beautiful lips. She pokes a little finger into Mrs Baker's cellulite, just once, as if she were testing dough. Which does nothing for Mrs Baker's raw nerves or painful cuticles. She turns her back and mends her own nail with One-Step, the nail rebuilding solution. She waits for it to dry, seething. The woman is a regular customer or she really would do something.

After Mrs Baker has staggered off into the noonday sun, looking as if she was in *need* of a beauty parlour instead of just leaving one, Tabitha's brow wrinkles. Chloe expected this. 'What happened?' asks her employer.

Chloe shrugs, looks at her now-perfect nails, is silent as any chastised adolescent.

Tabitha tries again. 'Usually Mrs Baker needs waking *up* after a treatment. When I came into the cubicle this time half the electrodes were on the floor and she was down on her knees trying to get dressed with the plug and two electrodes still attached. And you appeared to be *grinning*. Why?'

Still silence.

Tabitha sits down. 'This is not like you, Chloe,' she says coaxingly. 'I thought I had trained you well.'

For once, feelings overcome caution. Chloe will speak. 'Well how *could* she?'

'How could she what?'

'How could she be so cruel to her little boy?'

Tabitha asks for an explanation. Chloe gives it to her. Almost there are tears in her beautiful eyes as she speaks. 'I mean – blimey – I used to get a clip round the ear now and then, or a bit of a belting – but they never stuck me in the garden for the night, or put me in the cel-

18

lar. And I did some *really* bad things, I can tell you.' She adds this last as an afterthought, and with some pride.

The response from Tabitha is surprising.

She laughs. She laughs with unchecked glee. She laughs as she so seldom laughs. And Chloe is offended, astonished anew. Tabitha explains through her mirth. Mrs Baker was discussing the *puppy* bought for little Sonny's birthday.

The *puppy?*

Chloe's jaw opens, sags, trembles. They stare at each other for a moment and then Chloe laughs too. They laugh and laugh together, an event which has never happened before. On the whole, laughter is not the kind of thing promoted in a beauty parlour. When they are calm again it is not hard to see why Tabitha and the world of beauty parlours does not encourage feckless mirth. For Chloe observes, as she reconstitutes her own mascara in the mirror, that while on her own youthful face the lines created by the merriment have quickly vanished, on Tabitha's they remain delineated for a very long time and never – *quite* – fade away.

Poor Tabitha, thinks Chloe, not realizing that she should give her sympathy to the whole of womankind, including herself, including Helen of Troy. Poor Tabitha, she thinks, she is growing old.

But the sympathy does not last long. Well, well – she winks at the mirror — look on the bright side. She'll have to retire soon.

And she's been laughing.

And she could have been frowning hard – *very* hard. Chloe shivers. She could have said That Is It, Chloe. That Is The Last Straw After Mrs Pargeter. Now Out You Go.

Mrs Pargeter!

Now that *was* a close shave. Chloe giggles, despite the shiver. It certainly was *that*.

But Tabitha seems to have forgiven it after all.

Phew! Got away with it, she thinks. Thanks Mate. And she gives praise to her God-Mammon.

But Chloe is young and presumptuous.

Was either God or Mammon ever, really, a mate?

There were certainly women walking abroad, beyond the salon walls, who might one day testify that Chloe did not necessarily move through life with *God* on her side.

3

Women like Margery.

Until Margery had her little accident with some baclava she had lived a blameless life. She had taught music in schools, sighed for the conductor of the local choir with whom she had a brief but not altogether *conclusive* affair, and had, largely, been sensible. But now, as she began to move sluggishly from middle to old age with scarcely an adjustment, she had been given a quite shocking new breath of life: several thousand pounds, won on a premium bond. And instead of being absolutely sensible about it, she felt quite giddy.

The Baclava Incident, which revealed for her the path towards sin, occurred when she was out on her first spending sortie. During this she had been uncharacteristically silly: it was early summer, and she bought a gingham frock, lilac gingham, with puff sleeves, tight waist, full skirt and patch pockets. With broderie anglaise.

She did not understand the psychology of this, having forgotten that it was precisely the sort of frock she had craved as a child, instead of skirts, cardies, navy-blue Viyella with smocking and a very deep hem. It seemed it was a frock that was never to be. Her parents taught music, loved music and saw life as one long quartet, with Margery and her brother making up the correct tonal numbers. Her brother, who unknown to his sister had also craved a puff-sleeved frock (though primrose was more his choice), became choirmaster to one of the lesser-known cathedral schools. Margery, destined, according to her parents, to win the Hamburg Young Pianist of the Year, never did. And now she taught music in Kingston upon Thames, which was the nearest to London she dared live.

But when she wanted to go shopping for a gingham frock, crisp and lovely twenty-pound notes rustling in her purse, she ventured to Knightsbridge, heart thumping, cheeks flushing as she bowed and bowed again to the doorman at Harvey Nicks, the place to which, being female, her instincts drove her.

But the women of Harvey Nicks were not mere salespersons; they were aesthetes. They looked at Margery's short, rounded, fifty-one-year-old innocence. A woman who had knocked about a bit might have got away with puff sleeves and a frothy skirt by way of dashing contrast; Margery would merely look a fool. The women of Harvey Nicks were nice. They tactfully did not have the frock Margery wanted in her size.

That they had that kind of frock at all may need remarking. They had that kind of frock because of the Spielberg movie, *Anne of Green Gables*, which was heralded not so much for its campness, but because it gave the thirsting fashion world a new and exciting thrust. Super-models skipped down catwalks, grinning and befreckled, bringing a new kind of eroticism to Lucy Maud's plucky heroine; Jean Paul Gaultier did something with long frilled knickers that will possibly never be forgotten; while Vivienne Westwood opened up, quite literally, a whole new concept in cotton gussetting. None of this stylish *élan* touched Margery, however, who merely wanted the frock in a straightforward frock-wanting sort of a way.

En route for Harrods she observed, in a little side-street, something called a Dress Agency. Now a dress agency is a very polite term for a second-hand clothes shop, and even in fashionable Knightsbridge, a second-hand clothes shop it remained. Nothing wrong with that. But, alas, its owner Nanette felt demeaned. She could still remember the days when We Had An Empire, and was therefore not so disposed to be kind as the women of Harvey Nicks, who did, at least, serve royalty.

In Nanette's Nearly New she took delivery of sweat-soiled armpits, drink-stained bibs, collars smeared with face-powder – the lot. Which did not incline her towards sympathetic aestheticism. Nanette had just dealt with a particularly stubborn stain (which she fervently hoped *was* chocolate ice-cream) on a voile skirt, and was in no mood to view the world of frock-wanting women kindly.

Margery entered. A frock-wanting woman if ever Nanette saw one.

A benefit of the high-fashion movement to dress agencies is that one of two things usually happens. Either, carried away on a whim, a woman will buy a quite unsuitable garment and wear it once only, prove its unsuitability – and bring it with shamed double wrapping to Nanette. Or a woman with all the right equipment will buy a spectacular frock, wear it, and look so spectacular that she can never wear it again without looking cheapskate. Nanette had one of each category in puff-sleeved gingham hanging on her rails, and when Margery left the establishment, Nanette had only one.

With a small stirring of guilt, but only small, Nanette said as Margery was leaving, 'You need to wear a frock like this with a bit of a zing. Maybe you should try a makeover?'

Margery had no idea what a makeover was. It sounded like the sort of thing her mother used to say vaguely: 'Make do, dear, make do.'

And then she spotted a pâtisserie. And the baclava.

Baclava reminded her of being happy among the ruins of the Parthenon, in heat she had never experienced again. There she had been urged by a dark-eyed hairy man with gold teeth to take a little honeyed cake from his tray. He had then, on the thyme-scented hillside, made a woman of her. Something for which, in future years, and after infrequent couplings of a very English Choral Society nature, she was extremely glad.

Since then those honeyed cakes had been her weakness. Indeed, honey had been a source of constant delight in her life; she put it in tea, she sipped it with vinegar for hay fever, she spread it on brown bread, and she baked a gammon to take home at Christmas with honey as a glaze. Honey, she was happy to read, was one of life's great panaceas and as such, an allowable treat.

It was on her second cake, while sipping hot coffee and ruminating upon Makeovers, that she said 'Ooh' out loud and clutched her jaw. Seated at the next table were two women of Knightsbridge elegance who directed her to their own beloved dentist, Mr Reginald Postgate.

'Schoolteacher,' they remarked, feeling safe. 'Written all over her.'

Which was what Reginald Postgate said to himself as he pulsed through the waiting-room, wiping his mouth with a napkin to remove signs of the salade Niçoise he had been about to consume before Margery's urgent arrival.

Reginald Postgate had a way with women. And he was a dentist. This was an excellent combination, since all women have teeth and, on the whole, have been taught from an early age that it is good to smile.

'Teeth and eyes are the windows of the soul,' he would say to his elderly female clientele, who lapped it up and beamed forth their souls as instructed.

Reginald Postgate's wife enjoyed life. The children were at boarding school and she had a simply divine house. Why, the curtains for the front sitting-room alone cost two thousand pounds, not to mention the Peter Jones suite, and their pictures came from Harrod's gallery. Reginald took only private clients. The days of piece-rate toiling over the dental decay of a classless society were over, and he made a great deal of money from his elderly female clientele. Mrs Postgate was therefore quite happy that her husband had a way with women, and did not mind at all that he promoted his charm by emulating a Man of Sorrow.

In the surgery he would sigh a little, and let sorrow momentarily shadow his noble brow. This could be interpreted by his clientele as they chose. Mostly they chose to interpret it as sorrow in his private life and in particular, sorrow about his wife. Poor man.

As soon as women walked into his surgery, they were in his power, one way or another. Once they sat in the chair, popped on the shaded glasses and thrust their heads back with mouths wide, they were made weak and seriously disadvantaged. Short of lifting a hand to stroke his thigh, or tickle him under the chin, they could give no expression of their attraction to Reginald Postgate beyond the occasional gargling noise from the back of the throat and a rolling of the eyes.

Every woman knows this is not the best way to be viewed by anybody, let alone a dental Man of Sorrow.

His women clients struggled against this irredeemable facet of their relationship, and failed. They were all, without exception, to be seen agape, dribbling and from behind. The only comfort in this was that it was the same for all of them; even those of exceptional, if vestigial, beauty looked no different from those less well-blessed, in this position. A little ember of comfort, such homogeneity.

They quite often had this thought as they eyed each other across *The Lady* in the waiting-room.

Reginald Postgate was safe. His women were not the kind to go in for chin-tickling or grabbing a man's private parts by way of plighting their troth. The fantasy, therefore, remained fantasy, and he was perfectly and wonderfully in control of these obediently lacunal women.

23

Until Margery stood holding her cheek in the surgery and looking up, pleadingly, at his suntanned face, and into his concerned blue eyes.

He thought:

Schoolteacher.

Has she money?

Better check.

But his receptionist already had.

'MrPostgateisPrivatehowcanhehelpyew?' she said.

But pain-racked Margery stood her ground.

Karen gave him a teeny little nod and, with a faint whiff of tuna and dental rinse wafting in her face and an 'Oh you poor girl – ' Margery was led, simpering, away.

In the waiting-room the receptionist, Karen, put Margery's package safely behind her desk, taking a peek first, in case it was a bomb. 'Golly,' she said to herself when she saw its contents. 'Golly!'

When Margery came out of the surgery she could feel only one side of her face, which suited her very well, and she had a lovely new white filling.

'We could replace all the rest for you,' he said, patting her arm, 'and your smile would sparkle like new.'

He laughed in his dashing way, letting his fingers linger on her elbow for a fraction longer than necessary. 'We could stop those receding gums, tidy up here and there – a little cosmetic touch where necessary – a sort of makeover of the mouth.'

He chuckled, tapping his own perfect teeth. 'What a pity you live so far away.'

Karen winced into her appointments book at the standard routine. One day, she hoped, someone would take a real swipe at him and knock that syrupy smile for six. Margery sighed too. And looked into his tantalizing eyes for what she thought would be the very last time. He reminded her of Richard Chamberlain, even to his voice when he had spoken so directly, so gently into her ear.

She sat on the bus and heard him say again, 'A sort of *makeover* of the mouth.'

Makeover: that word again. And then, as she felt for her Nanette bag on the seat beside her, she realized she had left her beautiful new frock behind.

It seemed like fate to Margery. At least, once the dentist had pointed out to her that it seemed like fate to him, she had to agree that it did to her too.

'Wehaveyourparcelhere,' said the receptionist, 'andMrPostgatewouldliketospeaktoyew.'

That was all it needed.

'I think perhaps when I come to collect it, I shall have that treatment you suggested after all.' She hoped she sounded casual. 'The makeover.'

Reginald Postgate said, 'Good girl!' And behind him his receptionist squirmed. Punchhimonthenose, she urged silently, smackhimone. But no such luck. Sometimes she felt she could vomit.

'Teeth,' he said down the telephone, 'are the windows of the soul, as are the eyes ... '

Karen ground her own particular fenestrations.

'You can have as much honey as you like,' he said playfully, 'if you make your teeth a priority.' He cocked his head on one side, took a deep breath and Karen knew he would say it. He would, he would ... She waited, wincing, praying he would not. He did. 'But perhaps you are already sweet enough.'

Karen's stomach heaved. She could hear the girlish giggle on the other end of the telephone. It worked every time.

'Excellent,' he said. 'I will hand you over to Karen for an appointment.'

Afterwards, Margery moved as if in a dream. It would be an investment for the future. And she would save the frock until she could smile her perfect smile above its gingham and lace, until she could smile her perfection into someone's eyes. And she knew whose.

Whose, she knew perfectly well.

Mrs Pargeter was, in Chloe's opinion, very silly.

But there you are. Takes all sorts. And the memory of her is certainly as fresh and mortifying as if it were only yesterday. Just as well, thinks Chloe, for its lesson is best remembered if she plans to take over the salon. Quite where the money will come from is unclear. Bank loans came to mind, but she knows little of such places. Never trust them, her Gran said, and *she* kept her savings in a sock somewhere under her skirt. The way it's looking, she might need to know about that side of things quite soon. Given those laughter lines.

She winces.

Mrs Baker's little Sonny's *puppy*.

Mrs Pargeter's close shave.

Oh!

Chloe knows she must try harder to grasp the two fundamental rules. And she must remember that when she is here in this salon she is no longer Maureen and this is no longer home. Here you may not do as her Mum does and 'speak as you find', nor do you call a spade a spade: if you have to refer to one at all you call it an elegant scoop. Get that under her belt and the rules, which she now repeats to herself, and she would be fine.

Rule One, she addresses the tenderly curled rosebuds, is to avoid comment on any contentious issue raised by the client – including, if it comes to it, the locking of small boys in cellars for weeks on end.

Rule Two, is to *concentrate*. If a man runs naked through the salon while you are applying a face mask you *carry on doing it* … she smiles behind her hand … and only run after him when it's done.

These, at least, are Tabitha's rules. Hard to follow, and not very convincing for Chloe, who comes from a background where spades might be shortened to words of four letters, and where conversational gracenotes were about as alien as dining on tofu and mineral water. Women spoke plainly.

Her mother's large formica-topped kitchen table was witness to many long hours of female debate on a wide range of subjects, from her at Number Fourteen's black baby, to him in the butcher's, and his chopper – and any juicy titbits of a female gynaecological nature that might come tumbling in between. If it was the teapot and Gran it was fairly innocuous; if it was the Guinness, or port and brandy, and Gran it was usually quite highly charged.

Chloe, growing up, and tucked out of sight beneath the formica, listening hard, absorbed it all. At the same time it gave her a good opportunity to contemplate the hairy state of the two women's legs and to feel a very deep urge, fortunately restrained, to relieve them of their growth. Here, then, began her dreams of peddling beauty for a living.

Given such circumstances, and with the spade-like vocabulary well developed, it was hard for Chloe to tread the verbal eggshells now required of her. If she had an opinion she generally liked to share it.

Thus Mrs Pargeter.

Oh!

Chloe squeezes her cigarette packet through her overall pocket, and it affords some comfort. In *particular*, a Beautician should be delicate with the verbals in matters of a sexual nature. The language should gloss quite as delicately as one glosses one's lips.

That Mrs Pargeter should turn the conversation in this direction was not surprising – many women, lulled by the sensuous arts of the Beautician's couch, will blossom in their womanliness and find their minds turn to the glimmerings of eroticism, the flickerings of intimate desires. A good Beautician will remain serenely above it all, never disturbing the dreams or embarrassing the dreamers with comment. Theirs is to dream, the Beautician's to dispense. No more, no further than that.

Chloe – alas! – forgot the Beautician's Golden Rules.

Mrs Pargeter – alas! – never knew them.

She just lay back on the couch and suffered accordingly.

Oh!

In the matter of Depilation there is nothing more fundamentally important than a client who is relaxed. Depilation removes women

27

from the realms of the animal and masculine, and is therefore extremely fundamental, extremely important. But it is a strenuous and painful business, however quickly the hot wax is applied, the calico strip pressed to the offensive area, the hairs pulled and the Beautician's cool hand placed upon the angry, denuded follicles.

Concentration is essential, as is the initial inspection of the proposed area of skin. Hairs do all manner of devious things: they grow in different directions, curl up close to the flesh, or become weak and fragile so that they break instead of coming out cleanly and honestly.

The inspection of the skin prior to waxing gives the Beautician an opportunity to soothe the client by stroking the area with her fingertips and generally lulling both her and her follicles into a peaceful state. The most successful waxing occurs on a client who lies there gently smiling as the spatula strokes the warm, syrupy coating of beeswax across her skin.

Chloe got carried away with Mrs Pargeter, and it was through getting carried away that the Very Serious Incident happened: the one that nearly changed her life, and which undoubtedly *did* change Mrs Pargeter's – or kept it the same, depending upon your point of view.

Mrs Pargeter, a divorcee, was about to take her first holiday on her own. Mrs Pargeter had borne her husband two children, done good works and had never tried to shine brighter than her husband's own light. She had been a client of Tabitha's for years, having facials, manicures and her legs and under-arms waxed for special events.

Even during the worst excesses of the divorce Tabitha had maintained a constant air of calm, for which Mrs Pargeter – though frustrated by it at the time – was grateful. She had made too many humiliating scenes in other areas during the painful process of legal separation, not to be glad of the salon's respite. At Tabitha's she had never sunk lower than a few tears, a little sobbing and Tabitha's nodding, impartial sympathy.

Now she had come to be depilated for her trip to Tunisia. She was excited. She was afraid. She was convinced such a holiday was written in the stars of timeliness, for she could even celebrate to herself, as she sat waiting, that her period had arrived on schedule; its flow was nearly over, the flight to Tunis was the day after tomorrow, and she was not even going to have that irritating difficulty to overcome.

She would arrive at her hotel, strip off her clothes, put on her bikini and run down to the beach to lie on golden sands, rub in oil and look as perfect as a woman of not quite forty could look, which – thanks to Tabitha she was sure – was considerably younger than she might have otherwise appeared.

Mrs Pargeter was on an up. Privately, she hoped to meet a man and fall in love among the palm trees. She hoped she would share bottles of wine with him, that they would dance close together, and that at the end of the evening they would have sex. Mrs Pargeter had not had sex since her husband left her some two years ago, and she felt – though nervous – that she was now quite ready for it. The children were staying with Frank in Ruislip. She was looking forward to collecting them with a smug and dewy look upon her face. And she wanted it all to be perfect.

Which left the vexed question of her bikini line. Trying on the somewhat brief bottoms of the new ensemble, she had been embarrassed to see how much dark curly hair was revealed either side of the pink lycra. More dark, more curly and more apparent that most other women's, she felt sure, and much to her shame. No matter how she flattened the hair and tried to tuck it in, it sprang out in all directions, as if challenging her. Her new underwear accommodated such hirsute straggles because it was silky and billowy, and did not cling – but the bikini was quite different.

She was still anxiously considering this phenomenon when she arrived at Tabitha's salon for her pre-holiday leg and arm wax.

She was wearing some of her best underwear because it helped her continue to feel up. Before the divorce her underwear had been rather basic. Now she put on frills and lace, even if she had her period, like today, because nothing, as her counsellor assured her, should be seen as detracting from the whole person she really was. Menstruation was part of her womanliness, as was her desire to wear grey paisley satin next to her skin, and to deny one by the other could only mean that she did not value herself.

So, celebrating both aspects of her femininity, she arrived at the salon, a menstruating woman in search of boudoir ministrations. Here you could celebrate such things, for here it was All Girls Together.

Despite this sisterliness, Mrs Pargeter was sure that these two All Girls Together had perfectly neat triangles at the top of their legs, unlike her, and she hoped she could summon the courage to at least mention the problem.

Tabitha had a request. Tabitha was gradually moving Chloe out of Grade One general duties to some of the more intimate services. Would Mrs Pargeter mind very much if Chloe depilated her today? She had depilated Tabitha's legs very satisfactorily and also the legs and underarms of a couple of her friends, so Tabitha was quite confident she would do the job well. Since it was only leg and arm waxing, which Mrs Pargeter was quite at home with, it would be a great help if she agreed.

Mrs Pargeter put aside the anxious phenomenon of her bikini line and concurred. Here she felt safe. Here they were kind. Here they understood her. She knew Chloe well: a pretty, kindly girl, always there to hand her a tissue if her eyes spilled, always at hand with a cup of herbal tea. She nodded enthusiastically; it would be nice to encourage Chloe.

She removed all but her pretty knickers, wrapped a fluffy towel around her midriff and lay on the couch wrapped in its soft, sweet-smelling comfort. She waited, quite at peace, and could almost hear the lapping of water on warm sand, the shushing of westerly breezes in metallic palm leaves, the whisper of a masculine breath in her ear.

Chloe smiled as she tested the hot wax against her wrist. Tabitha stood to one side, observing the procedures and nodding. When the first leg was completed and Chloe's cool hands prepared to work on the second, Tabitha went away. She was quite satisfied Chloe was capable, and she had her own client for some rather urgent electrolysis.

The atmosphere was easy. Chloe worked deftly. The conversation centred upon foreign travel and Mrs Pargeter's proposed holiday, a conversational level in keeping with the salon's policy. Tabitha, nodding and smiling with her own client, could hear the relaxed hum of their voices, the relaxed hum that spoke of uncontentious matters. Good. Good. Chloe was coming along well.

The second armpit was all but done. Chloe was just giving the denuded flesh a quick going-over with the tweezers and feeling pleased with the way the session had gone, when Mrs Pargeter said, 'Do you know, I have not had a lover since my husband and I parted.' And Chloe, tweezers poised, said spontaneously, 'Fuck a duck, that's *terrible*.' Closely followed by, 'You'll never get over the bastard until you do.'

Mrs Pargeter was rather shocked.

But so was Chloe.

Shocked and completely uncomprehending.

She felt obliged to give counsel.

'There's nothing like getting laid to make you feel better about being dumped,' she said sagely. 'You should try it.'

Wise words. But from the tongue of a Beautician?

She paused, putting her hand to her mouth. Had she gone a little too far? She bent her head to her task, fixed her eyes, clamped her mouth tight, just in case she had.

Too late. Mrs Pargeter's eyes gleamed. Her tongue came out, pink and quivering, and she licked her lips. 'Getting laid?' she said. 'That's a very crude way of putting it.'

And Chloe, dabbing talcum powder on the newly raw armpits, could not resist such a point of view. She unfixed her eyes, unclamped her mouth, and said, 'Well, it is crude, isn't it, sex? When it's good. I mean, it's not something you do on your best behaviour, is it?'

Mrs Pargeter rather felt it might have been. Her mind was fired. Her heart went bump. 'Tell me more,' she said. But the treatment was ended. Legs bare, arms bare, nothing to wait for.

She took a deep breath and made the gigantic step. 'Chloe,' she said, 'I think I will have my bikini line done.'

And Chloe, who could see no reason to disturb the very delicate process of electrolysis next door, decided to Go For It and set about preparing everything, while Mrs Pargeter engaged her in conversation of a much more personal and altogether more *risqué* level.

She told Chloe about the loneliness of the nights, how the cuddles of her children were not enough, how she hoped to take a lover in Tunisia, how she had bought herself lots of lovely underwear and was beginning to understand that there was nothing more important under the sun than to make the physical best of herself and get some love. Chloe nodded, and looked askance at the springing tufts before her. 'Well, you won't be wanting these,' she said firmly. 'That's for sure.' And with some difficulty she tucked the filmy knickers up around Mrs Pargeter's groin so that the wax would not damage them.

What she should have said to her client was that in future she should wear plain briefs for such a treatment, that frills and froths had no place in the Beauty Parlour. And she should have steered her away

31

from the deeply personal towards the more generally impersonal.

Mrs Pargeter did not wish to be steered anywhere. She was absorbing this unaccustomed intimacy and enjoying every minute of it – so much so that she omitted to mention she had never had her bikini line done before and was quite nervous. The nervousness had reached her lower abdomen and the muscles were beginning to clench, both out of fear of what was to come, and on behalf of her vestigial period. Still, she could feel the tampon quite securely in there, which was at least a comfort.

The two women talked. Chloe kept her voice low, given Tabitha's proximity, but what she said was of high-pitched content. Mrs Pargeter's fascination became tinged with anxiety. Chloe talked about the ways of seduction, the ways of the one-night bed, the art of come-hither, the art of getting the best from the guy you chose.

Mrs Pargeter had not quite imagined herself doing the choosing. She had imagined it would all fall into place, with the man doing most of the courtship, taking her through the complications of the bed with gentle attentions. According to Chloe this did not generally happen.

As Mrs Pargeter listened she began to feel more tense, and slightly humiliated. After all, this girl leaning over her and scrutinizing her most private area was almost young enough to be her daughter. Tunisia began to loom as a place full of passive men who sat around waiting for women to come to them with challenge in their eyes and a list of sexual requirements.

'If you want good head nowadays,' Chloe said almost absent-mindedly as she stirred the wax pot, 'you have to be *very* clear about it. You have to come right out with it and say so.'

Mrs Pargeter felt even more humiliated.

Good Head?

She pondered.

Did that mean brains?

Stimulating intellectual conversation?

She looked at Chloe. Chloe did not look like the sort of girl who would find stimulating intellectual conversation a plus in a lover. Come to that, Mrs Pargeter was not convinced that she would either.

'Oh,' she said, as nonchalantly as she could muster and with what she hoped was a suitable hint of a leer, 'I am not too bothered about their *minds*.'

'Best way,' said Chloe, selecting a spatula.

Mrs Pargeter felt better. She smiled. 'I've never heard it called Head before,' she said.

Chloe smiled too. 'Well – better than saying Eating Pussy.' She smiled. 'I think that's *very* crude.' She smiled even more broadly to encourage the rather rigid fixedness of Mrs Pargeter's expression.

Mrs Pargeter had a sudden, not altogether pleasing vision of a would-be lover demonstrating his ardour by biting the head off a passing cat.

'Well – I suppose,' said Chloe cheerfully, 'eating pussy might do … ' She continued to smile, a *bon mot* having occurred to her. 'And now to tidy *yours* up a bit and wait for the hungry hordes.' She gave her client a wink. And ran the syrupy spatula over Mrs Pargeter's inner thigh, now drum-tense.

Mrs Pargeter felt the penny drop. 'Oh,' she said faintly, 'of course … You mean … ' And her hands were suddenly clammy.

'Hold the skin down here,' said Chloe, 'and when I say pull, pull tight – that way we'll have enough tension to get them out in one.'

Mrs Pargeter did not need to hold anything down to create tension. Mrs Pargeter, light dawned, penny dropped, illuminated, was perfectly, wonderfully, gold-medally rigid.

The frilly knickers got in the way a bit. Conversation was suspended momentarily as Chloe rearranged them. Then, with that firm deftness of the good Beautician, she took a linen strip, laid it upon the waxed section of springing hair, pushed at the thigh to get a little more purchase, and gave a good, firm, once-and-for-all pull.

With surprising results.

Mrs Pargeter, wrested from rigidity, shot across the room as if propelled by the blast from a circus cannon, giving a yell, as she went, to curdle the blood of the most hardened aggressor. Chloe stared in open-mouthed surprise – first at Mrs Pargeter, now altogether off the couch and cowering by the washhand basin, and then, still open-mouthed, back to the linen strip in her hand. This, as expected, contained a film of wax covered by a coating of hair. But alas! It also held something else: dangling from the strip, as pathetic as a mouse hung by its tail, was Mrs Pargeter's tampon.

Fortunately, Tabitha had finished with the electrolysis treatment by the time Mrs Pargeter suffered what she was later to describe as an experience very near to rape in reverse, and could therefore go at once to deal with the commotion. She calmed matters down, and with some persuasiveness encouraged Mrs Pargeter to lie back on the couch while she swiftly dealt with the offensive hairs remaining.

Chloe listened, and hung her head, for Tabitha talked with gentle banter until Mrs Pargeter was relaxed again.

'One minute,' said the pale recumbent woman, 'we were talking of the way men are in bed' – she swallowed more water – 'and what not' – more water still – 'and the next I felt myself turned inside out.'

Tabitha gave Chloe a long, critical look and shook her head imperceptibly. Chloe knew it would be some time before she was allowed to take on any high-grade treatments again. And it was.

For the first time in her life, as she waited for Tabitha to see Mrs Pargeter out, Chloe remembered praying. 'God,' she begged, 'God make me good at it. Don't let me screw it up again. Remind me, if I forget, that it is not done to bring The Streets Into The Boudoir. Remind me if I forget that Reality Has No Place In The Boudoir. Remind me and remind me that if I Bring Reality Into The Boudoir I Destroy The Dream. At least until the Dream becomes mine ...'

Mrs Pargeter left the salon feeling far less confident and a good deal more confused than when she had entered it. My *God*, she thought, is a stranger going to want to do *that*? When she reached home she undressed and stared at the newly denuded flesh. It looked very red, very angry, and as if she had been transformed into a plucked chicken. And though the memory faded a little along with the raised rawness, Mrs Pargeter could not relax. If she saw a head she thought of pussy. It was deeply confusing and she had no time left before Tunisia to get to her therapist to sort it out.

As a matter of fact, the very thought of any man coming near her made her nauseous, so in Tunisia she sat beneath the metallic palm trees alone – save for a bottle and the rolling of the waves. Any man who so much as smiled at her, even the rather nice and beautiful waiter, she looked away from, pursing her lips to show she was not ready after all. And she did not send her beautician a card.

Even thinking about it gives Chloe the shivers. She was put back on low-grade duties, and made to wear the humiliating plain buff overall that did not show the marks. Tabitha had always said she would train Chloe exactly as she was trained. One mistake of a substantial nature and back to square one. Like a Beauty Parlour game of snakes and ladders – and Mrs Pargeter had certainly been a bloody long snake. Chloe will never forget the weeks that followed. Indeed, it was during this exile from grace, and while she was on all fours in the window, in the disgusting plain buff overall and moving the Declarine products about, that she finally made up her mind. One day she would be the Boss. There is nothing like humiliation and degradation for spurring on those bitter twins of ambition and lust for power.

When Tabitha eventually persuaded Mrs Pargeter to come back, with an invitation for any free treatment she chose, Chloe gave her the best hand massage and manicure of her life. 'Going anywhere nice this summer?' she asked, in that neutral tone so inculcated by Tabitha.

'Scotland, I think,' said Mrs Pargeter firmly.

Chloe went on trimming the cuticles without so much as a blush to her face or a falter in her gentle grip. She was not going to get caught out like that again. 'Nice,' she said, delicately rubbing away the dead flesh from her client's fingertips. And she congratulated herself on resisting the urge to quip, 'Don't forget the tartan condoms,' which sprang to mind.

After a reasonable period in Salon Purgatory Tabitha felt cautiously optimistic about Chloe once more. And now little Sonny's puppy has nearly blown it. From now on, thinks Chloe, I really *must* watch it.

Tabitha suggests that the Baker incident illuminated a gap or two in Chloe's capability. It is apparent that she is not quite ready yet. Perhaps some sort of test should be devised? Tabitha will go home that night and Sleep On It.

Chloe, going home that night, cursed Mrs Baker in her Maureen tongue, and knew that she *was* ready. She was deeply frustrated, deeply cross and she told her boyfriend about the Baker's Puppy incident with many a spade-like expletive. He was very sympathetic until he had a lager too many inside him and then he looked at her, burst out laughing and said, 'Woof woof'.

Chloe smacked him in the eye, breaking another nail and this time glad of it, and walked out of the pub. She would never see him again, huh, and if he wanted *head* he could whistle for it. So saying, she whistled for a cab and asked it to take her to Mayfair, where she knew of a classy club. She had more skills to her fingertips than an ability to give a good deep kneading to the Anterior Tibialis. Time to use them.

In Chloe's book, when lovely woman stoops to folly she only does so in order to leave the youth carbuncular and seek out the rich Smyrna Merchant.

Tabitha, meanwhile, lay in bed considering the future with impatience. How can I be sure of her? How best to go about testing if Chloe is a suitable heir? For the truth was that, quite suddenly, in this sweet green springtime, herald of summer, Tabitha was yearning to be free. How could Chloe prove herself, she yawned, so that some other poor woman did not *souffrir pour être belle*? For unless she got it right, some other poor woman undoubtedly would ...

5

Some other poor woman like Caroline ...

Caroline always said to Bernie that if she could ever be of help to him, she would be glad to return the favour.

'More than a favour, Favour seems an inadequate word to describe the kindness and support you have given me,' she said. 'You, Bernie, have quite restored my faith in men.'

It had been a very messy divorce, a very unkind sundering, and Bernie's large frame had stood by her like a rock, sometimes quite literally sheltering her from the prying eyes in the staff-room when she got the shakes, or when the tears fell unexpectedly. He reminded her of Dobbin in *Vanity Fair* – solid, kind and reliable.

I hope, Caroline thought to herself, that he never finds himself in that kind of horror story. It didn't seem very likely – pretty little wife, lovely house, clearly settled in for life. Caroline sighed. Though whether for envy at Bernie's security, or whether for regret, she was not exactly sure.

She looked in the mirror and stuck out her tongue. Well, at least she was her own woman now. And her ex-husband's New Woman in high heels and a frilly red skirt at the back of the court. *Frilly red skirt?* Oh *really*! He used to love her freedom from all those silly constraints. That she could shin up a mountainside as fast as him, or take a little tumble off-piste without a murmur. Frilly red skirt, indeed. Absurd.

Ah well. No accounting for change. She shrugged at the mirror and her own ruddy-cheeked reflection. She kept forgetting to moisturize, though she had a bottle of stuff somewhere ... She leaned further towards the reflection, peered. Perhaps she'd better start.

Lucky old Rita, Bernie's wife, for he was devoted. And Rita clearly knew how to moisturize every day, if not twice; you could see, just from looking at her, that she knew how to take care of herself. No wonder they made such a perfect couple. But then, she had thought the same, once, about her own marriage.

You never could tell.

Nice man Bernie.

Lucky wife Rita.

Now where was that bottle?

*

Bernie and Rita were living as brother and sister. Rita had suggested it quite a long time ago.

'I think of you as a brother nowadays,' she said one day, bored in the bedroom, after which any remaining conjugal rights were spirited away. Bernie made the best of things. He convinced himself that it would change again one day, and carried on accordingly.

But around about the time he finished the Amazing Re-creation of their Victorian house in Putney, lovingly changing it from decaying ruin to four-bedroom, two-bathroom, architecturally detailed, landscape-gardened, hugely valuable asset, he realized that, despite the perfection of its family space, there were no plans for a nursery.

Rita was very snappish about it. Now they could sell the house, take the colossal profit, buy something cheaper to live in (Bernie could do it up), and spend, spend, spend … But separately. Meanwhile, she would do a cookery course – *haute cuisine*, cordon bleu – something with real status. It would give her a proper job for when the time came to part. Rita thought this might be quite soon.

Now, with the Putney house sold, they lived in a boring little villa in Maida Vale. Bernie had no heart for it, after the dream-that-was-Putney and had, indeed, found tears springing to his eyes when they finally moved. But he loved Rita. He still found her daintiness meltingly feminine, her ways lovely and desirable, her occasional bouts of helplessness quite delicious – and so he lived in hope. Besides, he feared loneliness. Disheartened but obedient, Bernie did up Maida Vale in mediocre, careless fashion, and suffered in silence.

He could not bring himself to tell anyone the truth. Sometimes he thought he might confide in Caroline, as she had done with him, but it would be a betrayal. Besides, he felt rather ashamed of living such a lie.

Rita took her cookery course and was highly successful. Now it was only a matter of time, and she plotted accordingly. Meanwhile, she fed Bernie upon the riches of her prowess, brought back from the cookery school – exquisite canapés, fluffy little cakes, beef Wellington, delectable breads, pâtés, compotes and moulds of sculptured artistry.

He was enchanted by her success, enchanted by the food, ate and grew large – the reverse of a Sultan fattening his concubine. She fattened Bernie, who ate, worked, and was entertained by her stories. She Scheherazaded him with herself as heroine, and he repeated her stories proudly to Caroline who said that *she* could not cook at all. Oh to be loved like that, was what she really wanted to say.

The Putney money was safe in the bank.

'When my course is completed,' said Rita firmly, 'we can decide what to do with it.'

'Go travelling together?' asked Bernie hopefully.

'We'll see,' said Rita.

He had a vague notion that once on the road they would revert to the passion of their youth. He hinted this to Caroline, saying as much as he dared about staleness and how liberating it would be to step off life's dreary treadmill. Pastures new.

'Ah,' she said, 'I shall miss you.'

'We're not going yet,' he laughed, patting her shoulder.

'You must both come to supper,' she said. But somehow she never quite got around to issuing a firm invitation. She felt just a little too depressed.

Thus it continued.

Rita cooked and schemed.

Caroline sat lonely, night after night.

Bernie ate and mourned.

And the once humble Kitchen Goddess Venus, nowadays enthroned and crowned as the mighty Queen of Love, perchance remembering her own distant connection with the simpler delights of domesticity, decided to raise her exalted head. Tiara or no tiara, she was bored. Perhaps her ancient connection with cookery and provender made her aware of her pretty little nonpareil below – or perhaps it was that Rita fitted so appositely the words that spring from powerful Venus's name: vain, venereal, fain and win.

Whatever the reason, the Queen of Love fancied a touch of the star-crossed. A little sport. A diversion. Thus was ruthless, calculating Rita selected; thus was ruthless, calculating Rita brought low.

He arrived in the form of a visiting lecturer in organic foods at the cookery school. Tall, dark and handsome – the very epitome of Heathcliff, Rochester, or Venus's own Adonis, though with peatbog under his nails and on his mind. He spoke with passion about real meat, real veg, and Rita could not keep her eyes off his strong hands, his chiselled features, his mane of black hair and his muscular thighs. A pushover, she fancied.

'I want to know more,' she cried. 'I want to know everything about organic farming and real meat and llama wool.' She clasped her hands beneath her little pointy chin, looked into his eyes and fell – disastrously – in love. The more so since he seemed peculiarly unresponsive to her feminine wiles.

She invited him to have lunch with her the next day at Maida Vale, at a time when Bernie would be safely in school. She made up the spare bed, carefully closing the door of the marital bedroom and locking it, and she removed all traces of husband Bernie from the house. She even remembered to hide razors, extra toothbrushes, letters addressed to Mr and Mrs.

Rita tripped and chirruped around, making these preparations, like a little golden canary, a very confident canary, flexing her pretty tail and sharpening up her fine little beak. He would be a pushover, just like all the rest. A twist of her burnished head, a pleading look in those wide blue eyes and they were sunk. Look at Bernie. Why this morning he had taken a box of her Viennese Fancies into school for everyone to share in the glory that was his wife. It was too easy really, candy from a baby.

The Organic Lecturer arrived.

Rita gave him smoked venison, artichoke hearts and crème brûlée, and afterwards lay across the settee as provocatively as she could. So far nothing had happened between them and he seemed impervious to her covert seductions. A conundrum, a frustrating conundrum.

And then, at her despairing inducement to 'tell me all about your farm', she understood. For immediately, in that irritating way of men, *he did*. He became fired with agricultural passion: hormones, free-ranging, and the beauties of a well-manured cabbage. He was expanding, he wanted to expand more, he wanted his piggies to go to their deaths with a smile on their faces, his lambs to bleat joyously with a view of the distant Nirvana hills, and his happy little peas to go singing arias into the pot. And he wanted to make llama wool freely available.

What he needed, quite simply, was the money to do it.

'I have some money,' she found herself saying, and she shrugged and fluttered as if money to her was as remotely understood as the properties of a good weaner pellet.

After this she ceased to feed Bernie with delectables, or anything much at all. Caroline noticed that he had begun to lose weight and she took to bringing him in a sandwich or two which they shared together, in these early spring days, while sitting in the park. He said he thought Rita was under a lot of stress. Caroline thought that perhaps Bernie was, too.

Venus worked on. Rita was hooked. A farm in Wiltshire and those thighs seemed too good, too wonderful to be true.

When she confirmed the loan, the Organic Dream kissed her resoundingly on the lips. 'We'll be very good together,' he insisted. 'And you must come and visit the place when lambing's over.'

Salt had been sprinkled on her little canary's tail. She waited obediently for the summons. And Venus chuckled.

'I want a divorce,' she said to Bernie that night. Love had made her foolhardy. Her pretty eyes, that used to beguile him, stayed cold. Her little hands were iron-fisted and quite still. Her body was rigid.

'Why?' he asked. And the eyebrow that she raised at his question, that little, perfectly plucked, enticing eyebrow, was cruelly dismissive. He reached out for her, put his arms around her and kissed her as, he now realized, he had longed to kiss her for years.

'No,' he said into her twisting head. But she pulled away from him.

'Yes,' she said, firm as a nanny and quite matter-of-fact, 'because I have fallen in love with somebody else.'

Which in Bernie's book was pretty final.

'You can join the Photographic Society,' she said. 'You always wanted to. And we can still be friends.'

No valediction to love more cruel.

Bernie felt a sharp pain in his diaphragm, something that no ointment or distalgesic was likely to reach.

His shoulders drooped, his face sagged, he needed a drink. He abandoned the light fitting and went out, blinking in the too-bright evening light. Everything seemed to hurt. He felt that he had sud-

41

denly lost his skin, the hide he had grown to sustain him all these years. He walked, but the pain in his diaphragm did not ease. He needed a drink, but the pubs were full of very happy people. He could not go to see their friends, the Couples, because he could not bear to see dual harmony.

He arrived on the doorstep of Caroline's flat because she had known the pain herself, and because – suddenly – he understood what she had been suffering when he helped her. She said he had been her rock. He felt he could claim the debt.

She came to the door looking dishevelled and grubby. Cleaning out the cellar, she said, because she was going to start making a few things. Keep herself busy. Then she looked up at him, directly into his eyes, and reached out her arm to pull him gently across the threshold. Caroline's flat. Sanctuary. He no longer felt ashamed, and told her everything, she not saying a word. She had a smear of dirt across her cheek, he noticed, but did not feel it was his place to rub it away. Her eyes were tender and encouraging.

He drank rather a lot of red wine and ended up staying the night in a wonderful, warm bed where the flesh was exceptionally willing and the concomitant spirit was joyfully weak. And he woke to find a face smiling across a pillow at him. A hand somewhere below the duvet's horizon did gentle things to his anatomy, while another fed him grapes from a wooden bowl. At that precise and darkling hour in his life a new light had entered.

They stared at each other across the pillows. He knew she was not beautiful, yet he liked to stare, and he wondered what was in those grapes since they had taken the pain away completely. He asked her, half joking, half serious, whether the homeopathy clinic up the road had been advised of their analgesic qualities. At which she laughed. Not a tinkling little laugh, not an eyebrow raised trill, not with a fan of dainty fingers, but a generous gurgle from the back of her throat.

Walking home in the morning he found himself singing. The air was bracing, his street looked cheerful, and as he let himself in the second-rate new pine door no longer irritated him. And as he met up with his wife he found himself smiling into her raised eyebrow, shrugging as she questioned his whereabouts, and he reassured her.

'Friends,' he said. And kissed her frowning forehead. 'I have found someone else too.'

Which made Rita feel piqued, for some odd reason, and took away some of her own newfound delight. *That* had not been part of the calculation.

Venus smiled while Mars shook his shaggy locks at her wickedness and thought about having a little fun himself. Love versus War, with Cupid well out of sight.

6

Tabitha and Chloe were spring-cleaning the Beauty Parlour. Late spring-cleaning, much to Tabitha's shame. Somehow this year she had been lax, a laxity she put down to the unseasonally warm, damp weather they had experienced throughout most of the winter. What she liked was a good biting cold (with plenty of aloe vera rubbed into the exposed bits) to get the circulation going and kill off the bugs. Winters like this one, a non-event winter, had no liveliness to it, no dash – and it was that pervasive sluggishness she felt now.

She could quite understand why people ran around naked in the snow in Finland, and rolled themselves in its cold purity. She almost said this to Chloe, who was on her knees at the reception desk polishing cherubs, but decided it was best not. Chloe had her own way of looking at things and – well – there was the question of being beaten with birch twigs afterwards. Chloe might have very forthright views on that. And express them to the Cathiodermie, who was due in a minute.

She made a note that they had run out of juniper oil and were very low on clary sage. Both particularly useful at this time of year for their stimulating properties. Best play that down. She was about to take Chloe off the foot massage and move her on to full massage. After all, she certainly had the technique. She was very good with her hands. But she needed to be aware of the *soothing* qualities of some of the thirty-two oils they carried as well. She was clearly very keen. Tabitha had found her jotting down the particular benefits of ginger root and black peppercorns – the one so good at fortifying and resuscitating tired bodies, the other so good for stimulation. All the same, an understanding of the more gentle uses of, say, tea tree, might be appropriate. At this stage, birch twigs were best completely forgotten.

She finished the oils and found, with some alarm, that the frankincense had almost gone: so good for rejuvenating and toning mature skin. Had she used that much? Then time was truly running out.

She looked at her assistant. Chloe was certainly putting her back into it. Straight as a reed. She was a lovely girl, really, if a little wayward at times. Tabitha moved on to sorting the metalware. Amazing the number of pairs of tweezers the salon owned, and the number of times she could not find *one*. What they needed was a new system. A new broom, when it came, would wish to sweep clean. She looked at Chloe again. But not, it was to be hoped, *entirely* clean.

Perhaps she should take this Sunday opportunity to do some more on the educational side? Chloe was certainly willing, *more* than willing, to be educated – eager even. Tabitha stopped sorting the metalware for a moment and closed her eyes. Very eager. Those books for instance. Hard to define what was wrong, because *nothing* was really wrong – only nothing was really quite *right* either.

And it was very odd to have her trainee waft in of a morning saying things like, 'Nothing can be beautiful which is not true,' and then adding derisively, 'Who is this John Ruskin bloke *kidding?*'

Then there was her detailed interest in classical subjects. After Helen of Troy, her views on why Ariadne was really tied to the rocks by Jason left – well – very little to the imagination. Quite a Girl, Chloe called her. And Cleopatra, who was apparently more likely to have been executing a snake dance at the time of her decease was just – well – *unlucky*.

Tabitha had begun to dread her arrival in the mornings And she had flatly refused to have the Ancient History book back in the salon at all. It made her uneasy, though she could not, exactly, say why. *All* of it made her uneasy. It was education, yes, but it didn't, somehow, feel *quite right*.

On the other hand, maybe she was just losing her touch? Maybe her mind was becoming as stiff as her hands? She returned to the aromatherapy cabinet and placed a drop or two of lavender oil on her fingers, rubbing it well in.

Last week, for example. She let the lavender oil waft about her to soothe the thought. Last week Chloe had started to talk about the Apple of Discord to one of the sunbedders, who was most surprised, and apparently quite interested. But then, once you were in a sunbed you were more or less trapped. If someone wanted to lean on their elbows and discuss the merits of Ancient Greek Beauty Competitions

45

you couldn't do very much about it. Except by being rude.

Chloe had got a bee in her bonnet over the whole Paris thing anyway.

'I think I could fancy him,' she said conversationally to the woman in the dark goggles. Hard to know what the woman thought, but she nodded.

What could Tabitha do while giving electrolysis, which needed a steady hand? She couldn't be forever leaping into the middle of Chloe's conversations with clients, especially when there was, ostensibly, nothing wrong with them.

'It seems to me,' Chloe had gone on positively, 'that the whole thing was a lot of hot air anyway. Those three girls had been eyeing each other up secretly for ages, feeling jealous – you know how you do?'

The black goggles, nodding, apparently did.

'Well, we all do, don't we? I mean, we say nice things but underneath we're thinking What a Tart with those small hips ... or, *she* fills *her* Wonderbra out a little bit *too* nicely – you know.'

Tabitha consoled herself. The sunbedder was young, too – perhaps this was the right kind of approach? Move with the times, she thought, and went back to her client's hairy chin.

Then Chloe's voice went dreamy. She was about to speculate. It was these dreamy speculations coupled with the Ancient History book that made Tabitha feel ill-at-ease, though again, she couldn't exactly say why.

'I wonder,' crooned Chloe, 'if it's the same for men? Is *anything* the same for men?'

The black goggles made a tentatively negative movement.

Apparently not.

'Well I'll bet it *is*.'

The black goggles instantly gestured positive.

Apparently it was.

'Only it won't be about all their bits and pieces. Biceps and what not. That's just cover. All they'd stand in a line to be judged on, the only thing that bothers them really, is the size of their, erm' – her eyes met Tabitha's – '*organs*. Who's got the biggest and is mine too small? I know that for a fact.' She nodded sagely. 'Well – we do, don't we?'

The movement of the black goggles indicated that they certainly *did*.

'Otherwise they'd have their own beauty parlours, wouldn't they? But they don't. Quite happy to be bald and blotchy as long as they pass the ruler test. And do we care? No we do *not*. Get out your wallet and –'

'Chloe!' called Tabitha.

'Anyway,' said Chloe loudly, 'all I was saying was that these three women with the funny names – you pronounce every letter by the way, give it all you've got – ,' she ticked them off on her fingers, 'Hera, Athene, Aphrodite – sort of Goddess Super-Models really – *also* known as Juno, Minerva and Venus for some reason –'

'Chloe!'

'Would you like me to tell you?' She looked down at the now prawn-pink creature. Who nodded. She looked up at Tabitha. 'I'll just finish this off,' she said good-naturedly. 'She wants to know.'

Tabitha took a deep breath. Generation gap? Perhaps she had grown dull? She let it go. Concentrate, she told her fingers, since you are just coming up to the lips.

'Paris *again*,' said Chloe. 'He doesn't half get about. Well – the whole point of the stupid story is that until this Paris came along with his Apple of Discord, on which someone had written "Let it be given to the most beautiful", they were all supposed to be good pals and never compared anything they'd got. I ask you. And then he dangles the old fruit and bob's your uncle. From then on he's supposed to be the reason we girls like to look our best. Once he'd given it to Aphrodite – or Venus if you prefer – I must say that's the only one *I'd* ever heard of – remember *Venus in Furs*? –'

She rolled her eyes. Very possibly the black goggles also rolled her eyes too. Certainly her eyebrows seemed to twitch a little.

'Oh, that book!' said Chloe. 'I remember when one of my boyfriends said he'd found it behind a lavatory on Waterloo Station – *honestly* – men – the *things* they say – I mean – why couldn't he *say* he was into all that –'

She paused to collect her thoughts.

Tabitha knew nothing of Leopold von Sacher-Masoch, nor his doughty heroine, and assumed the title was, very properly and philosophically, *Venus Infers*. She was therefore silent.

Chloe went on. 'Well – once this Paris had said that Venus was the corker, it was supposed to have let loose the Discord – that's to say Bitchiness to you and me – but it's all – erm – tosh. Because if those girls hadn't known what it was all about in the first place, and hadn't – really – always thought they were best – they wouldn't have stood in line. They *wanted* to win. All three – or is it six – of them. And it wasn't the Apple that was the prize ... Now was it?' The goggles were nudged and smiled weakly. 'Ha Ha. Oh no – it was the sodding man.'

She stood back, pretty hands on perfect hips. 'Well – am I right, or am I right?'

Tabitha looked at the naked chin before her and smiled. 'All done,' she said gently.

'Did I swear?' asked Chloe, catching Tabitha's look and widening her own lovely eyes. 'Sorry.'

Watching the sunbedder depart, and seeing that she was – perhaps – a little pinker than might be expected, though not fiercely so, Tabitha felt that creeping unease again. It was at that point she suggested, firmly, that the Ancient History book go back to the library.

'Right-ho,' said Chloe. 'I was getting bored with it anyway.'

But it still left Poetry. 'To His Coy Mistress': 'What's the point of having a mistress if she's coy?'

History of Art. Of the Venus de Milo: 'She looks armless – Ha Ha.'

And *A Beautician's Bible*: 'Skin lacking in moisture is often referred to as dry skin.' 'Geddaway – *really?* They must think we're all thick or something.'

On the whole, it was not quite the sort of educational programme Tabitha had in mind. She was extremely glad that the Ancient History went back to the library and sincerely hoped that Chloe had forgotten *all about* the Gorgons.

She had read out loudly, and with relish: 'Their faces and figures were beautiful with arching golden wings, but they were terrifying as they were lovely, with scaly skins, hair of hissing serpents and a gaze so powerful they could paralyse with a look.'

And then said, in that dreamy way of hers and quite devoid of criticism, 'Sort of *punk* really.'

But since then things have been calmer. Praise where praise is due, thinks Tabitha, and says, 'You have been very good this week Chloe. Not one piece of bad language since the sunbed. And you've done those cherubs marvellously.'

Chloe looks pleased. 'Ever thought of giving the Beauty Parlour a bit of an update?'

'Oh no,' says Tabitha, 'I like it the way it is. Peaceful, kind and caring. It will be for my successor to decide on alterations.'

'Successor?' says Chloe sharply.

'Why yes,' says Tabitha. 'We've all got to go sometime.'

'When the hour is nigh, we are called,' says Chloe, smiling.

Really, sometimes she had a beautiful turn of phrase.

Tabitha will educate. 'While you sort the cosmetics,' she said, 'I'll test you on your essential oils.'

Chloe nods. Very important. And she begins to go through the eyeshadows. All so pale and wishy-washy. Even the browns and golds. What this place needed was a bit of zing.

'Melissa?' calls Tabitha.

'Of honey,' replies Chloe. 'A gentle, soothing oil to balance the emotions.'

'Correct. Lavender?'

'A relaxing and anti-bacterial oil useful in skin preparations. Blends well with other oils. Can be used directly on the skin. Strong.'

'Well done. Black pepper?'

'Useful in massage to relax tired muscles, gives a sense of well-being, livens the mind.' She hides a little smirk. 'Stimulating.'

'Good – and –'

But Chloe is going through the lipstick display, which reminds her of a story she heard in the Dog and Duck last night.

Lipstick!

Better keep it to myself, she thinks. *Just* for the time being.

'Jasmine?'

'Has an exquisite scent and a sensual and luxuriant effect on the emotions.' Tabitha nods.

'And it turns you on,' she adds under her breath, 'if you use your *skills* right.' She runs her fingers over the display, from palest pink to vermilion. Oh yes.

You can teach anyone how to do it, she thinks, smiling to herself, if they want to know.

49

7

Even someone like Gemma.

Gemma had worked extremely hard in the eighties, which had brought her all the expected rewards: Gold Card, quite nice flat, Golf GTI, designer clothes, up-front sex with men of similar age who earned similar rewards, a little line of coke now and then, Barbados at Christmas and the happy belief that the gravy train never stops.

Then the eighties went away, taking the Gold Card, GTI, designer clothes, up-front sex, the expensive white stuff, Barbados at Christmas and hope with them. Gemma was left with the nice flat which she could just about afford if she shared it; a job selling financial services for a bank which gave her a Ford Escort and low basic; a very thin wardrobe; Christmas with her aged parents in Morden; and a deep, depressing sense of loneliness.

Sex was still available sporadically if required, but the men were no longer quite so young, nor quite so fleshy, and were certainly not up-front about anything much any more. Mention security to them and they would curl their lips cynically and maybe spit into the gutter.

Many of them had sought oblivion in humble jobs, marriage and babies. Some had sought oblivion in drink, or daytime television, or working out a computer scheme for winning on what they still called, shades of their past, the geegees. Their striped shirts were frayed; they had dark circles beneath their eyes that no longer carried the honourable stamp of too much champagne at Stringfellows; they were worried about genital herpes and AIDS; and they grew flabby for want of the tennis club and the gym.

They also did not want to be reminded of their more glorious days. Someone like Gemma was an embarrassment; where once they had wined and dined her, or she them, they could do so no longer. If their eyes met across a crowded pavement, they would look away.

She who had been dashing, thirty-something, desirable, was now moderate, forty-something, avoidable.

And Gemma felt the same about them. Those days were over, she counselled herself, no use pining for them. This is it, possibly for ever, and you'd better just get on with it my girl.

Life was now working for the bank, driving to customers as they directed, turning up on doorsteps, selling the mundane to the mundane, the new wave for the nineties. She knew she was lucky to have a job; she knew she was lucky not to have married one of those depressed City rejects; she knew she was *very lucky indeed* to have the plump and accommodating Megan as flat-mate and thereby have kept her home.

But she also knew she was *unlucky*, very unlucky indeed, in her loneliness. Even a woman in a low-key lifestyle (the kind reviled, ignored, dismissed in the time of Plenty) needs someone to share her misfortunes with. It seemed to Gemma that her kind of guy, whatever that was, had gone with a whole load of other suitable men to live on top of a mountain. A very remote mountain and one, certainly, that Gemma could never find on a map. True, she too worried about herpes and AIDS, but she worried more about being lonely, and most of all about not having any love.

Even flat-mate Megan had a boyfriend. The lookist in Gemma found this monstrous. The single in Gemma found it enviable. Megan had met him in the park one day when she was jogging – huge breasts pumping up and down, belly and buttocks jellying the air – and he went for it. He was the gardener, keeper of the municipal tennis courts, shooer-off of dogs. They spent the night together, and they were happy. So why wasn't Gemma?

The wretched man even tended their window-boxes with the most exuberant results. Now, looking out of the window across the roofs of Wandsworth on a spring morning was made perfectly surreal by the explosion of flowers as foreground.

With sighing frequency Gemma did indeed look out at those roofs of Wandsworth – and often came close to having a panic attack. Forty-one, she said to herself, forty-one and the looks have begun to go. And I AM FUCKING LONELY. She said this out loud, to the jonquils and narcissi that bowed and bobbed their heads in silent applause. In the old days, she thought acidly, one of her up-front lovers would have reached out, plucked them from the window-box and eaten them. Thus did they once have their fun.

Saturday morning, Megan in the park with Jim, Gemma on her own indoors. She stretched. She looked at the telephone which never rang for her. She looked at Megan's *Daily Mail* whose salacious moralizings failed to amuse. I want, she thought, a *real* newspaper – or rather, I want the newspaper I used to buy every day, along with my FT, the cost of which meant nothing to me.

For once she did not let her stringent budget prevail. Out she went, along the springlike street, and bought a *Times*, carrying it back as preciously as once she might have carried a new Versace jacket. She made coffee, pinching Megan's, sat cross-legged on the floor and leaned against the settee luxuriously. For a couple of hours she could forget everything and just be the woman she once was.

The Times on Saturday. Who would have thought it could end up being a luxury? She would read every bit of it, cover to cover, slowly, savouring every line – the sport, the classifieds, even – God help her – the *poetry* reviews. Those little boxy advertisements for men's underwear she would save until last; those, she thought with sour amusement, would just about be her only thrill this weekend – she'd have to make the most of it.

> *After the rise, the fall;*
> *After the boom, the slump;*
> *After the fizz and the fat cigar,*
> *The cigarette and the hump.*

Not even a packet of ten a week, so no early death. It used to be Marlboros all round – packs on the table – help yourself.

Oh for a glass of Krug and the beautiful people. Where, oh where, had they all gone?

8

Margery had begun to look at advertisement hoardings with a new eye. Wherever she looked she saw the bright and beautiful smiles of women whose teeth shone out unashamedly; with beauty and teeth like that you could be thrilled by anything – soap powder, life insurance, dog food. Soon she would be like them. Soon. Thanks to her beloved dentist.

Beloved?

Oh yes, no doubt about it, Margery now loved Reginald Postgate. And he nearly loved her. No man, thought Margery, could give a woman's molars such time and attention if he did not feel strong emotion. She lived for the moments spent in that dental chair, though once thrust back and mouth agape, communicating her feelings was not easy.

But Reginald was very good at finding things to say, one of which, fairly early on in the treatment, was about honey. So significant, since it was the very reason she had come to him in the first place. Honey, she thought, he is *interested* in honey. And he is interested in *me*.

She began to learn as much as she could about the subject. They discussed bees in between the drill and the mouthwash – how they feed on pollen and nectar from flowering plants, using their well-developed tongues to dip deep and long into the sweetness; how there is but one queen and all the rest mere drones (from unfertilized eggs) and workers (infertile females); how the queen bee who is lazy and indulged will one day be replaced by a younger successor.

Margery would lie there and dream. To be replaced, one day, by a younger successor … Mrs Postgate was bound to be old. The gingham frock waited for the moment, the appropriate moment, and that moment would most certainly come. She would be *Beautiful*.

*

Caroline was deliriously happy. She decided that she now knew what rapture was, and her students were surprised at the sudden upswing in her interest in the French Romantics. Suddenly, it appeared that Rousseau was God, imagination and emotion the high altar. And Voltaire was an unfeeling bastard whose form, balance, discipline and clarity of purpose made statues of us all. An odd swing of academic loyalty, but they accepted it. She had a certain wildness in the eye, a certain propensity to laugh very loudly at anything vaguely amusing, a certain dewiness when a line of Mme de Staël touched her deeply.

Bernie was also very happy. He whistled a lot, lost a little weight, and spent a good number of nights away from home. At first, in those early weeks, this had been very pleasant for Rita. He came home, worked on the house for two or three hours and then went out. This left her quite free to dream about her Organic Lover. Once she dared telephone, and a chap answered very crossly, saying that the Organic Lover was in the lambing shed; it was a hellishly busy time of year.

Bernie, not privy to the new lover's interests, was moved to say to Caroline that he feared Rita was being hurt.

Caroline, who loved the world at that moment, felt terribly sorry. 'Should we invite her out with us occasionally? If he's busy?'

They tried, but Rita was contemptuous. She would rather stay in and dream. One up for Venus: Rita was truly in love.

Seeing Bernie and Caroline so drippy all over the place made Rita decide that the time had come to separate physically. Rather than move again, Bernie bought Rita out – why move when all he wanted was a bit of peace to enjoy his new love with Caroline? She lived nearby, so it seemed doubly foolish to give the place up. She might even, one day (why not now?), move in with him.

The deed was done. Within two weeks Rita had found a rented flat. She was entirely pleased with the arrangement. She was near to Bernie should she ever need his assistance, and she was *free*! He helped her move and they drank a little champagne together for old time's sake. Best be nice, thought Rita, just in case – but she hardly dared think why.

They hugged.

He drove away with tears in his eyes but by the time he was round the corner he was already smiling again. Tonight he was going to cook Caroline a meal in his own home, and he had bought new sheets and pillowcases and a duvet as white as snow in which to bed her. He stopped at the corner and bought an armful of stocks, sweet williams and delphiniums; the woman at the stall winked at him. Back indoors he removed the large bunch of dried flowers from a vase and replaced them with the living blooms. For a moment his heart felt sad again: he had collected these now dessicated stems in a French field for Rita on one of their travels. That she could discard them so carelessly said everything, really. He swallowed hard, walked to the kitchen, and dumped the lot in the rubbish bin. All over now.

Venus smiled quizzically.

And Bernie, with the remaining pans and dishes Rita had left, set about preparing medallions of lamb, and fruit salad arranged in the shape of a heart.

Later, looking at Caroline's semi-sleeping profile – blunt nose, strong jaw, straight mouth, he whispered that he wanted her to move in with him right away. And she, stirring, and still having her residual common sense despite the flights of romance, said Not Yet Darling, and kissing him once, fell asleep.

A big mistake, thought Venus, shaking her mischievous head.

One up, thought Mars.

Bernie took one last look at her before closing his eyes. She was quite, quite beautiful.

*

Gemma sat back against the settee in the waning sunshine and narrowed her eyes. Her toes twitched. She was thinking deeply. The coffee at her side had grown cold, *The Times* was folded at a particular page and lay across her stomach, and the scrunched remains of an Aero bar gave the lie to her healthy resolve.

Megan had come back, all pink-cheeked and wobbly in sweatshirt and leggings, and vanished into the bathroom to emerge an hour later wearing a fresh T-shirt, black with a glittering diamanté pattern (designer-weaned Gemma shuddered), different leggings, and pumps instead of trainers. And carrying her sponge-bag which contained her Dutch cap.

Did Gemma imagine it or, whenever Megan set off for Jim and a night of passion, did she not wave that sponge-bag about just a *bit* too carelessly? Did she not sigh just a bit too ostentatiously as she twirled it over her head? And were not the words, 'Don't know when I'll be back,' flung over her exiting shoulder with rather more happy emphasis than was strictly necessary? It made Gemma cringe.

Of course, she did not begrudge Megan any of these pleasures.

Oh yes she did.

She begrudged her every sodding one of them.

In fact there was a terrible moment, after Megan closed the door and made her heavy tripping noises down the stairs, when the heavy tripping noises changed into a couple of thumps and a bang, and Gemma's instant hope was that she had broken one of her hefty ankles.

'It's OK,' called Megan. 'I'm all right. Just dropped my OVERNIGHT BAG.'

And the front door echoed with a cheery slam.

Alone. Nice. To have the flat to herself was always a bonus. Of course it would be a *real* bonus if she had someone to share the silence with …

It was now nearly six o'clock. Darkness looming, spring cheer vanishing.

Gemma looked down at the paper in her hands, absently reached for her cup, sipped it, spat in disgust, stood up, turned on the lamp, stuck out her tongue at the bouncing airborne flower arrangement, moved to the bureau, sat at it, stared some more at the newspaper, reached for a pen, shook her head, put the pen down, picked it up again – thought – smiled – paused, pen poised – and then began making question marks down the column in front of her. TIMES SATURDAY RENDEZVOUS, it was headed, and she made her question marks in various places down the column headed GENTLEMEN.

What's wrong with them? she said to herself.

What's wrong with you, come to that? she replied.

Oh, Go For It.

She began to read them aloud, hoping, as in the old days with race cards, that one name would leap from the page, one advertisement say I AM HE.

But they all sounded wonderful. This in itself was depressing. She took it to mean that she was so desperate, she had lost all notions of taste.

And then – miracle – one really did stand out.

Kind, caring, solvent, attractive, into travel, stylish, forty, lonely *and* owns half of a sixteenth-century château in the Loire.

Gemma giggled. Monsieur Le Château required a letter and a photograph, and she spent a delightful evening composing the former in what she knew to be her stylish hand. She still had the Mont Blanc from Other Days and was glad now that she had not sold it. Not that the recipient would *know* she had written it with such a fine pen, but *she* did. It was like wearing pretty underwear, a hidden boost.

She sounded all right on paper. Own home, single, lively with a serious side. And *loved* the idea of the château. It was a good letter, and she posted it immediately before she could change her mind. Walking back in the spring night air, she hoped he was, as he sounded, looking for companionship rather than a quick fling. Quick flings were easy to find. Quick flings, sex and nothing else, hardened you, made you not very nice to know. She had always liked being nice to know. At the end of the day – no matter whom she had cut up in the City – she could always come home and face herself in the mirror.

Hell, if she only wanted sex for the rest of her life she could always go down to the Dog and Duck tonight in a mini-skirt and say loudly to Gloria behind the bar that She Was Anybody's After A Couple of Pils. She had done so before with exactly the required results. Dreary after a time, and all those stilted morning-after conversations through the slightly bleary fug of lager. *If* they stayed. No, no – she felt, honestly, that she deserved better than that.

She felt she deserved to be cosseted, valued – but for that, she sighed, for *that* didn't you have to be young, or at least *beautiful?*

9

Tabitha's restlessness increased with the bright warm days of early summer. Clients were preparing themselves for the beach, for bare-legged trailings around exotic markets, for long scented nights sipping pina coladas and wearing not very much, and Tabitha, usually so involved in the process, so devoted to the requirements, made her own very first blunder.

It was during a pore treatment: stimulates skin in the facial area, desquamates, refines surface texture. Pore treatment is not a relaxing facial routine; it is, as Tabitha is fond of saying, a method of giving imperfections their marching orders. Background music of a peaceful kind is essential, and Tabitha's is a gentle Spanish guitar. The Beautician must concentrate – how often Tabitha has emphasized this to Chloe.

This particular Pore Treatment had the usual compacted surface skin, with glossy appearance, coarse texture and patchy coloration. Worse, blocked hair follicles had led to comedones and it would not be long before all this resulted in pustules, infection and discomfort. Tabitha looked on grimly while Chloe, under instruction and peering at the heinous display in a magnifying mirror, muttered in her ear that no one would keep their toilet in this condition. Though Tabitha tushed, she was inclined to agree with the rather brutal sentiment. The complexion before her was as messy as a seaside convenience in high season.

She had given a general cleansing, applied zinc oxide cream, and begun on pinchment (light petrissage) to increase vascular and lymphatic flow. She had placed her fingers gently under the mandible and was making firm rotaries on the nose tip – when her mind wandered off to a Spanish paradise with bougainvillaea, sea-spray and enchanting foods. In her yearning she forgot the client and the light petrissage completely. A Spanish Elysium where no beauty products dwell …

She could have been kneading dough. When she refocused she was startled to find not dough, but living flesh between her finger-tips. Her soft pink pads had become like iron pincers and the woman was gasping for air as Tabitha kept them too firmly pressed upon the comedonical nostrils. The woman presumably trusted Tabitha with her life, for she made no struggle as her body began to deoxygenate.

Tabitha slapped her gently on the cheeks, saw that she was breath-ing properly again, though with popping eyes, smiled reassuringly despite the panic, and continued. Fortunately, the client's skin was generally tough and rather coarse; had it been fine and delicate who knows what damage she might have caused? She might even have broken some capillaries. She shivered. The smile became harder to maintain. She prepared to apply a mask.

Chloe had quick eyes. A mistake. The doyenne of concentration had made a *mistake*.

'That woman,' she said later, nonchalantly, 'will think twice before she neglects her cleansing routine again.' Chloe sat down opposite and smiled into Tabitha's eyes, 'Won't she?'

Tabitha's fingers flew to her neck, a flush had begun to rise, and she could almost feel the snapping of the collagen level as the flesh mutated into crêpe.

It brought back the day that her own Cosmetics Muse, Betty, yield-ed to age. It was when she was using the small four-point electrode (quite a new thing in those days); one minute she was all concentra-tion, the next her eyes had misted over and she was planning the opening chapter of her book *A History of Beauty Treatments*.

Betty, holding the electrodes in position on the client's crosspatch lines, told her that before the war it was common practice in beauty competitions to cover the girls' heads with paper bags, lest their facial beauty should detract from judgement of their bodies. And didn't *that* say a thing or two about the Beautician's Art?

Tabitha agreed that it did, and it appeared that the client also agreed because she was nodding and twitching away with uncon-cealed enthusiasm. Closer inspection, however, showed that the client was less nodding and twitching with enthusiasm, than with the involuntary muscular spasm associated with mild electric shock.

Betty had forgotten to put glycerine on the four contact coverings. This scarcely mattered when placed between eyebrows, but when the instrument slipped down towards the molar region of the

Mandibular Ramus and made good dermal contact with the client's metal fillings it was, to call a spade a spade just the once, as hellishly painful as the finer elements of torture.

'That's it,' said Betty afterwards, 'I'm through.' And she practically hung up her Terylene tunic overnight.

Now it was Tabitha's turn to go. She closed her eyes. Imagined a vibratory treatment where she forgot what she was doing and the applicator heads gouged into the client's skin; imagined an oil mask on gauze where she forgot to cut holes for the mouth and nose. She shivered anew and looked across at Chloe, who was now completing old Mrs Spencer's manicure; the girl's youthful loveliness bent over the flaky liver-spotted hands and she was speaking in low, soft tones while the old woman nodded, half asleep.

Tabitha had several lonely old ladies as clients; they came, not to be made more beautiful, but to be touched, held, connected by human response again. Chloe had never seen the point, but Tabitha explained that, apart from the regular revenue, which was not to be sneezed at, it was also a kind of Social Service.

Chloe kept to herself the thought that old women did not need beauty treatments, and behaved impeccably. Nothing was going to trounce her. She was going back up that ladder again, and right to the top.

Tabitha watched the girl and the elderly client.

She had once seen a painting in a Venetian art gallery of a very old woman, all wrinkled and toothless, painted a long time ago by a man called Giorgione. 'It will come to this,' says the tag. 'Come it must.' Shocked at the old woman's obvious lack of forethought for skin-care, Tabitha was nevertheless impressed. She admired this Giorgione for his courage in the portrayal. But the Beautician has no right to become a symbol of *Vanitas Vanitatum*, as in that painting. A beautician who does so is no better than a butcher who eats no meat. You are what you sell. Tabitha sells Venus, Aphrodite, Helen – not Venus, Aphrodite or Helen's *mothers*. She, the Beautician, must not find, in leaning over her client, that the client is looking up into flaccid skin or a neck in serious need of a scarf.

She looks across at Chloe again. How sweetly she deals with the old lady. Tabitha reassures herself. Chloe is ready, of course she is ready. She just needs to prove it, that's all.

Later, while one of their regulars was undergoing the dimmed lights and gentle caress of ozone steaming (drying, healing, anti-bacterial and stimulatory) and another was on the sunbed (a pale-skinned client for whom fifteen minutes in the sun-roof solarium was maximum) Tabitha invited Chloe to sit with her and talk about the future.

'Do you remember,' she said, 'when you first came here and I asked you what was the function of skin?'

Chloe shook her head.

'And you said, "The function of skin is to keep the bits in," ' Tabitha laughed. 'Remember?'

Chloe laughed. It still sounded all right to her.

'And now, of course, you know that the function of skin is to control the body temperature – otherwise we should all cook or freeze.'

And keep the bits in, thinks Chloe, otherwise they'd be flopping everywhere. She nodded. 'Silly of me,' she said.

Tabitha patted her inward sloping knee, well hidden under the overall hem. 'But you've come a long way since then. Learned a lot. Haven't you?'

'Oh yes,' said Chloe, looking pleased, and tapping her *Beautician's Bible*. 'A lot.'

Tabitha feels that unease creeping up towards her neck again.

'Old Mrs Spencer just now.'

'Yes, Chloe – ' Tabitha's voice is a little high. 'What about her?' There is hope in the question.

'Well – while I was doing her hands I was telling her about collagen implants.'

Tabitha widened her eyes.

Chloe's smile was radiant with delight. 'Of course, she certainly couldn't afford those – but I sold her some of that new soluble collagen and an applicator.' Her look implied Didn't I Do Well?

Tabitha widened her eyes as far as they would go, which still did not seem enough. 'But she's eighty-two and living on a pension. It costs – '

'I know, I know,' said Chloe. 'An arm and a leg. But we all like to dream, don't we?'

You couldn't gainsay that. Tabitha knew you couldn't – yet it felt – well – not quite right. Something appeared to be happening in the salon, and she wasn't exactly sure what. Yet again, Tabitha felt she had been wrong-footed and didn't *quite* know why.

Fortunately the telephone rang and the moral dilemma was shelved.

Tabitha heard Chloe say 'Tabitha's Beauty Parlour.' Pause. '*What?*' Then. 'I think you must have dialled wrong.' Pause. 'Bernie? *Bernie?* No one of that name here. This is a beauty parlour. Tabitha's Beauty Parlour.' Repeat of telephone number. 'We do facials, massage, manicure, makeovers. You name it, we do it, but we don't do Bernies.'

Down went the phone.

'It's Caro here, honeybun,' mimicked Chloe. 'Just called to say hallo ... ' She returned to her seat near Tabitha.

'Why is it,' she said, 'that when you tell them they've got the wrong number, they never *believe* you?'

Tabitha, who had been lost in thought, nodded vaguely. She put down her cup and looked serious. Chloe was instantly on the defensive. Don't say there actually *was* someone here called Bernie? She waited, fingering the packet in her overall again, her talisman and comfort. As far as she knew she had done nothing wrong recently. She was ready. Ready to do lymphatic drainage massage. Ready to give a Makeover. Ready to be the Boss ...

Since her trip Up West the possibility was real. She had met a very nice businessman, a foreign businessman, one who seemed delighted by her fair, Aryan looks. He said his name was Otto, but she wouldn't count on it, and he drove a Mercedes which had apparently cost more than her newlywed sister's house in Barking. He was courteous, he was in need of a ladyfriend (he said) and he would never, she was sure, say 'Woof, Woof' at her. When he smiled he had a whole load of gold teeth; when he checked the time he had a watch to die for. And he did not mind her knock-knees, if he noticed them, which was doubtful in the position he preferred.

Chloe had high hopes that when the Beautician's Mantle was dropped from Tabitha's shoulders, he would pick it up for her with his wallet. He was very interested in the beauty parlour, asked her all about it, and they had even driven past it one evening and peered in. Chloe pretended that she did not have the keys with her, rather than never having had them entrusted to her.

He squeezed her bottom as they walked back to the car and said, 'A very nice little outfit, my dear.' Chloe told him she was looking forward to its being hers one day. She could do a lot with it. And he had nodded, squeezed again, and said, 'Yes, yes, of course.'

Couldn't say fairer than that, now could you?

Tabitha was still looking serious. 'I have been giving your final test some thought.' She fixed Chloe with a telling look, immediately bringing the Pargeter and the Baker back into focus.

'We need to be really sure,' said Tabitha.

Oh do we? thought Chloe, but she went on smiling.

'You will therefore apply every treatment and I will watch over you.'

Chloe, clever, kept right on with her smiles.

'Then, when I am sure you are ready, you will do a minimum of three makeovers, entirely alone. I will go out for the day.'

Tabitha's stomach churned at the thought.

Chloe's heart raced. Had she been among her own pals in the Dog and Duck she would have raised her fist in the air and uttered a mighty 'Yes!'

Meekly she folded her hands in her lap. 'Thank you,' she said. 'I shall try not to let you down.'

Tabitha stood up as the next appointment walked in. Manicure, pedicure and eyelash tint. She sighed. In tinting her own lashes the other day she noticed a grey hair menacing the rest. Truly it was time to move on. She turned to Chloe and raised a finger, 'But remember – you must walk before you run. These will be real, live women beneath your hands. And totally at your tender mercies. Each of them.'

Chloe looked downwards again, even more meekly. 'I know,' she said humbly, 'I know.'

Three makeovers, she was thinking, three women. She imagined them, long-limbed beauties every one. And she could not wait for the first ...

10

Margery felt depressed. She was on the bus going home and could hear nothing save the words in her head. Karen had spoken them. Karen with her big perfect smile and the little hint of pity in her eyes.

'Onlyonemorevisitrequiredandthenitsalldone.'

Oh misery. All done?

Never to be touched by those deft, masculine hands, nor observe the hairs on those strong tanned forearms as they went about their business? No more honey, bees, rinse now, open wider, did that hurt, are you comfy ... None of that ever again? Fantasies frozen with a last wave from the surgery door and no more new ones to squirrel away into her pillow at night?

Margery was not going to have it. She simply was not. And as the bus sped on she looked from its window at the passing shop-fronts, the passing shoppers, the endless imagery of what from now on would be an entirely empty life. Well, nearly.

One last appointment to go.

One.

And then?

Blankness, darkness. And still she had not worn the dress, to show him how beautiful she could be.

Oh that dress. How it held memories of that beautiful day when she ate honey cakes and met *him*. She re-ran the film in her mind, stopped it at the dress agency, remembered what the woman, Nanette, had said: makeover. Magical word. She had never understood what it meant.

And then, as if by chance, though Margery preferred fate, she looked out from the bus again and saw a sign: a beautiful sign, pink and vanilla, with golden stars surrounding it. She peered. Certainly the sign could not be offering two pence off a tin of Kit-e-kat; it was not that kind of shop. What kind of shop was it? The bus stopped, obligingly, at a queue for traffic lights. She was very close. She read the name, 'Tabitha's Beauty Parlour', and the sign in the window with its pretty stars and pastel colours:

Special Offer

Half-price on all treatments.

And then she ran her eyes down the list until, as if Gabriel had tooted his trumpet, and God himself had stuck a finger out of the clouds to point, there was the magical word:

Makeover.

The bus moved off. With the quick-wittedness of one who is seriously smitten, Margery breathed on the window glass and wrote the telephone number of the salon in the mist. Then she memorized it.

On reaching home, happy once more, Margery went to the wardrobe and gently stroked the lilac gingham as if it were a sleeping cat. Beyond her bedroom window and the rooftops of other houses, was a cerulean sky and a sinking golden sun, the perfect summer weather for wearing such a creation. With summer sun, pretty frock, perfect teeth, and a makeover to connect it all up, it would be bye-bye Mrs Postgate, Old Queen.

She did a very unladylike thing and whistled a few bars from the Beatles' 'Honey-pie'. Tapping out the rhythm with her fingers on the window-ledge. The sun was dropping towards the rooftops, slowly, slowly, and it looked for all the world like a large spoonful of golden sweetness slipping from the sky.

*

Caroline, recovering from the ignominy of having rung a beauty parlour instead of Bernie, decided on a surprise visit instead. Despite good sense, she was beginning to miss him very much on the days when she wasn't supposed to be missing him, and though the strategy of Not Getting Too Intense For Both Their Sakes was still perfectly valid – Own Space being a popular phrase with her – well – what was a little extra surprise now and then.

As she flung on the nearest T-shirt to hand and pulled on her boots, she was whistling. Whatever was happening between them made them both very happy. 'So I should think,' she said to the mirror, flexing her arms in body-builder style and remembering her assertiveness training. 'What a *fantastic* woman you are.'

She looked down and saw that she had scribbled the wrong number given by the beauty parlour on to the telephone pad, and next to it had written 'Tabitha's'. Better get rid of *that* before any of her friends saw it. But it remained there, forgotten, as she hunted for her keys.

Whistle, whistle, whistle, she went, not knowing that even now Rita was driving back along the M3, dangerously fast, and no longer, it would seem, in love. Whistle, whistle, whistle, Caroline skipped up the path to Bernie's front door, and let herself in, happy as a lamb, unaware that a dynamic little storm cloud was coming on fast.

An hour later the dynamic little storm cloud also let herself in. She gave a sob. And then another. The first was involuntary, the second to make sure that Bernie had heard the first. He did not appear. Nor did his tender concern, his tea and sympathy. She riffled through the mail in the hall, nothing for her, and then she remembered Wiltshire again and howled afresh. He *must* have heard that. Water gushed. Ah – he was having a bath. Up she went. She heard his laugh from behind the bathroom door. Odd. And before she could consider the thought 'Do Not Go In' – she had opened the door.

The first thing she saw was that Bernie had an enormous erection rather delicately emerging from a froth of suds which surrounded it like a sweet lacy collar. He was standing in the bath. He was not alone in the bath. The second thing she noticed was that Caroline was also covered in lacy froth. And she was holding on to the erection. Having absorbed this much, she looked at their faces and realized that there was only one thing to do. Rita opened her pretty little mouth, closed her enchanting blue eyes, and cried.

With excellent results.

Bernie hopped out of the bath, pulled a towel around his middle and having secured it, embraced her. She peeped around his shoulder. Caroline was standing in the bath, still naked, empty-handed once more and with such an expression of astonishment on her face that Rita felt a rising giggle which she quickly turned into a sorrowful hiccough.

'Do you mind if I stay here tonight?' she asked Bernie, looking up at him with spilling eyes. 'I am so afraid of being alone.'

'Of course,' he said.

'Bernie?' said Caroline behind him.

Bernie turned.

Caroline vacillated at the sight of her half-naked lover holding his

66

ex-wife tightly to him. Several options flew through her mind and out again as rapidly. One – tell Rita to Get The Fuck Out Of It – reigned supreme for a while. Two – Get The Fuck Out Of It herself – came in a close second. Three, four and five came and departed so rapidly that she could not recall them and six, the one that finally made supreme champion, was: 'How did you get in?'

Rita, snuffling into Bernie's damp chest, said, 'With my key.'

'Er,' said Caroline, afraid to ask. 'Your *key*?'

'Yes,' said Rita, snuffle, snuffle, snuffle.

Caroline was aware this was a tricky situation. It was not her house, and her lover had a right to dispense his keys where he chose. Monstrous.

Caroline looked at Bernie; Bernie looked back at Caroline. Caroline, contemplating this monstrosity, was an incredulous woman; Bernie was a dichotomized man. He was also aware that he should offer some form of explanation.

'I said she should have one, just in case.'

'In case of what?' Caroline kept her voice light, moved out of the bath and throwing a towel around her, sauntered to the door. She was fully aware that this was a sparky situation. She could roar with rage and very probably never darken this bathroom, or its owner's erection, ever again. Or she could box a bit clever and stay calm.

'In case of an emergency,' said Bernie. He made to move but Rita held on surprisingly tightly for one so small and dainty. By contrast, Caroline towered over her like an avenging goddess. Certainly her face, if not her voice and her manner, had a hint or two of wrath about it. Bernie had never seen that side of her. It was not, he felt, entirely feminine. By contrast, Rita looked very feminine indeed.

Little Rita cried afresh. She began to explain.

Caroline held up her hand. 'Not until we've got dressed,' she said, opening the door, 'and had a nice cup of tea. Bernie?' He hesitated. And in that moment's hesitation, Caroline had a very clear vision. Such a vision compared with which the eighteen sightings of the Virgin by Bernadette Soubirous were but comic-strip motes in her eye. Such a vision that Moses' burning bush was a mere prelude to a Scrabble game. Caroline's vision was more profound by far. She and Rita were at war.

Hostilities began immediately.

First came the ceremony of the tea. When Caroline and Bernie went down to the kitchen, Rita had already got the kettle boiling and three mugs set out. As she poured water into the pot she nodded at the mugs. 'Remember those? The Finches gave them to us. I always liked that kind of pottery.'

Bernie nodded.

'We had fun on that holiday, didn't we?' Rita's eyes went swimmy again.

Bernie smiled gently.

Caroline smiled much as Mrs Macbeth had smiled when welcoming Duncan.

'If you always liked them,' said Caroline, still smiling, 'why don't you take them? We prefer using our Divertimenti cups now. Don't we Bernie?'

And he, treading a thin line with difficulty, nodded enthusiastically.

It all approximated to no man's land.

Rita, sitting so prettily cross-legged on the floor that Caroline felt like kicking her, said, 'I shall cook us all something tonight. That will take my mind off – things.'

Caroline's eyes widened. But what could she say? Her cookery was appalling and they had to eat.

Bernie looked a little embarrassed and shrugged. 'She's a wonderful cook,' he said. Perhaps a little too heartily.

The Wonderful Cook explained over the meal that her Organic Dream had conned her. Of course, she did not mention how she had padded down the moonlit corridor of the farmhouse in her little cotton nightshirt, on the pretext that she had had a bad dream and needed comforting, only to tap on his door, open it and find the object of her passion fast asleep in the arms of Gilbert, his partner. Nor did Rita mention that he had never actually given her cause to think his intentions were anything but friendly.

Caroline suddenly understood territorial atavism. There is nothing more dangerous than an ex-wife in close proximity who is still held in affection and suddenly in need of tender care, especially if the ex-husband is a man of Bernie's mettle.

You fall in love with a man for his kindness, she counselled herself, therefore you cannot expect him to stint that kindness to others.

Oh yes you can, if the others contain an ex-wife.

Sex was the consolidator in this battleground and she had better get on with it. Rita, meanwhile, was perfectly content with the spare room and the sounds of their lovemaking disturbed her not at all. Caroline was welcome to that. For the time being.

*

Gemma, who had taken to whistling and humming around the flat after posting her letter, was moribund again by Sunday fortnight and playing Patience. She had placed all her hopes on one sodding telephone call. Which did not come. Clearly the Mont Blanc had lost its charm. The whistling ceased, followed a day or two later by a cessation of the humming.

At least, she thought, as Megan came in and flopped down on to the settee in front of her, at least she had the decency to keep her overnight bag out of sight during the crisis.

'You should get out more,' she said, folding her plump arms.

'Nowhere to go,' said Gemma, flicking the cards in that idle way that makes one wish to smack the flicker.

'They've opened a flotation tank at the local baths.'

'I don't want to lie around in the dark in lukewarm water and get in touch with my placenta again, thank you very much.' She flicked the cards more recklessly.

'How about some aerobics?'

'Yes,' said Gemma acidly. 'Care to come with me?'

'You'll feel better if you do,' said Megan, ignoring the insult.

'Do what?' Had Gemma pursed her mouth much further she would have looked like an accident with a silicone lip operation.

'You'll feel better if you get out more.'

Gemma grimaced.

'That beauty place is doing special offers at the moment.'

Silence.

'Tabitha's.'

'*Tabitha's!*' Gemma curled her lip. 'Sounds like an old pussy.'

'Everything half-price.'

'Everything? Like what?'

'Whatever you want.'

'Why don't you go then?' Gemma's chin came up and out.

'Because I'm quite happy,' Megan said through her cheerful piggy lips, 'and I don't need to.'

Megan had a man. She had no need of beauty treatments. It was the sponge-bag all over again.

'I am going to have a bath,' said Gemma.

'What you need,' called Megan, 'is some nice oil to soothe you.'

Gemma slammed the door. *Affording* sodding bath oil would be something.

It is a truth universally acknowledged that if a woman is waiting for a telephone call concerning her Private Life, she should have either a bath or a shower. Gemma did not have a working shower, so the bath was the next best thing. Nor was she aware of this particular piece of Sod's Law. The reason she sought the soundproofing of running water was because she felt like having a good howl. And she was sitting in the rapidly filling bath doing just that, when Megan started knocking on the door. Louder and louder.

'I'm all right, ' called Gemma, furious at having been heard.

The knocking increased. Megan sounded urgent. Above the roar of the taps Gemma suddenly heard two magic words: telephone and man. A galvanizing combination, she discovered, for she was out of the bath, wrapped in a towel and padding down the corridor to her bedroom before she was aware she had moved.

She sat on the bed, picked up the telephone, took a deep breath and said, 'Hallo.'

'Well, hallo,' said a male voice.

There were two distinct sets of breathing, neither of which belonged to Gemma. 'Megan,' she said, 'you can put the phone down now.' And she waited for the click which came.

'I liked your letter,' said the male voice.

You took long enough to tell me, thought Gemma. 'Oh good,' she said. And then, because it was necessary, she added, 'the Francophile?'

He laughed, 'Oui.'

They both laughed.

They were getting along famously.

'You speak French fluently?' she asked.

'Non,' he said again.

More laughter.

This was terrific.

'Do you?'

'Un peu,' she said, 'but you're the real Francophile. I mean – ' She paused, tried to sound casual, 'You've got some sort of house out there, haven't you?'

'Yes,' he said. 'You could say that.'

Gemma's heart gave a little leap. Le Château! Well – Le Demi-Château anyway! She banished thoughts of You Took Your Time and concentrated on sounding charming. And, she fancied, witty.

'In that case shall I call you Frank?' she quipped. It had sounded all right in her head. Frank, Francophile.

No laughter. 'You can if you want to, but my name is Keith.'

Perhaps it hadn't been *that* witty. Too obscure. *Keith*. Oh God. She nearly gave him her commiserations. She had always thought it went with Kevin as one of the world's worst names. She must try very hard to find it appealing. Like beer. Roll it over the tongue. Get used to it immediately.

'Keith. What did you like about my letter, Keith?'

She winced. Overdoing it a bit wasn't it? Calm down. It had tripped off the tongue reasonably well.

'You were the only one to answer up-front.'

'I was?'

'You said the thing that attracted you to the advertisement was part ownership of a château. Everyone else, bar none, said nothing about it except vague things like always loving France or some such. You were very honest. I like honesty. I put the château in as a deliberate attraction. And you didn't go on about deep and meaningful relationships – *you* know.'

'*I* know,' said Gemma, trying to sound bright. 'D'accord,' she added for emphasis.

He paused, and then said cautiously, 'Er – it gets a bit stilted if we talk in our second language. Save it for France.'

Her epiglottis responded equally cheerfully and she made a noise quite similar to the click-singers of South Africa.

He waited politely. She swallowed. 'Mmm?' she said, which was as much as she dared.

'Shall we have dinner?'

Oh thrill. None of her Dog and Duck encounters suggested anything more than a pub sausage.

She found she was nodding, which seemed a somewhat unconstructive response so she tried 'Yes', which came out all right.

She suggested a brasserie nearby. She had never been in it but what she said was, 'I often take my clients there. It's quite good.' She was thinking:

Dinner?

Bugger.

What could she wear?

What was the point of having a flat-mate several sizes bigger than her?

Ah well.

Sod it.

She was stalking a man.

Such things were too important for financial considerations.

Change the subject, quick. 'Um – what do you look like?' she asked.

'I look all of my fifty-one years. I have a suntan, close-cut greying hair, denim shirt, Levis and an MGB GT.'

'Parked outside or at the table with us?' Ha Ha, she thought.

'Will they mind casual clothes?'

'Oh no,' she said, praying they wouldn't.

'Only I'm not into dressing up.'

She thought of a blazer and flannels. 'You sound just my glass of Beaujolais,' she said, lowering her voice while wincing at the egregious wit.

'Nice photo, yours,' he said. 'And what will you be wearing?'

Cold clutching of heart. Something about five years out of date? 'Oh – um –'

'You women,' he said. 'So many clothes.'

If only he knew.

'Don't worry,' she said, 'I'll recognize *you*.'

'Now when?'

'Just get my Filofax.'

She made a scuffling sound with her bedside Edith Wharton.

He gave a date.

'That's fine,' she said, pretending to write it in with her finger. 'Can I ring you if anything goes wrong?' She didn't like to ask for his number directly.

There was a slight pause, and he said, as if thinking it through, 'No-oo. I'm not going to be in London that day. The best thing is if I ring you mid-morning to confirm.'

He was very positive. She liked that.

'Might ring you between now and then for a chat. Would you mind?'

Shin up a ladder with a box of chocolates if you want to, she thought. And said, 'That'd be lovely.'

'Well, I probably will then. I look forward to meeting you in the flesh.'

She crossed her legs rapidly. *Flesh!*

'A bientôt.'

'Si,' she said lamely, thinking 'merde'.

She replaced the receiver hurriedly and hugged herself, aware of stars suddenly back in the heavens. She pulled the towel around her, staring mistily into the mirror – Levis? MGB GT? Château?

Outside, a floorboard squeaked. Swift and silent as a laser she crossed the room and flung wide the door. Outside Megan looked nonchalant. 'Are you getting back in the bath?' she asked. And then she shrugged. 'And who are you meeting at La Gioconda?'

Gemma tapped her nose and said nothing.

Later, from the secret recesses of her undies drawer, she produced a new lipstick. Bought with the reckless abandon of a woman on an overdraft who needs something. Along with several hundred million other women around the world she had no idea why lipstick gave her a boost, only that it did. She had bought Evening Crimson because the name had the ring of a French summer's night about it. Magical sunsets bleeding into the paysage. Maybe she really would get to see them.

That beauty parlour, she thought, tapping her teeth with the golden cylinder thoughtfully. Half-price did Megan say? But even half-price it would not be affordable. To think that a few years ago it was a mere bagatelle to visit her aromatherapist for a de-stress. The only difficulty then had been how to find a window in her busy Filofax. She looked at Evening Crimson, thought about lips. Fellatio and Filofax. Every City man's dream. She looked at the lipstick and smiled again. Perhaps it still was.

Keith? Keith?

Ah well, beggars can't be choosers. Too bloody true.

She could hear Megan's snores down the corridor. *She* knew why her flat-mate wanted her to go out more. It was so she could stay in more with Jim. Whenever he came to collect her, or dropped her off, or had a reason to visit the flat, he behaved like a very large gangly bird on a very small pliant perch, and since the reason for this was his shyness, or fear, of Gemma, he could never be persuaded to stay over. Well – maybe he could now. Gemma, replacing the lipstick out of sight, suddenly felt she could afford to be kind.

In fact, suddenly she felt she could afford anything. Even a trip to the old pussy – just to see what was on offer. She felt her face with her fingertips. The skin wasn't *bad*, she thought. On the other hand, she felt it again, it wasn't *good* either. Beauticians were a caring bunch in her experience. Perhaps she would pop along there. Just to see.

11

Chloe had vowed to herself that she would persuade the next three women who came in to have a major overhaul – a real 10,000-mile service – a serious stab at true transformation.

So far, it seemed that the only thing most women were prepared to risk with a trainee beautician was massage. And Chloe was getting a little fed up with it. She did not mind effleurage of the face as a beginning to the more creative process of cleansing; nor did she mind effleurage and petrissage for the hands, arms, legs, feet as a winding-down service. But what she really wanted was to amaze, create, shock them with what she could do for their looks. She wanted to do *Makeovers*.

Fat chance.

It was all very well for Tabitha to smile sweetly across a mound of tensile customer and indicate that the customer is always right, but Chloe was not convinced. Let old-fashioned Tabitha think it, but Chloe had begun to contemplate a little persuasion, more firm than friendly, in future.

The First Three To Step Through That Door, she said to herself. After all, what was the harm? Tabitha did it all the time, gently and carefully, and persuaded many women to have a go at something a bit different. If she, Chloe, carried on like this she might as well turn up her toes and join a massage parlour and take the extra fifty quid for intimate practices.

OK. OK.

She *had* made another little mistake. Well – Otto was sometimes a bit demanding of an evening – and she couldn't afford to offend him – so she sometimes felt spaced-out the next day. But it was really only a little mistake. All that happened was that once, when Tabitha had popped out of the salon, Chloe persuaded her newly arrived client, while deep kneading over her medial arch (front foot massage), to have a pedicure.

Unfortunately, as Tabitha pointed out rather crisply afterwards, there are more ways to judge the efficacy of a pedicure than merely the state of the toenails. Like how much time the client has available. The pedicure ended up in a flurry of activity as Chloe tried to get the nail varnish hard with a hair-dryer in time for the woman to get to a vital lunch date. 'Stocking toes stuck to newly applied varnish,' said Tabitha, 'are no advertisement for salon skills.'

When the woman rang to complain, Chloe hung her head in shame and let a tear escape. Tabitha softened.

'Concentrate on the question of Initial Treatment,' she said. 'It is good salon policy. Begin gently – as if you were a lover.'

'You what?' thinks Chloe.

'When the client first visits us it is the wooing period. The moment the client has dared to step across the doorway the beautician must coax her into a future relationship. The Initial Treatment should be basic. It should allow time for discussion, diagnosis, homecare. It should allow time for thinking about available cosmetics, suitable products, for building up confidence so that the client will return. A client who goes home and removes her shoes to find her stockings stuck to her toenails, is not likely to feel a hundred per cent ready to come back.'

Tabitha looked enquiringly: 'Is that clear?'

Chloe thinks that it is up to the customer to know how much time they've got. The beautician can't be responsible for *that*.

Chloe knows that the real money is in the transformation of a woman. Chloe feels that Tabitha spends too much time in the psychology department.

Tabitha's view, and how Chloe yawns when she expresses it, is that the Beautician is to the Woman, as the Armourer is to the Man. And just as there is no point for a man to be put in the field, armour or not, until he has the head and the stomach for the fight, nor is there any point in rushing a woman into redefined eyebrows and moustache removal until she is quite, *quite* sure she can handle the results.

In Chloe's book women want to look beautiful, they want to look beautiful quickly, and they want to pull, or get money, and preferably both, before the wrinkles get too gross.

For instance, this wedding make-up that Tabitha is locked away with now. How Chloe would *love* to get her teeth into a wedding make-up. She watched the pale-faced, pink-eyed young woman cross the salon floor and her fingers itched. But Tabitha said the bride-to-be was far too nervous to have someone new, and whisked her away without further argument.

Chloe, still fuming, looks out at the world beyond. It is *full* of the most ghastly-looking people, particularly women who should know better, so why aren't any of them taking advantage of the special offer and arriving in *droves*?

She drums her fingers. Oh yes. The next three women, whatever they come in for, will book for a makeover. Tabitha is well out of the way for the rest of the morning. Chloe will give them the chat, and once they are persuaded, she will make them an appointment – each one on the same day so that Tabitha can go out and leave her to it, as she promised. People should keep their promises. You can't make an omelette without breaking eggs, she thinks vaguely.

And if she is quick with the throughput of these three women today – why – Tabitha won't know anything about it and she won't be able to *interfere*. Just to be sure, she puts the sunbed timer on the reception desk facing her. It has a nice little ping to it and is easy to set.

I'll make them beautiful all right, she thinks. She looks up and sees a round, fiftyish face peering in at the window, misting up the glass with its breath, pressing close with its yearning face. She wrinkles her nose, faltering momentarily in her resolve, or at least – she mouths 'Come In' to the worried moon face – as beautiful as possible given the raw material. And that out there, worse luck, was material about as raw as they came.

A challenge, she encourages herself. It'll be just like dressing up dolls. She smiles, even more alluringly. The face smiles back. Nice teeth, thinks Chloe, pity about the rest. Still, by the time she has given her the spiel, the woman will be in her power. Easy to persuade by the look of her. Nervous. Well – a bit *gross* actually.

You are Number One, she thinks, no matter what you look like. So, Number One, Come On Down ...

And in goes Margery, into sweet-faced Arachne's den.

She talks of love and honey and teeth and last chances.

Chloe adjusts the timer. Wouldn't do to overrun.

You want to be Queen Bee?

You want to be the sweetest?

You want to give him a buzz?

I can do that.

An appointment for a makeover and you can tell me your dreams.

Margery is thrilled. Margery is appalled. Margery succumbs.

'Well, this man you see –'

'Married?'

Margery nods.

'And I want him to know, that is I want him to see –'

Chloe pats her shoulder encouragingly. 'You don't have to say anything else. I understand.'

Margery thinks there can be no more rewarding word in the whole world right now – understand. How wonderful to be able to talk about it at last. She needs that so much.

Chloe opens the appointments book and fills in the first morning slot with Margery's name and her home telephone number. Now the client cannot renege no matter how unsure she becomes during the next week. Then she looks up with a beautiful, wide smile and says charmingly, 'Well, that's that then.'

'It is such a relief,' says Margery, 'to meet someone who understands about these things. I know that I –'

Ping! goes the timer.

'Sorry,' says Chloe, 'time's up, I'm afraid.' She hands Margery her appointment card and ushers her out.

*

Only two to go.

She sees another pale and anxious face peering in. Blimey – this one's not much better. Younger, of course, but – *shifty*. She has the collar of her denim jacket turned up and flicks occasional looks over her shoulder. Hunted. Better convince her she really is at the right place. Chloe peers. She could be – well – if not beautiful, *striking*. Heighten those cheekbones, whiten the ruddy skin, give the eyes more emphasis. The face retreats, almost floating away from the slightly misted window. Chloe smiles and does an unseemly thing: she beckons.

Caroline, deeply ashamed, retreats no further. She stares at the cherubs and the shells and the cushiony interior as a vegetarian might stare at a pie shop. But breathing deeply, remembering that

Rita never has an eyebrow out of place, she sheds her feminism at the doorway and enters. Feminism is fine, she thinks, but it doesn't keep you your man. Chloe beckons harder.

Caroline suppresses the memory of a postcard she recently sent to a friend which defined Post-Feminism as Keep Your Bra and Burn Your Brain. All very well, all very well – but the adage of Love and War also sprang to mind.

You want to wipe out a rival?

I can do that.

Make an appointment for a makeover and you can tell me your dreams.

Caroline, with brows beetling so much that Chloe's fingers twitch to get hold of some tweezers.

'You see, he has this ex-wife – and there is to be a dinner party – and I can't cook and she can and –'

I mean, you can tell me your dreams *then*.

Ping!

Chloe rubs her hands. Next!

*

One more needed, one more enters. This time a smartly dressed woman – deadly dull clothes – perhaps forty – whose face bears the marks of defeat and whose eyes are dulled and joyless, something of a victim. Nice figure, though, and nice face beneath the dismal sagging. Too much eyebrow, nice curly hair and, disguised by some pale lip sheen, a really good big mouth.

Could certainly do something there.

First question. 'It really is half-price?'

Chloe curls her lip a little. She nods. She'll be able to do anything she likes with this one too. A relief because she looked, at first, as if she was a woman of the world.

'There is someone I really want to impress.'

'Love or business?'

'Both,' says Gemma, surprising herself.

'No problem. I can do that.'

'You could look on it as an investment, couldn't you?' says Gemma, needing encouragment. 'I mean, you don't often get the chance of security and glamour combined in one man, do you?'

'Well –' says Chloe, thinking of Otto. 'Not at *your* age perhaps.'

Gemma is temporarily stung. Fucking cheek. And then she realizes. The girl speaks the truth. It is what, in the old days, she would have called shooting from the hip.

'There are rivals,' she says, thinking of the bag of letters he received.

'I'm at the top of the list but we've only spoken. He hasn't seen me yet.'

She puts her hand to her mouth, suddenly embarrassed.

Chloe's eyes do not even flicker. Nothing surprises her about the world.

You want to turn him on too much to resist?

I can do that.

Make an appointment and tell me your dreams.

Gemma smiles with relief as the date is written. Chloe responds. She looks at Gemma's mouth.

'We're meeting in a restaurant you see. And somehow I've got to get myself across – '

Chloe nods.

'When you get to a certain age and the opportunities don't … '

Ping!

'See you then,' says Chloe, and shows her the door.

Returning, she leans on the reception desk, fondles one of the cherubs, and dreams.

Come, then, into my Parlour, she winks at the golden babe. And I'll *teach* you how to fly.

And she strokes the appointments book as if it were living flesh, before shutting it with a bang.

Ping!

*

Over her shoulder Tabitha says in a gentle voice, 'No need to rush.' And she closes the door of her cubicle softly behind her. She is quite relaxed. There is something about pure concentration which removes the worries of the world and, in fairness, the girl had needed quite a bit of concentration. If only they would not take *Brides* magazine so *literally* …

'And how have you been getting on?' she asks Chloe.

Chloe smiles. The smile is bursting with pleasure.

Something about that smile makes Tabitha stiffen.

All over.

Nonsense.

She has only been in her cubicle for a little over an hour.

What can have happened in so short a time?

'I've got three makeovers lined up,' says Chloe.

That could happen in so short a time.

'*Three*?' Tabitha's voice cracks like Callas post-peak.

She coughs.

Puts out her hand to steady herself by clutching one of the reception desk cherubs, which comes off in her grasp. She looks at it. It smiles cheekily back at her as if pleased to be free.

'Oops,' says Chloe. 'Place is falling apart ... '

Tabitha swallows. And rallies. She looks at her watch. 'You scarcely had time to give them a proper consultation. You know how important that is to the Initial Treatment. How long did you talk to them?'

Behind the desk Chloe clenches her fists, counts to ten.

'You know, if you have not done a proper consultation then I shall feel obliged to be here while you – '

Chloe seeks, and finds, inspiration.

'They're all coming back. Didn't have time this morning. They were all a bit rushed – you know – just passing and saw the offer in the window sort of thing ... So I'm seeing them again *for a proper consultation* before they come in for the makeover. Next week actually. A sort of mini-appointment – free – because, after all, I *am* only a trainee.'

Tabitha looks relieved and anxious at the same time. Chloe looks relieved and angelic, a combination she has no difficulty with at all.

'Have I done right?' she asks sweetly.

'A good solution,' says Tabitha warily. At least she will see them for herself. 'When *exactly*?'

'Oh,' says Chloe airily, 'I've said Wednesday, but they've all got to ring and confirm. You know how it is ... '

'Did I hear that the sunbeds are in use?' Tabitha looks at the timer on the top of the desk. Chloe picks it up.

'No, no – ' she says, 'I was just dusting it.' She peers at Tabitha's hand, still holding the cherub. 'Shall I stick that back on?' she asks.

'You can try,' says Tabitha, sadly, 'but I don't suppose it will ever be quite the same again.'

Behind her the door of the cubicle opens. Saved by the bell, thinks Chloe, whipping the timer out of sight.

The bride-to-be issued forth. She was certainly a radiantly beautiful creature now. Her eyes shone and she had the look about her that said Queen for a Day. Despite her sweatshirt and jeans she moved as if she were the very Goddess Hymen herself, impeded by the heavy silvery satin and pearls of her gown. Of the pink mouse there was no trace.

'Blimey,' breathed Chloe in both awe and envy, 'we *can* do magic in this place.'

'Not *quite*,' said Tabitha with a snap. 'She brought her own happiness from within. Remember that. The glow of beauty can never be entirely imposed.'

Chloe said 'Mmm ... ' noncommittally, thinking that Super-models had their photos taken when they were under the weather or the boyfriend had been a bit uppish, so happiness had nothing to do with it. Necessarily. But she was wise enough not to say so. She had those makeovers organized and that was the main thing.

Well, *nearly* organized. There was still the matter of getting them back again for a Proper Consultation if Tabitha was going to keep her bargain and go out. She wrote down their telephone numbers and tucked them into her bra. She'd do it tonight: call them from home, tell them they had to come in. Give them the summons.

'Yes,' said Margery unhesitatingly.

'I'm not at all sure about any of this ... ' said Caroline cautiously.

'She who dares, wins,' said Chloe.

'Oh, I don't know that I need to,' said Gemma crisply.

'You'll be charged full whack if you don't,' said Chloe.

Ping! Ping! Ping!

12

It is an odds-on certainty that the three women who on this beautiful clear summer's day prepared to make their second trips towards Chloe and the salon would, at that precise point in their lives, have eschewed all other attributes in their quest for the elixir of beauty.

None would have stopped to even consider the offer of The Top Job; Do Me A Favour their expressions would say. Margery would have spurned Hamburg Young Pianist, Caroline would have rejected Head of the French Department and Gemma, if offered it, would have declined quite easily the opportunity to become a Director of Hambros. Towards the Beauty Parlour they travelled, in hope and expectation. Two very dangerous modes of transport.

*

'Now remember,' said Tabitha, pacing a little too rapidly back and forth across the eau-de-Nil carpet so that she felt quite giddy and had to sit down, 'in a proper consultation you talk about skin type, their usual beauty routine, what kind of life-style they go in for, etc, etc. And you get a picture of what the client requires. You take your time and you let them talk. You are allowed, just this once, to express an opinion on their beauty habits, which you will almost certainly find unacceptable. In this way you will know your client and be able to give her what she wants.'

Chloe smiled. 'Thanks for the reminder,' she said, and looked at her watch. Nearly blast-off. Her head fairly ached with this manipulation and effort. She had managed to get Tabitha completely booked up that morning, so that she would only be able to watch from a safe distance.

And not
hear anything
at all ...

What she had to say to her three had best not be overheard. What she had to say was not *exactly* correct salon procedure.

*

'Men are very stupid,' said Chloe, keeping her voice low. 'They see beauty only as a road towards lust. It is no good,' she tapped the appointments book, 'expecting them to recognize your other unseen qualities like ... '

For a moment Chloe was stumped. She was also running out of elegant language, which she always found a bit like taking a run at a hill – fine for the first hundred yards then it tended to teeter off. Tabitha could go on for ever. Chloe dredged through her brian. Mustn't teeter now ...

What qualities? What qualities were there? Big eyes, small nose, good cheeks – flauntable knockers as a bonus – what qualities were going to overtake that lot? She looked at the hopeful pair of eyes which looked back at her expectantly. She thought harder. Qualities? What did they used to say about the Virgin Mary at school?

' ... like kindness and goodness ... '

The pair of eyes blinked.

What did they used to say about Chloe at school? Qualities she lacked? Went on saying it until she became thirty-six, twenty-three, thirty-six, no pimples, and then fell silent.

' ... like brains and good typing ... '

The eyes blinked anew. Their owner was not much of a typist.

Chloe took a run at the hill again. 'Exactly. No good being kind and good and brainy and qualified ... ' here the run at the hill failed 'until they've got a direct message ... ' completely ' ... from dick to brain. And *that's* what you want the makeover for. Right?'

The eyes looked hopeful.

Well, thought Chloe, well – Tabitha said much the same: Make the Best of Yourself. Chloe was just a little more blunt. She was convinced that if Tabitha had a sex life, she wouldn't be half so wet – talking about the women who came to the salon as 'having something of their own to bring' or 'challenging' (too bloody true, thought Chloe again, looking at this one), but none of them was going to set the world ablaze even when she'd finished with them. When the Beauty Parlour was hers she wouldn't need to take on dross like this lot.

'You've got to understand *lust*.'

Silence.

'Oh,' she said, suddenly wearying of the linguistic struggle, 'please yourself. '

Margery squeaked, and put a hand in front of her mouth apologetically. This was all far too important to interrupt. If Reginald Postgate was going to get a message from – Oh crumbs – *that* bit of himself down there to brain – she had to concentrate. Margery wished to become initiated in the Ways of a Woman of the World, which clearly this young woman was.

'When he is with me he sings, he hums, he smiles into my eyes. That, surely, is love?'

'I wouldn't count on it,' said Chloe. 'They are wriggly things, and if they can find a hole to slip through, they will.'

Margery clutched at her heart. She must woo, win, secure him. It wasn't that *he* would wish to escape, but if Mrs Postgate, Old Queen, made trouble he might feel obliged to buzz off? In short, and remembering the Bruch opera, she realized that she must embrace the Lorelei and turn herself into a Dental Siren.

She leaned forwards and concentrated on Chloe's pronouncing face. She was not going to end up like a drone, she was not going to end up as just another worker bee – she was going to be Queen. She had never seen such tenderness in a dentist's eyes before, nor really had she ever seen such tenderness in any man's eyes before. But this was possibly due to most of her previous encounters taking place in the dark.

Never again.

Sunshine. With her new teeth and new face and new frock she could embrace Reginald with confidence, in a blaze of sunshine. A makeover, and Reginald would be hers. She trills a line of Bruch. Chloe winces.

'Now remember ... ' says Chloe quickly, reading aloud from *What Sex Means for the Intellectual: Bedside Trinkets for the Mind*: 'remember that the *sexual embrace* can only be compared with music and with prayer.' She closes the book with a bang and winks. 'Bugger the singing,' she says, 'go for the body.'

'Oh,' said Margery happily, 'I fear no lust. You have no idea how exciting it is when he snaps on his thin rubber gloves. He does it *so* expertly!'

Chloe pretended she had not heard. The thought of this person getting into rubber wear was vomit-worthy.

She smiles demurely at Tabitha who is engaged at the far end of the salon. Tabitha smiles back.

So far so good.

Margery is hers.

*

'I don't think that is altogether true,' said Caroline, considering Bernie. 'Some men can eschew sex for the greater good of their marriage.'

Chloe blinks. 'In that case they've either got no balls, *literally* ...'

'This one has,' said Caroline, the smugness irresistible.

'Or they have other women on the side.'

'Never, he says.'

'In that case,' said Chloe without a pause, 'he's seriously damaged as a human being and you should have nothing to do with him. I mean, that's why the brain and the dick are directly connected by the arterial nerve. It's the Ever-Ready Factor.'

Chloe had done rudimentary physiotherapy and had an alarming way of suddenly using the right terminology for something entirely bogus.

'Are they?' said Caroline, confused.

'Of *course* they are.' Chloe felt utterly confident on this one. 'That's what dicks were put on the outside for – so they were Ever-Ready for the slightest hint of a parking-place.'

She put her perfect little hand over her mouth and nose to simulate Ground Control. 'Dick to Brain, Dick to Brain, tits ahead, tits ahead ...' and then laughed knowingly. She really was very convincing.

Caroline, both fascinated and repelled, decided that this young woman knew a thing or two that she didn't, and might have some useful battle plans.

'What was his wife? Paraplegic or something?'

'I wish,' said Caroline.

'He's a bit of a nerd then?'

Caroline bristled. 'Certainly not.'

Chloe sighed. 'I can just about understand a bloke staying with a frigid woman if he looks like Quasimodo – but if he looks even part-way reasonable – he's likely to be Very Damaged Goods. In fact, like

86

I said, the sort of bloke who suggests a little bondage now and then? Or rubber sheets? Next thing you know he's got nine of 'em under the floorboards.'

'She said he felt like a brother to her, so they gave it up. I'm not so sure she still feels that way now,' she added miserably.

She was remembering the previous night, when she went round to Bernie's house and found Rita sitting all tucked up on the sofa cushions eating little white grapes and looking like a kitten in clover. Bernie had looked at his wife fondly several times, much as if he would like to stroke her. Caroline was pretty sure that unless she did something dramatic, he soon would.

Rita had once said to her that sex with Bernie made her feel sick, but on the sofa last night, nibbling those grapes with her sharp little teeth, she did not look like one who would let a little post-coital biliousness spoil the repossession order.

'Beautifying Action is definitely required,' said Caroline in a pure shaft of Zen understanding. 'He's worth fighting for.'

Tabitha, looking up, thought how charming the two of them were with their heads so close together. Clearly Chloe was getting it right.

'Ah,' said Chloe conspiratorially, 'going to war, are you? Then you'll be needing warpaint. And a motto.'

She opened *Bedside Trinkets* gravely and consulted it. 'Here we are. You should also remember what Voltaire said ... '

Caroline blinks. *Voltaire?* I do not believe this, she thinks. Out loud she says 'What?'

'It is not enough to conquer; one must know how to seduce.' Chloe closes the book. 'Is he right, or is he *right!?*'

Caroline reels. A Beautician quoting the King of the Neoclassicists? Oh my God, she thinks, half-excited, it'll be high heels next. She can feel them growing on her ... She leans forwards to hear more.

*

With regard to the dick to brain issue, Gemma said, quite briskly, she thought it would be best to pursue the line of thinking that said *all* men respond in that Pavlovian way, and act accordingly.

The few out there who genuinely didn't – Gandhi came to mind – would not object since they were quite clearly on another spiritual planet altogether.

'And should bloody well stay there,' says Chloe spontaneously.

Gemma feels desperate, keen to get back to the flat and relieve Megan from Phonewatch (Ansaphone on the blink – male God). She is convinced that if he doesn't ring by today he will have forgotten her. She had, on the purchase of a quarter bottle of mediocre Martell, vowed that if so, she would do something drastic. Seducing Megan's Jim came to mind.

Surely the God of such a devout chapel girl would intervene to save His lamb from the painful experience? I'll do it if he doesn't ring, God. You bet I will.

'I feel this is my last chance.'

Chloe scrutinizes her. She nods. She notices the creep of low self-esteem, of bitterness – what her Gran calls Sourpussitis.

'You were a looker once, weren't you?' She puts her head on one side and screws up her eyes. 'You can still see traces of it ... '

Gemma, feeling somewhat akin to an Ancient Site and just about resisting the urge to slap the irritating loveliness of that face, says, 'Yes, well, I haven't quite got down to the Roman Level yet; so what are we going to do about it?' Her fingers crossed, for in her heart, that much-depressed muscle, she did not believe he would ever ring again.

'Well? What do I get for my money?'

Chloe made an arc with her hand as if she were wielding a wand. 'The Works. We can do magic you know.' And she winks.

'I want to look so good he throws all the other photographs away ... '

'Photographs?'

'I mean addresses ... ' Gemma lowered her voice a little.

Chloe recognized deception when she saw it. 'No more porkies,' she said. 'Just tell me the truth.'

Gemma does.

'The makeover will last through the night,' says Chloe.

'What happens in the morning?' said Gemma guardedly.

'That depends on how good you've been during the night,' Chloe replies, very seriously.

And it is a serious business. Gemma's heart sinks at just how serious she is. Chloe beckons her closer.

Tabitha, gazing from afar, congratulates herself. She has trained her assistant well.

'And finally,' pronounces Chloe, turning to the Great Book, 'you should remember – um – ' She reads, discovers, smiles.

'Might use this for myself. By someone *completely* unpronounceable again. They are *never* British.' She pushes the book towards Gemma and points. 'How do you say that?'

'Giraudoux,' says Gemma wonderingly.

Chloe peers. 'You do?' And shrugs. 'Amazing they ever learn to pronounce it.' And reads: 'If a woman goes everywhere with a crowd of admirers it's not so much because they think she is beautiful, but because she has told *them* they are handsome.'

She closes the book. 'See what I mean?' She scrutinizes Gemma, who is momentarily lost for words and smiling rather hazily. 'You've got a good mouth somewhere under that lot,' she adds. She leans forwards, drops her voice and says, 'I heard a very good lipstick story from my friend Jo-Jo – '

And she tells it to Gemma. With gusto.

'Amazing, eh?' says Chloe with satisfaction.

It certainly is. The Somewhere Under That Lot falls open. Gemma, if no longer hazy, is to say the least – staggered.

'Good eh?' says Chloe. 'Trust Jo-Jo – she comes up with them every time. Tell him that at the right moment and he'll love it.'

'He will?' says Gemma cautiously.

'Sure,' says Chloe. 'Sure.'

*

Chloe sells the dream; the dream is bought. Power, Chloe feels it within her hands. She is not going to relinquish it, despite Tabitha's disapproval. After all – she'll never know.

'Tell me what you want,' she urges, 'and I will make it happen. Come closer, closer.'

They do. They impart. They absorb.

*

'Slap on the mascara and get the skirt hitched up a bit, whatever your romantic dream of him is,' says Chloe, 'because it's the only truth he'll know.'

'What about changing them so that they revere higher things?' asked Margery, secretly sure that Ronald did – mostly. And also thinking that the gingham frock wouldn't hitch all that well. 'Some might.'

'Some what?' asked Chloe, puzzled.

'Er – men.'

Higher things? Chloe shook her head, confident in her wisdom. 'Nothing,' she said, 'is higher than a prick in erection. While that's buzzing about we are talking Snowdon, Everest … ' here her geography ran out 'Er … Box Hill.'

A little surprising, this latter, but Margery accepted it.

'Prick?' said Margery wonderingly.

'Well, you'll have to get to grips with it,' says Chloe.

Margery tried to imagine what Reginald's was like. Something akin to an elongated beehive perhaps? Filled with honey. And in return she would give him honey, too, and she would take him into the countryside, away from his cares, and she would give herself to him in gingham and clover. She left the salon as if the deed were accomplished – pink of cheek and light of step. Chloe's eyes met Tabitha's, clear and innocent as a summer pool.

*

'Prick?' thought Caroline. 'How inadequate a term for what that wonderful creation actually *does*.' She was thinking sadly of Bernie's noble erection which was seriously under threat, and had even wilted a few times recently as he recalled the sadness of his wife. She was also thinking sadly of his wife. She would, she thought, quite like to poison her.

'Not a bad idea,' said Chloe, tapping thoughtfully at her beautiful cheek.

Rita had even wangled herself into their dinner party.

Bernie had insisted Rita be invited and at first Caroline thought that she herself would not go. She just would *not*. That would teach him. But – ah – *would* it?

'You'd be cutting off your nose to spite your face,' said Chloe firmly.

'She'll cook. She'll cook *successfully*.'

'So what?' said Chloe. 'It's what you give him after the pudding that counts … '

'It'll have to be on the same day that I see you.

'No probs.'

Whichever one of them cooked the wretched meal, she would have to look as good as she could. Either by way of apology, or by way of diversion.

She felt afraid of the battle, but Chloe had an idea. An idea which offered Strategy, Timing, Artillery, in a rather outrageous form. It was devoutly to be wished, quite suddenly, that Rita would flex her cordon bleu talons after all.

*

'Can be applied both to name the sexual member *and* its owner,' said Gemma absently, still thinking hard about friend Jo-Jo's lipstick story. And then she put such deprecating thoughts behind her. If he turned out to be a prick, she just wouldn't notice, that's all. Chloe was encouraging. Make-up could give you any image you wanted.

'How about a cross between Madonna and Grace Kelly floating around the turrets of a château?

Sure.

'Definitely the mouth,' said Chloe, scrutinizing her as if she were palaeolithic.

Gemma said nothing. She would come back here, with all her archaeological promise, and grit her teeth at such impudence. And afterwards? Afterwards? Why, on with the dream. Forgetting entirely her promise that once she turned forty, she would have neither dreams nor expectations again. But still, she could not wait to return.

*

Tabitha feels heartened. She will have her lovely day of leisure. Perhaps even visit an art gallery after the Spanish Embassy. It was a long time since she had looked at painters' views on Beauty. She would have fun. She would. And anyway – she looked at Chloe – she had to keep her promise.

Only one thing niggled.

One very small thing.

Hardly anything at all, *really!*

Why did Chloe give each of them the *Thumbs Up* as they left?

She looks at Chloe. Chloe looks back innocently. Maybe thumbs up is the modern way?

'Well done, Chloe,' she says.

Chloe smiles, so sweetly.

'May I read you this?' she asks, holding up her *Beautician's Bible*.

Tabitha sighs.

'Of course, please do.'

So the trainee reads, in a firm, clear voice: 'Part of the responsibility of the beauty specialist is to sell what is needed to the person who needs it, and not decide for clients what they should spend, or how much they can afford, otherwise she is robbing the client of the pleasure of purchase ... '

She nods her head, heavy with significance, as she closes the book. 'Ann Gallant said that. I think she's blooming marvellous. Don't you?'

Tabitha nods.

Chloe has just quoted the Guru, so why this unease?

Mrs Spencer's collagen?

The Thumbs Up?

She traces the wonky cupid with her fingertip.

She shivers.

But the air in the salon is not remotely cold.

13

Now or never, Margery told herself as she approached the surgery. The days were continuing warm and golden, but they would give her no pleasure until her plan had been accomplished. She hoped he would set aside honour for the greater good – she certainly would. She clutched her cardigan tighter around her; it was the colour of honey and soft as a bee, and wearing it gave her courage.

Through the dear, familiar doorway she stepped, the beautician's voice in her ear: *'Give it all you've got.'* She fully intended to.

Reginald Postgate felt the unfamiliar pall of boredom. Sometimes his irreproachable gentlemanliness got him down and he yearned to brush a knee or touch a hand – dentistry being so tantalizingly intimate. This is why he had decided to specialize in older women, for he had once found himself looking yearningly at a plump young rosy throat and thinking it would be fun to bend and kiss it – with all the horrors of professional mayhem such an act could bring.

Even now, waiting for Margery, he shivered at the memory. But he still, dammit, felt *bored*. Mrs Postgate was rather more into curtains than she was into his body. Come to think of it, *he* was rather more into curtains than he was into *her* body. And mostly, given the golf and tennis and the adulation at work, that was acceptable. Today just seemed like the kind of day for having a little bit of fun. Nothing serious. He whistled. He found he was whistling 'Where the Bee Sucks' because it had been on Radio Two that morning – a rather nice, easy-listening version by the Mike Sammes Singers.

Margery heard it as she came through the door, and it was the signal she sought.

'I shall miss you – er – Miss – ,' said Reginald, as he came out to the reception area to greet her. And there was something in the placing of her feet, something in the curve of her proferred hand, something in the light in her eyes – which all added up to a little, a *very* little bit of fun.

'Margery please,' she said boldly. And she smiled at him so broadly that it made her ears ache.

Reginald Postgate nearly lost his resolve at the sight but he rallied, took her hand and looked into her eyes, 'Margery then.' He paused and said, more softly, 'Margery. I shall miss you very, very much.'

'And my teeth?' she found herself saying. It sounded rather odd.

'Those too,' he said, slightly puzzled at the somewhat offside nature of the statement.

Karen seemed to be having a mixture of a gargle and appendicitis.

Sometimes he could wish for a change of staff in that department, but she was his wife's niece and he would not under any circumstances disturb the domestic status quo. Generally, life was good. A little society, a little golf and tennis, and he was content. All he ever had to do was give Mrs Postgate another couple of catalogues to peruse, a free hand with the Visa card, and he could be gone for a week almost without her noticing.

But today Margery's adoring gaze tickled his boredom.

He ushered her into the surgery and sang 'Where The Bee Sucks' as he closed the door. Margery flopped into the chair. Now or Never, she told herself, and joined in with the words. She must startle him into submission. The pretty little beautician said that she should.

'Now lie back' he said when the duet was over, 'and let me take a little teeny look at you.'

He said it as if she were naked, and felt the throbbing of her pulse as his hand rested gently on her neck. He tested the teeth and then he tested the throb.

'All in order,' he said as he tapped. 'What a dear little honey hole.'

Eroticism is a strange phenomenon to the uninitiated.

Why the phrase honey hole should make Margery pull her knees together with a jerk was a mystery to her, and where Reginald got just the right words at just the right time, would, had he thought about it, have been just as much a mystery to him (and very possibly to Mrs Postgate too) – but so they both did, and it fused into an erotic thrust which made Margery pink with pleasure, and Reginald a good deal less bored than when he had first arrived at the surgery.

A little flirtation works wonders.

'I shall miss you too,' she said, emboldened by the knowledge that there was no going back. 'And I shall never think of honey or bees again without thinking of you.'

She looked into his upside-down eyes and he read the seductiveness of victim in hers.

'Oddly enough,' he said, looking into all her naked longing for him, 'oddly enough in olden days they used honey as a healer. The village tooth extractor would come along, pull the offending one, and then stuff honey in the hole to help it heal.'

He tapped her teeth again playfully. 'Not knowing, of course, that while it healed the hole left by one, it was already beginning to eat away and damage all the others. Either that, or he was a very shrewd practitioner ... ' He laughed, much taken with the idea. She loved to hear him laugh, watch those shoulders heave up and down, hear the bass notes; it was very masculine.

She sat up. 'Very amusing,' she said enthusiastically, seeing her cue. 'And did you know that bees read shapes and can pass on the information?'

Reginald had grown a little bored with this bee stuff of late, but today he was prepared to embrace it; anything to keep the game going.

'Tell me all you know,' he said, deepening his voice and speaking directly into her ear so that she squirmed with pleasure. He watched the pulse in her neck with fascination. He had never dared go quite this far before – it was thrilling – made you feel powerful – took you to the edge.

He forgot it was Margery at this point and went into a fantasy world where the woman in the chair beneath his hands was someone quite, quite different – all Margery saw was the light of something excited in his face. She thrust on.

'Yes, yes. An experimenter put sour food on a square shape and sweet food on a round shape, and the worker bees learned which was which and went back to the hive and told the others, so that they only came and took from the round shape. And then, when the experimenters swapped it around so that the sour was on the circle, the sweet was on the square, the bees continued to feed from the round.'

'How obedient,' said Reginald Postgate. He liked the idea of obedience.

'Very,' said Margery. And in that atom of a second she decided to go over the top. 'Narbonne or Sicily or Minorca are said to produce the best honey, *wild* honey that is, but I think the best honey to come from around here is clover.'

Not surprisingly, Reginald's eyes popped with surprise. 'In Knightsbridge?' he said.

'Not exactly – but not far, not far.' She put her hand beseechingly on his arm. 'Not far at all. Just a little way down the M4.' She dared to squeeze his forearm. 'I know a field where clover grows. We could go there, you and I ... '

Reginald was uncertain if this was the line of a song or not, and very nearly said, 'You hum the tune and I'll pick it up.' But instead, he brought his hot breath close to her neck and said, 'Tell me why' – closer to her neck – 'clover' – within lip-brushing distance – 'is the best.'

Margery very nearly passed out. This was a great deal easier than she had thought.

'Clover makes the best honey,' she began, and then she stopped and smiled. 'Ah no,' she said, 'you should judge for yourself.' Clever, she congratulated herself. 'Will you come?'

'Is it far?' he said, leaning wickedly against the wall and crossing his manly arms.

'Not far as the bee flies,' said Margery happily. 'And I would feed you hydromel in a horn and honey in a cake – if you would come and be my guest.'

The hydromel had been a bit tricky, but she had finally found a reasonable recipe for it in an 1883 encyclopaedia which also quoted it as Odin's favourite beverage. That it should be the number one favourite of the God of the Dead was not very edifying – apparently it was thirsty work keeping a charnel house – but she put this to one side in pursuit of the greater good: Reginald.

You needed water, egg whites, honey, cinnamon, ginger, mace, cloves, rosemary and yeast – all of which made quite an interesting fragrance in Margery's house. But it seemed to be bubbling all right in the airing cupboard. The horn, she would have to tell him when appropriate, was merely a romantic figure of speech. She beamed at him anew.

He gave her the benefit of his profile.

'It sounds wonderful,' he said, and then shrugged his usual sad smile, slowly turning his face towards her, 'but I have no time – busy, busy every day – '

'After surgery on Friday,' said Margery promptly.

'My wife ... ' he shrugged.

Margery winced.

He looked long and deep into her eyes, from the right way round, and almost laughed out loud. Margery hyperventilated. Reginald Postgate knew what it was like to be Errol Flynn.

'I shall take everything there by taxi. You would not need to bring a thing.'

'Sounds like – *heaven*,' he said, and gave another of his self-deprecating shrugs, which said, 'If only ... '

'It is very near the honey farm where we can Tell The Bees together. And they will tell *us* if anybody comes.' She fished around in her pocket and took out a piece of paper. 'I have drawn an exact map. You wouldn't go wrong. Will you come?'

He looked at her and smiled. 'I should love to,' he said.

'Oh *good!*' said Margery, and sat back relieved.

And then the buzzer of his intercom went.

He answered it.

Karen discussed a broken bridge with him, rather an urgent one.

'I'd better come out and have a look,' he said, dumping Errol Flynn and donning Reginald Postgate again. He turned to the smiling Margery.

'Rinse and spit and I'll see you in reception,' he said.

After she had rinsed and spat she put on her coat, humming happily to herself, 'You are my honey, honeysuckle ... ' and she knew the little beautician would be proud of her.

Out in reception Reginald was already scooping his arm around the frail shoulders of a woman of pensionable age.

He gave Margery a bright smile, the smile of one whose mind is elsewhere.

'See you on Friday at four,' she said softly.

He assumed it was an appointment. Then recollected it was the evening of the annual Practice barbecue, held at his home, for the best of his clients. Either way he nodded – his mind on the tricky bridgework.

Margery was perfectly happy.

'Will you come?' she repeated under her breath as she signed her last cheque at the reception desk. 'I'd *love* to,' she replied, remembering his every inflexion. She handed the payment to Karen and went on her way.

This time, waiting for the bus, she found she was humming 'The Bee's Wedding' – which, quite suddenly, seemed to be her most favourite piece of Mendelssohn in the whole world.

'I'd love to.'

He agreed.

Ah Margery, sorrow, sorrow.

For what he had forgotten to add, of course, was that little, all-powerful, all-destructive word – 'but'.

Followed by.

'I can't.'

14

At least, thought Caroline, they were on their own, even if Bernie did have that hunched look about his shoulders that boded no good. She was sitting on the window-ledge, staring out, waiting; he was standing by the kitchen door holding several plastic bags and looking decidedly miserable.

In the old days when Bernie had hunched shoulders like that she used to help him out. 'Come on,' she'd say, 'tell me about it.' She didn't this time.

His shoulders had gone up as soon as he saw her, and as soon as he saw that she was holding a cookery book. And her entire set of vertebrae had seized when *she* saw what he was holding: the plastic bags full of dinner-party food; the perky tail feathers of two brace of pheasants poking up; pink little onions pressing tight against the plastic. They had not even discussed the menu yet. Rita's *fait accompli.*

And she knew that he knew that she knew. That was what the shoulders were all about. People first, food second was her dinner-party motto. He knew that and would say that this dinner was too important to be ruined. She heard him put the bags down in the kitchen. She waited. He returned and came towards her, trying to look at ease.

'You're early tonight,' he said.

She swung off the window-ledge and kissed his mouth. Tense.

'I thought we'd better discuss the food for Friday,' she said, deciding to be cruel. 'See – I've brought my *Larousse.* What do you think they'd like? There's a wonderful starter in here made with lemons and yoghurt and tahini. What is tahini I wonder? And for the mains – we could give them a whole baked salmon – easy – '

He moved away.

There was a trilling of the doorbell, followed by the sound of a key in the lock and a little 'yoo-hoo', and Rita was in – fresh from the gym, golden hair shining, smiling face all rosy, every symmetrical detail of her perfect little body outlined in neat black lycra and finishing in dainty pristine trainers.

Caroline, instantly depressed, studied her. And suddenly perked up. This woman hadn't been anywhere *near* the fucking gym – she had just dressed the part. She was clean and sweet-smelling as if from a bath, and her make-up was exact, subtle, fresh. Caroline went to a gym. Caroline knew how women looked after a gym. This woman looked fresh as a morning daisy – a morning daisy one would willingly tread on with one's not-so-fresh boot.

If she had ever doubted the efficacy of booking a makeover at that beauty salon, those doubts now vanished. She needed every ounce of help she could get. This – this *creature* before her was *lethal* – absolutely *lethal*. Still – she might have a *little* bit of a game with Bernie now, before giving in. Who, she thought, could blame her? Not that tough little beautician, that was for sure. Why, she could almost feel her clapping her on the back and telling her to Go For It – a favourite phrase of hers, it seemed.

Rita was certainly setting up hostilities and Caroline would have to be swift. Even the trilling of the doorbell was a part of Rita's pincer. It was the concession Rita had made to Caroline's request, put through Bernie since it *was* his house, that his ex-wife should announce her presence before being let in, like anybody else.

Now all they got was the sharp noise of the bell, which usually made them jump, followed by the swiftest entry possible. Bernie had done his best. Dark thoughts might lurk in Caroline's heart, but she could do nothing about them. Except walk away from Bernie of course, and she was not prepared to do that – yet.

'Why hallo,' said Rita to Caroline, with infuriating surprise, 'you're early.' She turned and smiled at Bernie, caught her reflection in the mirror, and stood on tiptoe to pat her hair. Tiptoe to remind him of her weak and female tinyness. All Caroline could do was cheer herself up by reminding her brain to be on guard because scorpions, those deadly arachnids with lobster-like claws, could be female and tiny and there was nothing weak about them, nothing at all.

'Tea, Rita?' she said lightly.

But Rita was already there, saying, 'You sit down – I'll make it.'

And Caroline, who until then was unaware she had a violent side, gave a passable shoulder tackle and managed to win the try.

'No, no,' she said sweetly, '*I'll* make it, you sit down. You look *exhausted* after the gym.'

Rita's little smile sagged. 'Do I?' she said, and hopped to the mirror.

'Mmm,' said Caroline, filling the kettle. 'I think you may have overdone it. Don't you, Bernie?'

He agreed wholeheartedly, feeling it was safe.

'A bit drawn,' he said.

'Perhaps a spot more rouge?' called Caroline. 'Maybe it all came off on the aerobike?'

She refused to look at the bags and their contents. Waiting for the kettle to boil she kept up a cheerful chattering with Bernie that would not be easy for Rita to penetrate.

Rita popped her head round the kitchen door and gave a little Oh! of delight, clapping her hands. She fell upon the plastic bags as if they were Christmas stockings. Caroline had never seen such a disgustingly amateur piece of quasi-paedophile's delight. Rita went from thirty-five to about eight in less than a picosecond: Violet Elizabeth Bott could have done no better. All she needed was the lisp.

She knelt at the bags and took out celery heads, pimentos, the fronding herbs, an artichoke – and called to Bernie, 'Well done! How lovely, *lovely!*' And then to Caroline, *sotto voce*: 'He was always so good at doing the shopping ... '

With shaking hand Caroline poured out three cups of tea, wishing she had the odd spoonful of strychnine about her person, and shoved one steaming beverage as close to Rita's nose as she dared, sloshing as much as possible on to the lycra. In the sitting-room Bernie smiled at her nervously, took the proferred tea, and sat down in a corner of the room, as far away from her as possible.

Caroline pursued him. He cowered. She knew that this was no way to win this particular battle. Bernie was not one for arguments, let alone the pyrotechnics of a hearty row. Rita might step down and not come to dinner, let alone cook the sodding thing, but it would be a Pyrrhic victory.

Caroline took the only route possible under the circumstances. She cradled Bernie's cheek in her hand, bent and tickled his ear with her tongue, and said in a voice warm with affection: 'So, what is Rita going to cook for us on Friday?'

And Bernie, looking as relieved as if he had an excess of air let out of him, reached and squeezed her thigh and said, 'You don't mind?'

Caroline crossed everything and said, 'Not at all.' She felt Rita's presence as her hackles rose.

'I'll need him to help me in the kitchen,' said Violet Elizabeth Bott, a little too sharply.

'I'll need him for about a couple of hours in the afternoon first,' said Caroline firmly.

'Oh that's all right,' said the munificent Rita. 'We'll get everything done the night before and leave it ready. I'm in Bournemouth on Friday, cake icing. I must say you could have chosen a more convenient date.'

Bernie sat there looking from one to the other as they doled out his time. He sipped his tea, and tried to concentrate, which was hard after what Caroline had done to his ear.

'I'll bring the wine,' said Caroline, wanting to contribute something that could not go wrong.

'No need,' said Rita, 'I've ordered it from my wine-merchant friend. He gives me a very good deal.'

'Fizzy fucking water, then?' Caroline muttered under her breath, but out loud said, still smiling, 'Remember last time I cooked, Bernie? Those awful crabs, the gloopy gnocchi?'

He smiled and nodded, and added cheerfully, 'Those dreadful sunken islands,' so that Caroline nearly brained him.

But she took a grip. This was no time for self-indulgence.

'And remember afterwards,' she said, 'when they'd all gone home? How you laid me down on the table and covered me with the whipped cream and then licked it off very slowly? You said I was the best pud you'd ever had … '

Bernie took at pull at his tea as if it were raw whisky.

Rita gave a little chirrup that could have been amusement but might have been disgust, and returned to the food bags, exclaiming as each new item was brought forth.

'I'm so looking forward to cooking for you properly again,' she called. 'Remember how you used to love it when I brought my little offerings home for you, Bern?'

Little offerings? thought Caroline, wishing to vomit.

Bernie could not reply, for in Rita's absence Caroline had taken the opportunity to drape herself across his lap and clamp his mouth very positively to her own. Battle Plan A seemed to be moving along satisfactorily.

She could hear the little beautician urging her on.

Give him more tongue, she seemed to hear.

So she did.

15

No phone-call for Gemma. And Megan's sympathy had become sickening by the time Monday morning arrived. So much so that Gemma was glad to climb into her neat navy suit, button her white cuffs and drive off to the clients on her list.

As soon as she got in the car she felt, if not cheered, at least liberated. If Megan had given her one more sympathetic grunt, or offered her one more milky cup of cocoa, she would have thrown up. One thing to tell a friend you are feeling vulnerable, quite another to pretend you are not and have them realize it anyway. Especially after that bloody little beautician talked about her as if she needed excavating.

Just about the only thing that kept Gemma from going off the deep end was her pact with God (or the Devil) to have Jim for retribution. As she negotiated the traffic on the South Circular she hoped with all her heart that the deed would not be necessary. Apart from anything else, she didn't remotely *fancy* him, and she rather wished – as the likelihood of the required telephone call grew more and more remote – that she had chosen crawling to Canterbury barefoot as penance, which she would have much preferred.

She closed her eyes and pictured Jim and herself At It. It was not a pretty thought.

M. Le Château. She would be really good for him; she just knew it. Mature with a sense of fun – just what he needed. She braked for a woman with a pushchair. Always amusing the way they shove those things out into the traffic first, she thought. If the children survive, it must be safe for the parents to cross.

She had even begun to dream about him. Curious dreams in which she appeared in floaty white frocks or gorgeous taffeta gowns, walking along the crenellations of a building. He held her hand, speaking low. In each dream Gemma's newly beautified face glowed in the moonlight, perfectly lit, not a line in sight and clear-eyed with happiness. Quite obviously he had not only taken her to his château and made a woman of her, but he had paid off her credit cards as well. In the dream she was happy; when she woke she was miserable.

Hence Megan's overweening sympathy. *More Fool You*, she read in every line of her flat-mate's expression, *for I have a man, and you do not*.

M. Le Château, telephone me please.

The day, like all days recently, was slow. Well, it was hardly an inspiring job in the first place. You were trading on other people's hopes or fears when you did what she did; either you sold them a golden future, or you insured them against the loss of one. Either way, it was to do with hope, and hope was always in the future. Hope was never now. And there were too many bloody couples in the world – look at them all out there just *Being*.

She drove aggressively to see if that would buck her up. Sometimes she played a game, selecting a particularly pompous-looking young male driver and nudging right up close behind him so that he had to drive a bit faster than he wanted – than the traffic in front of him allowed – and check his mirror constantly with a nervous, darting look. Or else he had to grow horns and Not Take That Sort Of Thing From Anybody and be even more aggressive than she.

Amusing. Dangerous occasionally – but life was too bland – and it was never seriously dangerous – not in London traffic where thirty miles an hour was speed.

But today she could not even raise the steam for that, and she let a perfectly selectable Vauxhall Astra with coathook and jacket go dreaming on – of the area manager's job, the little house in Chorley Wood, and the holiday to come in Benidorm.

In the secret recesses of her soul, even that lot didn't sound too bad.

The Loire, though! That, of course, was the insidious thing about hope – it fed the arteries of desire, swelled the veins with dreams and pumped up the capillaries all ready for action. And she'd got it circulating through her, making her perk up at the thought, die away when she suppressed it.

Telephone please.

Swinging off the South Circular at last, she thought that if she were going to cede the joy of life, she'd rather do it stuck in a loveless marriage amid crenellations in the heart of the Loire, than in Chorley Wood.

She indicated and moved into the outside lane. South London, here I come, she thought grimly.

Deeply depressing thought.

The *Today* programme was discussing the Equal Opportunities Commission. Such poppycock! All it meant was that in the office you had to be ready to swing a right hook when a chap spotted the unmistakeable outline of a bra clasp beneath your shirt, and had the liberated thought that it would be fun to twang it. This game had become noticeably more prevalent since the resurgence of Wonderbras. Gemma knew exactly what she would do when the time came and her bra elastic went Wham! After the right hook, and while his mind was on his throbbing proboscis, she would twang the elastic of his underpants and smile winsomely as she cried out Snap!

She switched off the irritating pronouncing voices. Of course she wouldn't. Not really. Jobs were too scarce. It would have all been so different with M. Le Château. Only it wouldn't now. She sighed. Let the day begin. First call a Lambeth woman, recently widowed, needing pension advice. Dizzy, glorious heights. If she has dark hair, he will ring. If she has light hair, he will not.

The woman was grey. 'Damn,' said Gemma when the door was opened to her.

'I beg your pardon?' said the elderly client.

And so you should, thought Gemma sourly. Perhaps she should pass on the card for Tabitha's Beauty Parlour. Might as well – it was beginning to look increasingly as if she wouldn't need it after all.

Lambeth, Mitcham, Raynes Park, Streatham and home. A real touch of the Eldorados. She climbed the stairs. He would not have rung – he was not going to ring. And she might just as well abandon all thoughts of having a makeover to go for the kill. Depressing. She had not realized how *very* much she missed the whole business of pupa into butterfly and wearing the ornaments of seduction. But you couldn't clap with one hand.

She knew that if she went and had a makeover just for herself, and then came back to the silent, empty flat (devoid of Megan's overnight bag) she would merely be pathetic. Somebody famous once said To Be is to Belong. True, she thought, and pushed open the door.

There are some to whom bells are merely the sound of the Angelus, the summons to prayer. There are some who would mock poor Quasimodo as he swings through the belfry, crying with pain, in search of a way to be as beautiful as the sonorous sound. And others, of course, who will deny the rumour that each death knell in the land Tolls For Thee and say they never heard one.

But those effects are nothing in comparison with the profound experience awaiting Gemma as she turned the key in her lock, pushed open the door, and heard that first, familiar, beloved ping, that denoted the machine was about to spring into life.

She stopped, then, galvanized, she ran, took three full breaths and let it ring three times, before picking up the receiver and saying, cool and languorous as any couch-curled female, 'Mmm? Hallo.' And giving her number.

He did not apologize. And Gemma decided this was not rude: it was cool. A man at ease. He had been busy. Which explained everything. Busy, of course. And he was just checking everything was still on.

'Oh yes,' she said easily. 'And I can be late. In case we want to – um – go on somewhere afterwards.' Why beat about the bush?

'So can I,' he said.

She dropped her voice and said, 'Good.'

'I'm looking forward to it,' they both said in unison, and the telephone receiver was replaced.

Technology.

Wonderful, beautiful thing.

When Megan arrived with Jim in the kitchen, Gemma dared to look him up and down. He, stringbean, staring floorwards, cords still muddied at the bottom over large black outdoor boots, had the air of a man condemned. But not, Oh not, by me, thought Gemma. Thank you God, she muttered. I will be good in future.

Last chance, last chance, came whispering through her mind. 'Did you speak?' she said testily to the voice.

'No,' said Jim, who was sitting rather cautiously at the other end of the kitchen table, about as far from her as he could get.

'Sorry,' she said. 'Just thinking out loud.'

Later, when Megan returned, she found Gemma grunting her way through crunchies and sit-ups on the floor, with weights from the kitchen scales sellotaped to her ankles.

'Christ,' was all Megan could find to say. 'I hope he's really worth it.'

Gemma smiled to herself, despite the pain. Of course he was.

If she'd had any puff left she might have said that he was a good deal more worth it than Jim. But she couldn't speak. A crunchie too far, she thought, and laughed her socks off.

Life.

Hope.

Go for the burn.

Go for the *Beauty Parlour!*

16

The cupid has been stuck back crookedly. Tabitha pushes at it idly with her fingers but it is held fast, apparently blowing its trumpet up the unsuspecting dimpled rear of another little cherub in front. She pushes again, feebly.

'Superglue!' calls Chloe proudly from the other end of the salon. 'No end to its uses.' And clatter, clatter, bustle, bustle she goes, Preparing The Way.

Tabitha could wish it had been employed momentarily on all the other items in the salon which have been moved, turned, placed awry in Chloe's current efforts to Be Prepared. She whisks her dainty self around the place like a shining pin-ball, hitting her target, moving on, hitting the next, until Tabitha feels quite dizzy.

There is a fan of magazines on the low table where once the jade plant stood; cushions that offered themselves as a delicious nest of artfully arranged marshmallows were now scattered haphazardly in the manner Chloe calls *casual*.

Tabitha, resisting interference, nevertheless balked at the cassette entitled 'Up Yours' and whose songs seemed, largely, to be all about sucking. Chloe substituted Madonna for three bars, but this was even more swiftly rejected; sucking was tame by comparison. Chloe gave in to Tabitha without a grudge. Perhaps Tabitha had a point – it would be no good if the client started tapping her toes or getting into the rhythm while she was wearing a mask or having her nails painted. Sometimes it paid to listen.

'Thanks,' she said, 'for the advice.'

Have faith, thinks Tabitha, your protégée is *all right*.

Chloe now begins the final joy, busying herself with her trolley, which she calls her vanitory unit, and the rattling and clunking denote serious activity. Tabitha watches her and realizes that Chloe is like a child with a doll's house.

Towels are pulled out of cupboards and the remainder pushed back indiscriminately. Three robes hang over a chairback, draping their empty pink sleeves forlornly across the eau-de-Nil. Tabitha has a momentary, terrible vision of them actually containing forlornly draped clients – a vision she banishes. Those three women looked perfectly capable and realistic. They knew what they were coming here for, and they knew what they were getting. A Makeover. Nothing more, nothing less.

Besides, Betty had agreed to come in and stand by. An offer which did not please Chloe at all; in fact she sulked for a while.

She wanted Jo-Jo to come. But on this, Tabitha stood firm. A bad influence that one. She shudders to think of it. Betty might be a bit ancient but she had the right gentility. Jo-Jo was to Beauty Parlours what Alternative Comedians were to the Townswomen's Guild. Maybe even worse. Thinking about it, *certainly* even worse. She would prefer not to think about it and puffs up the satin swathes of the blinds vigorously. Outside it is another glorious summer's day. Lucky her to be out roaming free.

She looks around the salon. Perhaps warm ice-cream does hit the mark. But it is pretty and feminine, and flatters all the senses. The chandelier catches a sunbeam – so fetching that Venetian glass – so charming the little angels in the frieze – just like a bit of paradise. But even as she thinks this, out of the corner of her eye she notices again that cupid and the cheeky obscenity of its trumpet. Thank God Jo-Jo is *not* coming – she'd spot it straight away and point it out to the customers.

Jo-Jo! Oh *dear*.

Jo-Jo is Chloe's Antipodean Beautician friend. Originally here to do a Remedial Camouflage Diploma for her fellow-countrywomen's rocketing carcinoma rate – and more's the pity, never gone back. Now settled here, she speaks proudly of her homeland's beauty salons and thinks Tabitha should Get Real. She has many stories to tell of a Getting Real nature, apparently, which Chloe absorbs with relish. Tabitha considers her a youthful incubus so far as the gentling services of the Boudoir are concerned and would, if she could, ban Chloe from the taint of her, just like the curry. But that would be tyranny – it is not in her nature.

Hence Betty. Rather go back in time than forward to one such as that.

'Jo-Jo was really sorry she wasn't needed,' calls Chloe.

Can the girl read minds? Her beauty is certainly particularly ethereal today.

'Really?' says Tabitha noncommitally, giving the immutable cupid one last hopeless yank.

'I said she shouldn't mind.'

'Quite.'

'She told me a good story about lipstick.'

'Chloe,' says Tabitha warningly.

'I wasn't planning on telling it to the clients,' says Chloe defensively, crossing her pretty fingers.

'Just remember Mrs Pargeter and Mrs Baker.'

Chloe still looks defensive. '*Quite*,' she replies, finding satisfaction in the mimicry.

Tabitha raises an eyebrow. 'Not to mention Miss O'Rourke.'

That's not fair, thinks Chloe, who casts down her beautiful lashes and looks the perfect picture of contrition.

'That's where your Jo-Jo stories can get you ...'

Poor Miss O'Rourke.

The unspeakable Antipodean was banned from the premises after that.

Poor, *poor* Miss O'Rourke.

Her of all people. A twice-a-month manicure who sold whisks for a living and who, being a young woman of startlingly pure mien, was not up to much excitement and even found the Bible too raunchy. She was also a good Catholic; sexual aberrations were not part of her conversational agenda and were certainly not the kind of subjects she expected to learn about in Tabitha's Beauty Parlour. To her Tabitha's Beauty Parlour was as much a sanctified retreat as her church.

But this was a little on the abstruse side for Chloe who, much taken with Jo-Jo's tale, felt obliged to pass it on. She had always thought this particular twice-a-month manicure needed a good laugh. She would give Miss O'Rourke the full blast and benefit; a little earthy good humour was just what was needed to tickle her up. If the Antipodean Beautician spared nothing in the telling to Chloe, Chloe – a generous girl in many ways – spared nothing in the passing of it on.

Miss O'Rourke, who had arrived looking slightly sleepy and with eyes of a standard shape and size, gradually developed an ocular paleness and circularity not dissimilar to polo mints. Chloe took this as a remarkably good sign that the tickling up was a success. It was, after all, a very good story. Even if Chloe said so herself.

Antipodean Jo-Jo, newly come to Sydney from the Wild and Woolly West, was working in a salon in that city. One day the salon's owner said that they were going to be working flat out on depilations for the next couple of weeks, and if anyone wanted it, there was plenty of overtime. Jo-Jo, already intent on coming to London, did indeed want it – and put her name down. Only to find that instead of the rarified feminine atmosphere usually prevailing in Diana's Dainty Box, the place was suddenly swarming, after hours, with men.

Not, it is true, Real Men. Not men who would be ashamed to be caught eating quiche, and certainly not the kind of men whose realness in terms of their desire for women might encompass a few beers on a Saturday night followed by stallion notions with rubber duck reality. No – *these* were men who loved men – or at least men who loved to attract men – and they wanted to attract in the most aesthetic and delightful way that they could – with a view to cramming in (sic) as much sex as possible, while having the time of their lives in the Sydney Carnival.

According to Jo-Jo the Sydney Carnival is legend. The Sydney Carnival makes the Rio Mardi Gras look like a pub with no beer; the Sydney Carnival is for Real Gays with plumage on their minds and a great deal of interest in physical gratification. Rubber shares soar. Tourists and straights come to snap, camcord, goggle. The male participants come to look like the Bluebell Girls and to behave like rabbits. The links between the desire and the spasm were the overtiming beauticians, hot wax at the ready to smooth, so to speak, the Gay Bluebell Path.

Jo-Jo told the giggling Chloe, and Chloe passed it on to the goggling Miss O'Rourke, how the Antipodean Beautician would wax the backs, bums and legbacks of queues of beautifully proportioned men, all of whom lay face down on her couch and none of whom, surprisingly, required anything but their rears rendered hairless. The Antipodean Beautician offered to do their fronts too – but the men, gritting their teeth at the removal of a rich growth of buttock hair, stoutly refused.

They had, Jo-Jo assured Chloe and Chloe assured Miss O'Rourke, every inch of hair removed from their rearward viewpoint and were stoical about the pain. 'Now!' they would cry, and their buried screams would vibrate through the couch, throughout the salon. Waxed, plucked and lotioned they left the salon as smooth and shiny as mythological woman. But only from behind.

Jo-Jo being an inquisitive Antipodean, a commendable Australian trait, finally cracked. 'Why?' she asked a particularly Ramboesque pair of haunches, 'do you only have your backs done? Why not your fronts? Don't you want them to be smooth and beautiful too?'

She had, you may remember, just come to the city.

Ramboesque haunches shifted on the couch, twisted his neck, looked up at her with fluttering eyelashes that hid eyes heavy with sarcasm and said, 'Because, dear, they never look at the fronts when they're fucking the backs. Why take more pain than we've got to? Silly bitch.'

At which point both teller and listener were both supposed to fall about laughing. Chloe certainly gave it the full Scheherazade treatment. But Miss O'Rourke, instead of falling about laughing, went completely white and absolutely rigid, feeling she was in the presence of the Anti-Christ. Despite having one hand stuck in the cuticle softening pot, she rapidly made a sign of the cross and began invoking quite a lot of Latin.

Chloe, to whom Latin was not second nature, mistook this for lack of comprehension and was just spelling out the main thrust for a second time when Tabitha, fortunately now free, passed by cubicle number two. On the fairly sound assumption that – generally speaking – clients tended not to go casting out devils in a salon situation, she came to the rescue. Comfrey tea was produced, the jungle music turned up, and the manicure finished in silence, and on a pair of hands that were going to wobble with their whisks all day.

Tabitha recoils. And now Chloe says she has heard another one, about *lipstick!* Tabitha shudders. No more tales of Jo-Jo. Never again. But can she be sure? Just for a foolish moment Tabitha thinks that maybe she could hide herself away somewhere, perhaps in the broom cupboard, so that if anything untoward *does* occur she can come to the client's rescue.

But reality shakes its head. She could hardly leap out at the first intimation of anything unseemly, now could she? One thing for a makeover to be lying on the couch feeling a little on the wound-up side because the Trainee is cutting a verbal dash with raunchy Jo-Jos; *quite* another to have the Beautician suddenly leap out of a dark cupboard screaming '*J'accuse, J'accuse.*'

No, she must leave Chloe to it as promised. And it will be All Right.

'Remember,' she says to her protégée as she wheels her vanitory unit towards her for inspection. 'Remember that within the intimacies of the boudoir there is a veil of silken knowledge between Server and Served. The true Beautician will read her client as a living book – she will know her – she will not impose gauds where there should be subtleties, nor constraints where there should be freedom. And above all, she will know that the bond begins and ends at the salon door.'

Chloe, eyes flicking back and forth at the display she has just created, nods. Her mind is only half engaged. She is building up to telling Tabitha something Very Important. Otto has been kind. Well, in *some* respects he has been kind, though there were *certain* practices of his ... However, he was prepared to be generous if she was, and everything was a trade really. She rather felt she had the better part of the bargain. She smiled and cleared her throat.

'Tabitha?' she said in a sweet, clear voice, 'I have something to tell you.'

Tabitha immediately thinks Chloe is pregnant and sits down. To begin all over again with someone new, just when she is ready to retire. Just when 'Una Paloma Blanca' coos to her, when 'Viva Espagna' clicks its castanets, when Time has turned porcelain to paper. Cells that do not renew. Now this. It is too cruel.

'What?' she says sharply. But she is sure she knows.

'Tabitha – if you were ever – I mean – should you decide to – that is – if you are going to sell the salon – I would like to buy it off you.'

Perhaps, thinks Tabitha, I do *not* know.

'What?'

Chloe repeats it more succinctly: 'I have enough money to buy the salon.'

'How?' says Tabitha, amazed.

'Tightened my belt,' says Chloe. That bit at least was true, she thought.

Tabitha is touched. Chloe seemed the kind of girl for whom belt-

114

tightening would never be invoked for anything, save the illustrating of a neat little waist.

'You're not pregnant?'

'Oh no,' says Chloe unabashed. 'We use – er – ' She realizes what the question was, draws herself up with dignity. 'Certainly *not*.'

Tabitha thinks she must be losing her grip. How could she have thought such a thing; how indelicate to have mentioned it.

'Shall we check your trolley?' she asks.

'Yes please,' says Chloe humbly. 'And you'll think about the other?'

'I certainly shall,' says Tabitha. And she certainly will. It would be the perfect solution to everything. *Perfect*. She looks at Chloe. Chloe is beautiful. She smiles at her. Encouragingly.

Pink cards?

Chloe nods.

These strawberry-pink cards look as official as medical records. They are divided into categories so that no possible skin condition, aberrant or otherwise, can escape detection. When a client sees these she understands, perhaps for the first time, the seriousness of her case:

Name of doctor
Smoke
Drink
On medication
Asthma, Hepatitis, Diabetes, Allergies
Skin assessment
Seborrhoea
Open pores
Blocked pores
Comedones
Acne
Delicate
Dry
Dehydrated
Mature
Ageing (not above fifty to be written down even if they are)
Suntan
Pigmentation

Dilated capillaries
Skintags
Moles
Scars
Slack
Superfluous hair

This is Tabitha's invention. In order for it to be completed the client must be stretched out on the couch while the Beautician pinches a little of the facial skin to feel its elasticity, judge its sheen for collagen levels. She will then cleanse the face, scrutinize it under bright lights with a magnifying glass, at which point every client will become deeply apologetic. Here, Tabitha suggests, it is allowable for the Beautician to tut. Tut tut tut. And they will be ashamed.

The Beautician will then smile encouragingly and explain that the condition of the skin is controlled by both physiological factors, such as diet, skin-care routine, poor health, bad work environment; and emotional factors, such as stress, anxiety, general depression, fatigue.

The categories of diagnosis being:

Age
Pigmentation
Skin imperfections
Skin balance (natural oils and moisture)
Skin temperature
Acid/Alkaline

The main assessment of emotional factors being:

Age
Need to please
Loneliness
Insecurity
Vulnerability
Low self-esteem
(Sex/Love/Men not shown)

Once their pink card is filled out they will exist in salon terms. And they will feel a touch of humility about themselves, the first step towards redemption.

Why then, Tabitha finds herself wondering as she looks at the strawberry-pink cards, did those three women go away so light of step, with smiling faces. Where was the humility in that?

The Thumbs Up?

Worrying.

She will never know. The broom cupboard not being an option, Tabitha reconciles herself to never knowing. Out she must go, and soon, and leave the girl to her clients. How delightful she looks as she counts off the contents of her trolley on the tips of her pretty little fingers. Hands, perhaps more than any other part of the female body, save elbows and knees, denote the passing of age. Tabitha's have just begun to show signs. Chloe's sparkle in their smooth whiteness. To everything there is a season, and a time to every purpose.

Chloe mutters to herself as she checks each item:

Cleansing milk for dry skin (nutrient emulsion)
Cleansing milk for greasy skin (cucumber, lemon)
Cleansing cream for mature or delicate complexions
Tonic for refining, normal
Tonic for refining, delicate
Astringent for oily, unblemished
Astringent for disturbed, blemished, seborrhoea

On it goes, so much to get right:

Lash extension kit
Foundations
Powders
Lipsticks
Eye make-up
Cheek blushers
Shaders

'All done,' she says.

'Sure?' says Tabitha.

Chloe looks, checks, nods.

'And your mask mixing lotions?'

Sod it, thinks Chloe. Out loud she says, 'Oh dash!' another of Tabitha's favourites, and collects them up.

Time.

The salon is silent save for the musical tinkling of water on foliage.

The air smells prettily of verbena.

The pink and cream surroundings glow in the diffused sunlight.

The Venetian glass gleams, eternally beautiful. Tabitha looks from it to Chloe, remembers for a fleeting moment the Venetian Giorgione, has the sensation known colloquially as someone walking over my grave – and waits for Betty to arrive.

The hour is nigh.

Escape.

At any price?

Ping!

Tabitha jumps.

But it is only Chloe moving the timer aside to open her *Beautician's Bible*:

Demonstration is a wonderful way to promote the beauty therapy business … A technically qualified beauty therapist with a full knowledge at her fingertips can make the audience believe that almost anything is possible. This feeling can then be converted into real salon or cosmetic sales revenue if the opportunity is grasped.

'Yup,' says Chloe happily. 'I'll go with that.'

Nothing wrong there, thinks Tabitha firmly, nothing wrong at *all*. *It is* a business they are running, after all.

And the other thought that crosses her mind is that it is not too late to ring the three women up and cancel them. But of course she doesn't.

I must be getting jealous in my old age, she decides. After all, these women are only coming in to have their *faces* made over, not their *lives* …

17

Margery crossed to her wardrobe. Somewhere in his house Reginald Postgate would be waking and dressing and she wondered what he would wear. She had never seen him in anything but his Dental Regalia and it was hard to imagine him in shirt and trousers.

Or, as the little beautician had said with a wink, *out* of them.

From the wardrobe she at last took the gingham frock. It rustled and floated as she swung it off the rail, swished seductively as she gave it a whirl around the room, crackled excitingly as she held it up to her chin before the mirror. When she smiled she saw that she was really quite beautiful against the pretty lilac checks. As that young lady at the salon said, 'Give It All You've Got. Wear something exciting – married men get into a rut. Leave me to do the rest.' Margery was very happy to oblige.

The taxi was due at any minute. She folded the dress very carefully and placed it, with as much reverence as if it were a bridal gown, into a large plastic bag. The hallway was almost full. Baskets, bags, boxes lined the way to the front door.

Margery went over her list one more time: pots of honey, the honey cakes, special honey to sweeten his tea, and the hydromel, which looked a bit funny but fizzed encouragingly and smelled wonderful – all yeasty and sweet like a warm summer's night. There were honey sandwiches, honey biscuits and honey-glazed ham; she had even found little golden tomatoes, honey sweets, and a circular white tablecloth with a motif of honeybees.

All this, she thought happily, was Giving Him What He Wants. The next best thing to having a hive to nestle in.

Beaming at the sunkissed world she gave the name of the Beauty Parlour to the taxi driver and said, leaning back, that after today she would never be the same again.

*

Caroline had not slept well. The night before she had been to see a film – part of Feminist Fortnight at the NFT. The film was about women bandits, living in the Indian hills, who selected only male travellers as their robbers' meat. Literally. For not only did they steal from them, but they also salted them down and, apparently, ate them. The point being that these bandits were now liberated women, free from the domestic drudgery of washday in the Ganges or sweating over a hot khali.

All Caroline could do was think of Bernie and Rita sweating over a hot Le Creuset together. There was much to be said for domestic drudgery. Certainly as much as might be found in salting down a bloke or two for the rainy season, or using his rendered grease for hair lotion and facial moisturizers. Which, apparently, the bandits – in a heartwarming display of liberated good housewifery – did too.

Bernie had rung to wish her goodnight, ending the call abruptly by saying, 'Well, I'll go now. You need your beauty sleep.'

Needed her Beauty Sleep? He was beginning to find her unattractive already? He had never said such a thing before.

The little beautician was right. Her plan was brave and perfect; so wicked it took your breath away, so daring it made those Bandits look like Rupert Bear.

She sank back on the pillows. Daring it was. But did *she* dare?

And she sat up again.

Did Boudicca dare? Did Boudicca hit the Romans where it hurt?

She did.

Did those Indian woman, crunching on the odd male femur, fight back?

They did.

Who then was she, Caroline, to falter? Shouldn't she, Caroline, follow her sisters and Have A Go?

She should.

The telephone beeped. That would be Bernie. On the dot of eight, so he must be feeling nervous. She answered it in a friendly, sleepy voice and he sounded relieved.

He was relieved. The fact that he had been preparing a dinner party with his ex-wife and without his lover the night before, had not escaped him. The fact that this was not, perhaps, the most tactful way to carry on with one's lover, had also not escaped him. Far from escaping him, it had settled round his neck like a millstone – the very pheasants themselves might have been a couple of brace of albatross, so heavy did he feel as he sewed up their bottoms.

And now here was Caroline being her usual nice, friendly self. Phew!

'Get everything done?'

'Yes. Rita's very efficient.'

Caroline chewed the pillow.

'What's the final menu?'

Bernie told her, beginning with the ceviche.

'Sounds heaven,' said Caroline, making pencil notes. 'And then?'

'The pheasants. We – well, she –' – Caroline did not help him out – 'stuffed them with grapes and walnuts and made a kind of paste.'

'Mmm,' said Caroline, writing fast. 'I see, STUFFED them.'

He swallowed.

'Vegetables?'

'Cold roast peppers in olive oil, baby peas, new potatoes, then an artichoke salad with balsamic dressing.'

I'll balsamic her, thought Caroline, saying loudly 'BALLSamic'.

She scribbled away. 'Pudding?'

'My favourite,' he said, without thinking.

Her heart twisted, because she did not know what it was. 'Really?' she said, voice as light as thistledown, and she waited.

'Pear and almond tart.'

'Pear and almond TART,' repeated Caroline, writing furiously. 'Anything else?'

'No. She's got the wine. Red and white burgundies. Left it up to her. She's good at that sort of thing.'

'FUCK HER EYEBALLS,' Caroline found she was writing all over the page.

'We may run out.'

'I'm sure we won't.'

'Don't bet on it,' she muttered.

'What?'

'Oh good,' she said. 'What fun.'

Even to Bernie's willing ears, this sounded odd. He did not really understand Caroline's attitude to what was, after all, just friendship with Rita. Rita had done a brilliant job on his behalf and, as she pointed out, if Caroline was going to be jealous then it wasn't a very sound basis. He could be *Chairman* of the Photographic Society if he liked, Rita said. Responsibility. Good for him. After all, life couldn't be all fun.

'Fun?' said Bernie cautiously.

'Fun,' said Caroline positively. 'Much more fun.'

'I'm glad you understand. About the Chairmanship. Rita suggested it.'

So those are her battle lines, she thought. She smiled. Wickedly. '*Il faut cultiver notre jardin!*' she said. 'Darling.'

'Pardon?' said Bernie.

'Voltaire, *Candide*. You should read it.' She remembered the little beautician. Voltaire from her mouth certainly had a new ring to it. One could slip back into him any day.

'I'll see you this afternoon at the house,' she said. 'Can't wait.'

The truth was, neither could Bernie. There was no doubt one felt the slightest bit hampered in matters of the bedroom if an ex-wife was likely to pop in.

'Me too,' he said fervently.

At least that was on target.

She leapt out of bed. She would do it; she would do it. It was a waste of a very good idea otherwise. And she had better get going because she had a little bit of shopping to do before school.

Clutching a small plastic bag, she let herself into Bernie's house about an hour before he was due home. She went straight to the kitchen. Later, she let herself out of Bernie's house, still clutching the small plastic bag, which she squashed down deep into a litter bin. She then returned to Bernie's house, arriving on the doorstep just as he did.

'Come and see,' he said excitedly. And he showed her the food with pride.

Such a prettily prepared ceviche, all innocent in its clingfilm.

Such plumply stuffed pheasants, coldly awaiting roasting, neatly stitched-up tight little bottoms.

The peas, so prettily snuggling up to the pearly little potatoes.

The salad so daintily arranged, with its jug of balsamic dressing standing sentry – aromatic perfection.

Miraculously pretty the tart, with its pears so fat and white, the almonds so evenly browned, the crust so crisply glittering.

Made your mouth water.

'It all looks splendid,' said Caroline enthusiastically.

'Oh it will be,' said Bernie. 'Rita's never let me down yet.'

'No?' said Caroline indulgently. 'Well, that's good.' She shut the refrigerator door. 'Something about those pheasants' bums,' she murmured in his ear, 'reminds me of her. Now let's go to bed.'

Surreptitiously she looked at her watch. Wouldn't do to be late for the Beauty Parlour.

*

Gemma sat in the bath singing. Something told her that tonight she would win. Even her naked body looked perkier. Gravity, that nasty thing discovered by the misogynistic Mr Newton, seemed to have developed another law all of its own, and retracted a little. Nose, chin, breasts all appeared to be uplifted once more. Amazing, she conceded to the sponge, what a bit of hope can bring.

Who, she had asked the Wandsworth skyline when she had indulged in that ropey Martell, will close my eyes and hold my hand and miss me when I go? And the bobbing daffodil dead-heads had not had a satisfactory answer. If Jim had dared to spend more than half a minute in the flat he would have refitted the window-box – but he hadn't, and so they wobbled about in the various breezes on offer, desiccated *memento mori*. No longer. From tonight it would all be different.

Megan banged on the door. Gemma sang louder. Usually it was Megan getting ready for a night out with Jim, and Gemma who sat around having no one to get ready for. 'Up Yours', she sang to the tune of 'My Way', and sank further under the bubbles. Nothing could go wrong. As the little beautician said.

Megan banged again. Gemma knew she was miffed. Not only because of the bathroom being occupied but – well – because Gemma had not behaved very well the night before.

Jim had arrived early, and just for once he had to wait while Megan finished changing. And if she hadn't settled him down on the settee so smugly – a human version of the sponge-bag really – Gemma would have more or less ignored him. As it was, with his hands clutching and unclutching his knees and his whole manner being one of desperate unease, well – it was too easy really.

Gemma began talking about the beauty parlour. Describing its pinkness and its smells, describing some of the intimate practices on offer. Jim's eyes began – she could swear – to revolve.

'You shouldn't really be privy to any of this,' she said knowingly. 'It's girl talk.'

Megan being out of the room, Gemma moved the pouffe a little bit closer to his stolid brogues and described the Beautiful Chloe. Described how the Beautiful Chloe had pinched and stroked her flesh and then moved on to the much more interesting subject of the way women, and Gemma in particular, should handle their men.

Basically, the message was to keep it light at any cost and don't say you have hopes or dreams or feelings. Pretty Draconian, but she had argued the case convincingly.

She felt like teasing. Was the Beautiful Chloe right, she wanted to know? His eyes picked up velocity. 'Tell me,' she said, 'would you run a mile if Megan told you she felt deeply about you?'

'No,' said Jim.

'Or showed signs of fear that you might go away?'

'No,' said Jim.

'Or said she wanted more than just fun, she wanted commitment?'

'No,' said Jim.

'The girl in the beauty parlour wouldn't believe you. She said that if – er – Keith – starts saying lovey-dovey things I should still stay cool. Be desirable … ' She edged a little closer. Short of standing up and immediately falling over her, Jim could do no more than go on sitting and clutching at his knees. '… but distant. Or he'll run a mile. Would you?'

'No,' said Jim.

'What would make you pull out?' she asked wilfully.

But just then Megan came back into the room.

'What's she saying now?' she asked, as if Gemma were a gaga geriatric.

'I was just telling him about the beauty parlour.'

'Oh – ' said Megan. 'Not the sort of thing *you're* interested in. Is it?'

'No,' said Jim.

*

Bang, bang, bang she now went on the door. Big hands, thought Gemma, riffling her own through the bubbles. Sausagey fingers. People could be so unattractive. Like the little beautician said, you had to really care about your looks if you were going to get anywhere.

Looks were linked to demographics. No doubt about it. The Beautiful Chloe probably came from somewhere like Barnes, or Reigate. Whereas Gemma had a fight on her hands, coming originally from Morden. But she had overcome. Morden was drab: fifties boxes; neither country nor town; neither soul nor sense of humour; stultifying. Most people who remained in such an area looked like extras in a Fellini. Most people who remained in any of those areas *deserved* to look like extras in a Fellini.

All those South London places she recently visited, for instance: the Streathams, the Mitchams, the Tolworths. Full of unpleasant-looking people emulating their surroundings. Quite unnecessarily. Look at Gemma: down to her beam-ends, but she was still pitching. Interestingly, none of those dreary places had boasted a beauty parlour. Hairdressers of course, run-down-looking affairs – but no Tabithas in sight. Which backed up exactly what the little beautician had said. People who aren't interested in improving their looks aren't interested in improving their lives either.

And out there, banging on the bathroom door, was the living proof. Port Talbot and Chapel. Yuk!

All the same, she shouldn't have told them the little beautician's lipstick story. It was unfair. Nor should she have told it as enthusiastically as it had been told to her. But she had. She had winked once, and begun:

'An Australian called Jo-Jo had a friend called Mike who told her this story about *his* friend Pam and Eric ... '

Neither of them could speak afterwards, as indeed Gemma had been struck dumb in the salon. But she did notice the gleam of interest in Jim's usually deadpan eyes. Satisfying. And if it worked on him, it was bound to work on M. Le Château.

Eventually Megan had stood up, made a magnificent rally for dignity and swung her overnight bag on to her arm, as usual, just a *little* too obviously.

'Don't want to be late, Jim, now do we?'

'That'll give you something to think about, on your stroll through the park,' said Gemma innocently. 'Will it not?'

'No,' said Jim.

But whether he spoke in reply to Megan or herself, she could not be quite sure.

Gemma pulled out the plug. Better get out of the bath and face the music she supposed. Or the banging. Besides, if she didn't get going she'd be late for the salon. The last appointment of the day, she was to be, and she wondered what, exactly, the Beautiful Chloe had in store. Any more lipstick stories? Exciting! *N'est-ce pas?*

18

Chloe had a real urge to shout 'Fire!' or something, just to see what desiccated old Betty would do about it, but she probably wouldn't even see the joke. Couldn't see anything very much, let alone hear. If you wanted to know about the sauna arrangements on the Ark, or about giving a face mask to Mrs Methuselah, she could oblige – but if you wanted anything more lively, forget it.

Last time she was here she'd offered the meter-man a forearm waxing, she was so blind. He'd whipped his shirt-sleeves down quicker than a bride's knickers. How Tabitha could prefer her to Jo-Jo was a real mystery. There she was sitting at the reception desk, still writing her history book, past sell-by date, definitely no advert, best ignored.

Whereas she – Chloe looked in the mirror and cracked her fingers – *she* looked great. Tabitha had been pleased at the healthy, shining, natural look and had left for her day out looking better than she'd looked for weeks.

It was so easy. You just opened a magazine, and there it was – Tweed and Silk *Can* Combine in the Country. Makeover Number One was going into the country, so Makover Number One would look like this. Chloe's resolve faltered momentarily, remembering what Makeover Number One *really* looked like – but then she rallied. Here they could do magic. Or even *miracles*.

Crack, crack, crack.

The foundation was pale gold, the blush tawny as if the sun had made its mark, the lashes curved sweetly, apparently by nature, and there was even a fine sprinkling of pale amber ephelides (false, fortunately, thank *you*). It looked *natural* , though of course, it was Art.

Those of us who have strode across morning-wet fields in the misty sun generally come back with flushed cheeks, red noses, hair in damp tendrils and soggy eyelashes; Chloe looked as if she had just stepped out of a Laura Ashley catalogue, and that is what she would attempt with Margery. A bloody hard slog, though, she said with distaste into the mirror. But if she showed each of her clients how *she* could do it, it would give them a bit of confidence. And then – she cracked the other hand – then they would come *back*.

Without Tabitha in the way she could put her own theories into practice. This one was the Carrot, and the client was the Donkey – and she'd keep *that* thought to herself. But clients needed a show. Not Tabitha's Calm Centre of Unity – another of her incomprehensibles – but *Tricks*.

Chloe was not entirely clear about Margery's proposed outfit, the description being very muddled, but she knew the date was out of doors and had planned rustic demureness for her accordingly. Clever, thought Chloe, admiring herself in the mirror. Clever. And she pouted, pleased.

It took a lot to make Chloe's pretty jaw drop. Yet, on hearing a taxi and sauntering to the window, and looking out, her jaw – so pretty – did indeed drop quite dramatically. Number One Client was unloading what appeared to be her *home* on to the pavement, while a taxi driver sat in the cab, staring straight ahead, as if he were bravely paraplegic.

Chloe rallied. This was no time to falter.

She hitched up her jaw, strode out on to the pavement, stepped around picnic hampers, bags, vacuum flasks and boxes, went up to the taxi driver's open window, and said very sweetly into his ear:

'If you want paying, let alone a tip, mate, I'd give a hand if I was you.'

The taxi driver turned, stared coldly, got the return equivalent of an icicle up his bum, and got out of his cab. He recognized, despite the charming simplicity of her rural get-up, a dirty fighter when he saw one. Movement instantly returned to his legs.

The belongings were taken into the salon and stacked in the Client Corner. The taxi driver was dismissed, grumbling at the smallness of his portion and staring about him in fear and wonder at the unequivocal femininity of the surroundings. It confirmed all his worst fears about women: they were nothing less than a ruddy secret society. He held his breath against the thickly perfumed air, glad to get out unharmed.

'And what,' said Chloe sweetly, folding her hands, 'are we going to wear?'

Margery started rummaging among all the stuff. 'Hope it's not creased,' she said anxiously, and pulled out the gingham frock. She shook it so that its ruffles bobbed and swung, and smoothed it so that the full skirt hung to best advantage. She held it up against herself.

Chloe stared. She had not in all her wildest imaginings (and they could be wild) considered being faced with a gingham cream puff. Oh no. She had not anticipated this. Frankly, *no one* would have anticipated this. And she wondered briefly whether Reginald Postgate had also not anticipated this? Had this woman *seen Whatever Happened to Baby Jane?* She could be sued for copyright.

Chloe took a deep breath. She smoothed out the towels and adjusted the head of the couch. She beckoned. I'd like to be a bee in their hive when he cops that lot, she thought.

'Lovely!' she said, and still smiling sweetly, she settled Margery on the couch.

She looked again at the swinging monstrosity. And reverted in crisis. Fuck a duck, she thought. Someone walking down the High Road in a rubber wet-suit and dog muzzle is considered barmy, while someone walking down the High Road in that frock is considered *respectable?* Didn't make sense.

'Very nice,' said Chloe quickly again. 'Charming.'

As she lay wrapped in a large, fluffy towelling robe, Margery felt a spasm of happiness. It was like being a child again, and she surrendered her neck and face to be washed with little damp sponges that were deftly and firmly applied.

Between wipes she told Chloe, 'I have asked him out and he has accepted.'

'Good,' said Chloe, who was now applying cream (quite a lot of it) to Margery's face and neck. 'This contains thyme and lemon – can you smell it – very good for your particular kind of skin.' She began the effleurage, gently roll-patting, hands following each other from left to right clavicle across the sternum in the approved manner. She paused for a moment, and winked, in a way that Tabitha would certainly *not* have approved.

'I said you should take the initiative. Where are you taking him?'

'To a field,' said Margery happily.

You had to hand it to Chloe, the roll-patting hardly wavered as Margery unfolded, secrets of the boudoir, her honey plan. Nor did it waver as she followed the line of the left superficial cheek muscles, crossed the chin, and followed the superficial cheek muscles of the right.

Margery continued, in between the facial motion, 'You said I could even have a honey face mask if he liked honey so much – that a little sweetness worked wonders; I liked what you said ... '

Chloe felt a slight unease, but banished it. She concluded the massage with a light, slow lifting of the Occipito Frontalis muscles.

'That's right,' she said, shrugging away the doubt. 'If honey's his thing, give him honey – '

The doubt reared itself again. 'But of course there are other things, aren't there?'

She began mixing the mask, averting her gaze from the appalling lilac concoction.

'What?' said Margery happily.

Ker-ist, thought Chloe, better come up with something. If Jo-Jo were here instead of Old Betty, she'd have some ideas. Chloe racked her brains. She gave a sweet little smile as she squeezed a few droplets of orange juice into the warmed honey and stirred the pot, daring a quick peek at the gingham monstrosity.

'You are wearing that?'

Margery nodded. 'He'll love it,' she said simply.

No arguing there, thought Chloe, testing the heat of the mask with her finger. She had a sudden and very terrible picture of long frilly bloomers.

'What are you going to wear under it?' *Someone* had to help this thing along, poor bloke.

Margery, a little surprised, hazarded 'underwear', hoping that was right.

'Why?' said Chloe, winking. 'It's a hot day. No need. Give him a thrill. Don't wear anything. Believe me,' she gave the pot one more stir, 'I *know*.' She certainly looked as if she did.

Margery blinked.

Chloe shrugged again, smiled again, holding the honey pot, about to apply the contents. 'Except maybe a dot or two of the honey he likes, strategically placed. Know what I mean?'

Smile, wink, shrug.

Margery gave a little shriek, but Betty wrote on.

She had just found a cosmetic corollary between the bold, wide-eyed, lip-less dollyrocker of the sixties, and Tertullian's reference to the prominence given to Roman women's eyes circa 200 AD 'by that black powder itself wherewith the eyelids and eyelashes are made prominent'. And was cross-referencing it with Pliny's recipe for mascara, consisting of bear's fat and lampblack – or, for those special occasions, crushed ants' eggs and squashed flies. Absolutely *fascinating*.

Strategically placed?

Margery apologized for the noise, swallowed hard, lay back to receive the face mask, and surrendered herself entirely.

'After all,' said Chloe, applying the smooth unguent, 'who needs knickers? You've only got to get them off sometime.' She paused and her face took on that dreamy quality so feared by Tabitha.

'And just remember, even if it's the size of a prawn you tell him it's a Moby Dick. And if he's no good at it you tell him he's The Best you've ever had. *Particularly* if he's no good at it – otherwise he'll never get any better.'

'Oh, there won't be any problem there,' said Margery, beginning to dress.

Chloe looked at the ruffles as they swung over her matronly shoulders. 'I wouldn't be too sure about that,' she muttered.

The taxi driver grumbled. He grumbled at the length of the journey before him, he grumbled at the amount of stuff he was to pack into his cab, he grumbled at the delay while his customer stood at the salon desk paying.

'People are usually ready,' he said defiantly to the bossy young piece.

'People pay you to wait,' said she, and turned her beautiful head.

Margery, in her gingham at last, stood proudly by the desk paying her bill.

Betty peered at her, very closely, and then moved her head away, squinting.

'Good Lord,' she said. And gave the blurred outline of Chloe an enquiring stare.

Margery gave a twirl. 'Good Lord,' said Betty again. But she had learned to be philosophical. After all, women had once considered the farthingale flattering ...

The taxi driver went out to his cab, pausing on the way to whisper to the beautiful young bossy girl in the eau-de-Nil overall, 'I hope she's going to be accompanied.'

'Get knotted,' said Chloe evenly, still smiling at her creation.

Betty said to Margery, 'When would you like to book?'

Margery giggled. 'No – I've *been* done.'

'Really?' said Betty, thinking that was more than true. '*Really?*'

Margery twirled anew. 'She said it would look natural.' She put her hand to her mouth to simper a little, remembered her fine teeth, and removed it, letting them blaze away.

'Good grief,' said Betty, returning to the safety of her manuscript. Some cosmetic surgery was carried out on Romano-British women, apparently. The raising of slack eyelids, the patching up of mutilated ears, lips and noses were recorded, although the lack of efficient anaesthetics must have limited such surgery cases to dire need.

Dire Need? She watched Margery swinging out of the salon door. Fortunately it was a very blurred image, but she could have sworn that, just for a moment, as a ruffle swung high, she saw a pair of dimpled, quite naked, buttocks. Impossible.

From the taxi, waving, issued a happy little hand, perfectly manicured, nails irridescent in the sun. And above it was Margery's face, a work of art to behold, as Chloe reminded herself. Betty might react unenthusiastically, but then, she wasn't a man, now was she? And the taxi driver might react unenthusiastically, but he wasn't much of a man either. No. She had created a positive statement. She was just a little hazy about what the statement was exactly …

That was the way to do it, no matter what Tabitha said: give the punters what they wanted, after you'd told them what it *was*.

The taxi turned the corner. Chloe loosened the ribbon in her hair. It was to be hoped the next one would be a bit easier. Love triangle, ex-wife? Piece of cake!

19

'Beauty is the power by which a woman charms a lover and terrifies a husband. Ha Ha.' Chloe's parting shot did not exactly settle Tabitha's unease at leaving her in charge. She hopes this visit to the art gallery will, and takes herself off swiftly to begin with the Master, Giotto.

His Madonna's eyes slant and woo beguilingly. She is the difference between pretty decoration and genuine beauty. Something only becomes beautiful when the imagination is engaged.

That, she thinks, moving on, is why Giotto is considered a Master, and why this earlier panel is not. Here are female angels and pious women (it is painted by a woman) who do not take their place in real space, in the real world, but float through it, expressionless. Beneath their stylized coiffures all their faces are the same – formula beauty as decreed by the Byzantine Church.

Giotto's mother looks beautiful in a real way; her child may be a God but she holds him securely; baby gods can take a tumble; her child might be doomed, but she is proud of her achievement, enjoys him while she can. She has a soul. She holds Tabitha with eyes that look out and confront her woman to woman. The artist has lit her well. She is radiant. And Beautiful.

Tabitha loves the mix of spiritual and practical in this painting. She smiles again at Giotto's sweet, masculine confusion at practical female matters. The bevy of angels surrounding the Virgin Mother's throne wear their golden auras like hats. And according to Giotto these hatlike haloes must needs be fixed in place with *halo pins*. How else could they withstand a rushing angel wind?

Perhaps they fix each other's during one of those all-girls-together beauty nights, draping themselves over celestial couches, raiding the heavenly refrigerator for paradisiscal snackettes, swapping stories and giggling into their feathers as they lined up for under-wing waxing. Trust in God up to a point, but don't go flying around without your halo secured.

The Boudoir. The Secrets. Eternal, wherever women congregate. Safe with Tabitha, but with Chloe? She shakes her head. Wrings her hands. Of *course* it will be all right. She wrings her hands some more.

She lingers so long with the Giotto Virgin, looks so agonized, wrings her hands so much, that the two attendants become suspicious. They hover nearby, pointedly willing her to move on which, eventually, she does. Pleased, they sidle over to the painting and take a good look themselves. What's to stare at? They peer more closely. Perhaps she was planning to pinch it? Or even more exciting, to *damage* it.

Tabitha leaves the Giotto behind and walks on through the deserted galleries. If it was a beginning, it was also an end, she thinks. Beginning of realism, end of the comfortably unobtainable ideal. She passes Madonna after Madonna, thirteenth century, fourteenth century, fifteenth century, each with the beauty of a real woman in the real world. From Cranach's pure white-skinned celestial mothers, with their ghostly bellies and bee-sting mouths – as frail as porcelain and just as rare – to Bellini's rustic simplicity: round ruddy cheeks, downcast eyes and pretty dimpled chins.

She walked and gazed, reflecting again upon the perfect female Chosen By God. Never an ugly one. It was poor old Brenda all over again.

She turns the corner, much to the interest of her stalking attendant who has left his companion still staring at the Giotto Madonna and tuning his walkie-talkie just in case. The Stalker can *definitely* see her lips move. He knows he must be on to something. You don't talk to a load of old, dead pictures – and they certainly don't talk back to *you*.

Stretching before her, there they all were, the Beauties of their day. So much beauty was exhausting, really.

'Of course,' she muttered, bringing her Stalker closer, eyes a-gleam, '*of course*. Don't you see?' She turned to the Stalker with troubled, importuning gesture. 'It was when Giotto said Enough Of The Stylized Female – Now Let Us Paint Reality that we were doomed. Doomed! You do see that?'

The Stalker saw only too clearly. This was madness. He knew better than to engage those eyes and discovered quite a large blob of something on his tie which he went to work on with a will. Made a change from 'where's the toilets?' anyway.

'You see, what *Giotto* said was You Can All Be Like This – and then he painted *Beauty*. And whereas before when women looked at those Byzantine women, who bore no resemblance to the world and were not meant to, they went away feeling jolly relieved because they did not have to compete, now, post-Giotto, they were looking at *Possibility*! See?'

'She's getting wound up to do something,' he said into his radio. 'Over.' But his fellow huntsman had nipped off for tea. He tapped the machine, blew on it, fiddled until it made a crackling noise and picked up a taxi asking his base for directions.

'Some bloody honey farm off the M4 she says,' crackled the voice. 'Funny farm more like. Over and out.'

He looked up, annoyed to see that she had moved through into the next gallery. He skipped after her, torn between a desire for blushing honours and tea with ginger nuts.

'Oh, those painters had a lot to answer for,' she was saying, standing grim-faced before a reclining nude. He came as close as he dared. Go on, he urged her silently, touch the bloody thing – tread over the wire – *do something!* But she only waved her arms about and there was no particular law against that.

'The secular, the classical – mythology offering more apparently attainable beauty – an elongated Venus emerges from the sea and women racked themselves to emulate her. Three Graces dancing in a wood, hair tumbling in golden curls, so that raven-haired ladies went either bewigged, or doused their heads in acid, weeping with pain and vexation. Aphrodite's unblemished skin in the days of the pox, her perfect breasts defying gravity like the breasts on a fairground cut-out. Six, five, four hundred years ago. Yum yum said the patrons, and hung them on their walls.'

The attendant lurked. 'Do you see?' she said.

Frankly he wished she wouldn't do that. No, he didn't see, hadn't got a clue – and anyway she should not try to engage him in conversation. He had read somewhere that the best thing to do if you were captured by armed guerillas was to strike up a conversation with them as soon as possible. Apparently, they found it much harder to torture you if you'd been chatting to them about the wife earlier in the day. Not necessarily a vital piece of information, but you never knew. He glared at her.

Tabitha did not blame him. Here she was, deconstructing feminine beauty and sexual enticement – blowing the poor man's conceptions apart – yet she would persist.

'And all through the ages women have obliged. Dissimulating from little state to little state, even in this tiny bit called Europe. If you cannot achieve this look, you good women of Florence, Ghent, Venice, Burgundy – you have failed. And you – sisters of the Flatlands – no use looking at your Franco-Italian cousins – you're *Dutch*. It's different. You've got to be big and bouncy, you have ... '

'*Dutch!!*' she said loudly.

He came closer. Was she spitting?

'*Dutch!!*'

Alas! She was not.

'If you were Dutch you needed serious amounts of cellulite: Rubens laid it on with a heavy hand, every nymph a strapping wench, thighs like fleshly pillows. Rembrandt feathered it in delicate folds of paint, his adored Saskia's rippling nether regions, contriving a complete reversal in his countrywomen who had gone bulimic in order to supply the slender suppleties of Dürer.

The faces, she observed, matched the bodies – florid, full, with luminous popping eyes. Not surprising, she thought, sniffing, as she walked on. Given that weight they must have had grave heart problems.

The attendant, moving ever more shadowily behind her, stared as she stared, and stared particularly hard at this last image of bouncing pink-nippled breasts. Now why should a woman spend so long looking at *that*? Middle-aged women did funny things. Take his wife. Please. Ha Ha.

Tabitha was shrugging and fluttering her hands in vexation.

Bronzino. Sinister deceiver. Venus, Cupid, Folly and Time, painted as a warning against lust my eye, says Tabitha, half aloud. Painted as an invitation to it, more like. Soft porn. How honest Giorgione would have despised his fellow-painter.

'What do you think?' she says aloud.

'Not paid to think,' he mutters. More dirty pictures. Woman's a maniac. At any rate, he hopes so. He fingers his walkie-talkie just in case. Mutter, mutter, she goes. He stays very close.

The Beauties no longer soothe. Tabitha tuts as she walks.

Spain – different again – Velasquez requiring dainty little limbs, sallow, olive skin. What was a woman supposed to do when travelling, asks Tabitha? Metamorphose at each border town? No wonder they mostly stayed at home. You couldn't have kept up with the dieting, for a start – and then there's the taking in and letting out of seams, the raising and lowering of bodices while the border guards stood around waiting to check cellulite levels – hopelessly muddling. She shakes her head, moves on quickly, passing Tintoretto, Veronese, Poussin, Van Dyck.

Coming up behind her the attendant peers at the Velasquez. So what's wrong with this one? He wonders. Then he knows. *This* one's got a frock on. Oh for a cup of tea and a sit down.

On and on through the galleries. Tabitha is scornful, she curls her lip. The attendant, behind her, does so, too. She moves swiftly and he knows why – she moves swiftly because these pictures have got their clothes on. And this woman on whom his eye is glued, is a *pervert*. In his opinion, half the people (or more) who come in here are *perverts*.

As she goes she thinks, here are Chloe's Super-models of their day – picked from the gutter, picked from the court, picked only for their beauty to hang there, as safe in the bright light of day as in the soft glow of the evening candle – hanging in their ornate frames, the loveliness never diminishing, making women ashamed, men dissatisfied.

Tabitha flinches, stops. She stares at a sleeping Venus, naked – perhaps a harlot from the streets but the painter knew a thing or two – Beauty in every feature, every line – Beauty to Die For – and given the poison in cosmetics she probably did. How many women did he send to despair with this image?

She peers at the name on the card by the picture.

Giorgione.

'Bastard!' she says.

'What?' says the Stalker, who would really need witnesses.

'He never really meant it after all. See?' says Tabitha. '*Vanitas Vanitatum*, nothing to do with our vanity – do you see? It meant – quite simply – here is my clever painting.'

She looked at the attendant's blank, don't-try-and-be-friendly-with-me expression. And stamped her foot. 'Oh, you *men*!' she cried.

Oh-ho, he thought, one of *those*.

And how many women had Tabitha sent to despair with her Liposome would do this, Cathiodermie that, Collagen the other? She denied it – she had made women happy, she had brought out their beauty, let them celebrate what they could, disguise what they could not. She had passed on the art, as it had been passed on to her. Today was the beginning of Chloe's era.

She feels quite faint.

Go on, implores the attendant, go on, *touch it* – just once – one little tickle from your fingertip. Wouldn't harm. Liven things up a bit. He could see that she nearly did, he was almost sure that she would and then, in that infuriating way of women, she suddenly developed a teardrop on her cheek and dabbed it instead.

She moves towards a bench, brushing at her other cheek with the back of her hand. She wishes she had stayed in the broom cupboard. Things don't feel right. Too late now.

She pauses at Goya's smiling portrait of Isabella, full of life, aglow with vitality. She reaches out and touches the warm, red lips. They are cold and silent as death. Illusion. All Illusion. She removes her finger pensively.

The attendant walks away sorrowfully, refixing his walkie-talkie, and looks round one last time. But she is just standing, staring at her fingertip. Harmless. Quite Mad. Thinking. But thinking *what?* You're no oil painting. Ha Ha.

Suddenly she sees the whole absurd sham of it. The salon! Chloe! She must get back. Past picture after picture she flies, with the Stalker emulating winged Mercury himself and coming on strong behind.

Past a little Elizabethan lady, so young, and yet she is no more natural than the roses embroidered upon her gown. Swamped by artificial colouring, with eyes that look as if she has been up all night weeping – Tabitha peers again – henna – dropping a little into the eye to make the rims pink. Ouch!

Seventeenth century: a middle-aged woman forced by Court protocol to strut her stuff. Elizabeth Grey, Countess of Kent, resembles a pantomime dame. The Beautician has painted some blue veins on her skin to give a suggestion of its translucence – lost youth, lost dignity.

Eighteenth century: Lavinia Fenton, actress. Full red lips, finely drawn brows and plump pink cheeks – the Beautician spent time enough on her toilette. Clever this one, out to get her Duke. She knew a thing or two about looking respectably natural. On the wall is the painting's label: Later Duchess of Bolton. Tabitha laughs. The pay-off.

Age of enlightenment, *except* for its beauties. For the sweet-faced girls with glazed white faces, those little enamelled beauties created from poisoning white lead that ate its way through rosy cheek, unresisting bone, towards gum, teeth and finally the crumbling of the jaw. Lavinia Fenton, Duchess of Bolton, RIP.

RIP, too, for those pallid, indoor, well-bred beauties whose claim to the Age of Enlightenment was to have their front hair stunted with walnut oil or shaved, to make the home of the brain, the skull, look larger.

And romantic Rousseau lovelies in pursuit of the ultimate, ever tightening the curling tongs, having their noses broken and reset to resemble the Greek ideal. Long necks, created by sleeves set so far down their arms they could scarcely lift them high enough to scratch the lice.

Picture after picture.

Women obliged.

Their Sin.

Eve in every one of them.

She stares so greedily, thinks the attendant. What does she see in it all? Just a load of old, long-dead tarts?

The salon, the salon, she thinks – she must stop Chloe now, this minute, at *once*!

20

Exactly what kind of image does a female poisoner present?

Chloe was a bit stumped.

'Betty?' shouted Chloe, on the way to get changed. 'Know any lady poisoners?'

'Not personally,' said Betty.

She is very wary of Chloe, ever since the last time she was left in charge, and the girl helped her complete an ionithermie treatment. The poor woman was stretched out like a fish, completely covered in sea kelp and bandages, and asked Chloe how long she would have to stay like that for maximum cellulite reduction.

'Oh, about six days,' was Chloe's casual reply, at which point the woman sat up – well, wriggled up, really – like an injured mermaid and demanded to have it all taken off immediately.

And it was no good saying, 'Only a joke,' as Chloe did. The woman was very distressed. They had not told Tabitha about *that* one. All the same, Betty was going to have to keep a sharp eye out – if only she had one.

'What do you think a lady poisoner should look like?'

'As self-effacing as possible, I should think.' Betty said crisply, without looking up, and wiped a hand over her tired eyes. She was cross-referencing the war years, and sometimes it seemed she would never finish. The war years when you scooped out the last of your lipstick with a spoon handle, and smeared it on with a fingertip. No different, really, from the Romano-British women who used their dainty ligulae.

'Well?' said Chloe, and then came right up to her and shouted, '*Well?!*' so that Betty jumped. 'Lipstick,' said Chloe. 'Want to hear a good story about lipstick?'

Betty firmly shook her head.

'You'll love it,' said Chloe. 'Everybody does.' And she began.

'Well – there was this married couple, Pam and Eric, friends of Jo-Jo's friend Mike, and they had come adrift a bit. You know – *he* was carrying on with someone else, she was pissed off about it, and this Mike chap was somewhere in between sort of thing – one night he'd see Eric, and Eric would moan on at him, the next night he'd see Pam and *she'd* be having a go – know what I mean?'

'Poisoners?' said Betty rapidly. She had come across Hecate poisoning the bread of neglectful housewives, and a water nymph called Telphusa, with prophetic powers, whose fountain of knowledge was so bitterly cold it killed whoever drank from it. She doubted if Chloe meant that sort of thing.

Chloe also doubted if she meant that sort of thing. 'Something a bit more – er – strong than nymphs and whatnot – more colourful maybe? Sure you don't want the rest of the story?'

Betty closed her eyes. 'Pale as the moon, with a large, purplish mouth that looks bloodsoaked. Secret eyes – dark, thick-fringed, like jungles into which the seeker for truth cannot penetrate … lids blue-black, lashes midnight blue, brows thick and shapely … ' She replaced her glasses. 'Will that do?' she asked. But Chloe had gone. She had just remembered the Gorgons.

'Why poisoners?' called Betty after her. She would have pursued Chloe, but the book held her. Lots of those ligulae still found wherever women went – streets, baths, shops. And huge numbers of hairpins. Women were no different then than now – hair and face being considerably more important than war and politics. You could safely leave those to the men.

'Custard powder,' she wrote, 'if you could get it, made a reasonable dusting for the night-time face – but you had to dash for cover if it rained.'

Chloe reappeared.

From the neck down the eau-de-Nil overall looked comforting and harmless, but from the neck up Chloe was transformed into someone it would be ill-advised to meet on a dark night.

'Well – how do I look?'

Betty saw a beautiful mixture of vampire and sharply-lit Mary Pickford.

'Lovely, dear,' said Betty vaguely. Usually that was best.

'I mean – do I look enticing, do I look sinister, do I look like a

141

woman who would take her destiny in her own hands with any means, even poison?'

'Yes,' said Betty. 'Oh yes, indeed.' She had just remembered that she once made her own false eyelashes out of gum and horsehair. Those were the days in which glamour was a *triumph*.

'Just ticketty-boo,' she said.

*

Caroline arrived at the salon with a smile of exhausted satisfaction on her lips. But she was not half so exhausted as Bernie, she consoled herself.

She had left him deeply asleep, nose down in the pillows, and with the duvet over him. So who needs to cut hair? The longer he slept, the less time there would be for him to investigate the food in the kitchen. Now, weakened from a fairly dramatic attempt at going for gold, carnally speaking, and also from the sheer terror of what she had done *au cuisine*, she sought the balm and refuge of the Beautician's couch. She had to say that the Little Beautician did not exactly look the part.

She looked *dangerous*.

'It's rather *strong*, dear,' said Betty.

'It needs to be,' muttered Chloe, and took Caroline off to her little cubicle, shutting the door tight.

'You'll look like this when I've finished with you,' she said cheerfully.

Caroline swallowed. Chloe knew best.

'Did you manage it?' she asked, settling her client on the couch. 'Did you do what I told you?'

Caroline nodded, and made a silent pointing gesture.

'Oh, don't worry about the old bat. She's past it.'

While Chloe did all the uncomfortable bits (squeezing comedones, tidying the brow line, clucking over stray hairs like a Cruella de Vil shepherdess gathering up the strays) Caroline described what she had done, a sin committed being a sin shared. She was grateful. She would never have thought of it on her own. She settled back, ignoring Chloe's shaking head as she mourned the way those eyebrows grew so free and untamed.

'First,' said Caroline, 'I took out a little of the ceviche … '

'The what?'

'Ceviche: raw fish marinated – soaked for a while – rather than cooked.'

Chloe thought it sounded quite disgusting enough.

'And put it on a saucer out of sight. Then to the rest – a rather good marinade of lime, ginger and soya – I added a drop or two of iodine and tasted it again. It was horrible, but only *faintly* horrible, as if the sea had suddenly developed an oil slick – then I replaced the clingfilm.'

Chloe, negotiating one or two stubborn chin hairs, smiled evilly.

'Next?' she asked viciously, feeling power in every movement of the tweezers.

'Tricky,' said Caroline, barely feeling the plucking in her elation. 'It was two brace of pheasant.'

Chloe thought hard, tried to work it out but couldn't, reminded herself she was a Beautician not a Blooming Mathematician and said, 'How many's that?'

'Four.'

'That's a lot for four people.'

'Five,' Caroline reminded her, 'with *her* joining us.' Her eyes were filled with vengeance. Vengeance! She laughed, glorying in the pain as the tweezers plucked away. The bitter taste in *her* mouth was as nothing to the one they'd all have tonight.

'So – pheasants. What did you do?'

'Well, first I had to unsew their bottoms – '

'How disgusting,' said Chloe, back to squeezing Caroline's nasal comedones with gusto.

'Then I had to take out all the stuffing. I set some aside and hid it with the ceviche, and put the rest in a mixing bowl.'

Chloe wiped the little pockmark clean.

'What was it made from?'

'Oh – wonderful things: walnuts, grapes, a little orange flesh and peel, breadcrumbs – and I think a little dash of whisky.'

'Mmm,' said Chloe, thinking sage and onion and licking her purplish lips, 'sounds bad enough already. What did you do to it?'

'I tasted it and it was – actually – delicious. So I added some anchovy essence and washing-up liquid, and then it wasn't. I packed it back into the birds and sewed up their bums again.'

'Washing-up liquid?' said Chloe rapturously. 'Cle-ver.'

'Well, yes,' said Caroline modestly, 'I thought so too. Because it made it all ever so slightly *slimy*. Oh yes – and in one of them I added an unwrapped though not used Durex Fetherlite.'

Chloe's shriek was worthy of an old-fashioned train passing through a tunnel. Even Betty, deep in a struggle to remember what she mixed with Vaseline to create eyegloss, was roused, shaken, and moved to hobble across the salon to identify the noise.

'Well, if you had a johnny what would you do with it?' asked Chloe innocently.

Betty went rigid. So, for that matter, did Caroline.

'*Pardon?*' said Betty, cupping her ear with wrinkled hand.

Chloe took a deep breath and spoke directly into Betty's ear: 'I said OH HELL JUST A BIT OF STUBBORN ARMPIT,' shouting so loudly that the glass droplets on the chandelier went tinkle, tinkle, tinkle.

'That told her,' said Chloe, when Betty had made her considerably frailer jouney back to the reception desk.

Betty was baffled – one minute she could hear so little with Chloe, and the next it was like being on the Somme.

Chloe closed the cubicle door again, put a finger to her head in a screw-loose gesture, and began massaging Caroline's face with a light moisturizer. 'Deaf as a post,' she said, 'or she will be now, ha ha. Now relax.'

Caroline tried.

Setting the delights of good humour on one side, Chloe returned to the issue.

'Of course, I love the idea of sticking a johnny up its bum,' she said, 'but it's a bit *crass*, isn't it?'

'Oh, I took it out again. Much as I'd have loved to see the Chairman's face as he unravelled it from his walnuts.'

Chloe nodded and prepared a warm peel-off mask.

'But at least I know it's been *in* there,' Caroline said smugly.

'Don't get found out. Just make her look a complete tit. Show her up. Right?'

'Right.'

As the mask was applied, she wondered, uncomfortably, if her actions that day had shown her to be any better.

'Sod that,' said Chloe cheerfully. 'To win is all. That's the way it is, her or you. Any pud, before it dries?'

'Pear and almond tart, injected at intervals with bitter almonds –

the stuff you use to stop yourself biting your nails. I left one bit blank though, and I know where.'

Chloe smiled, smoothing the spatula with the last of the setting mixture. It was the basic mask. One part kaolin, one part fuller's earth, a little water and – 'Guess what?' she said. 'By coincidence, into this exotic and very special face mask, made with the finest ingredients from around the world, I have added a little – go on – smell and see if you can guess.'

Caroline sniffed, the smell was familiar, not unpleasant, though it made her feel ill at ease and rather tense. She shook her head.

Chloe tapped her cheek playfully. 'I've added almond oil. Nice touch, eh?'

Behind the pads, Caroline squeezed her eyes up tight and tried not to see the innocent-looking, doctored food.

'Relax now,' said Chloe, dimming the lights. But somehow Caroline couldn't.

While the mask dried and, as she fondly thought, her client relaxed, Chloe prepared the make-up tray with the same colourings she wore. This woman would look dangerous *and* beautiful. And be as tough as the Terminator.

Caroline, overcome, finally released her muscles into softness and snoozed.

The mask began its work.

Later, when Caroline stood at the desk preparing to pay, Betty asked her, peering closely, if she felt quite well. Caroline, who was actually feeling quite sleepy, and beginning to understand why footballers, athletes and suchlike slept alone before important dates, smiled lazily and nodded, eyes half closed.

Betty blinked, refocused, and recoiled. She turned to Chloe, whose face had an expression that would be referred to around the formica table as Swank. Keeping her ears well out of range, she lipread Chloe's words, which issued from a mouth that might well have been sucking blood:

'Well,' asked the girl triumphantly, 'is that Drop Dead Good-looking or what?'

Betty, flinching, peered hard once more, shook her head thoughtfully, leaned back and said 'Drop Dead *something*, dear – certainly Drop Dead something ... '

The client showed all the hallmarks of a very fine snake.

Thus did they wave Caroline out of the salon, the one with perky confidence, the other wavering, uncertain.

Very uncertain.

Chloe clapped her hands.

On with the show.

21

Tabitha was exhausted. All that running, all that looking, all that thinking – all that *Beauty*. Nevertheless she pushed her way out of the swing doors, to the top of the gallery's steps, took a deep breath and plunged on. She had been in there longer than she knew. It was the evening rush hour – queues at bus-stops, tube line closed because someone had done the dance of death, taxis at crawling pace.

How to get back quickly? Nothing was moving – only Tabitha herself it seemed, running from point to point and stopping at each, like a beetle trapped in a box. She looked back at the gaunt exterior of the gallery. She had gone there for reassurance and found only falseness. Even Giorgione had let her down. Now she must atone.

Back she raced, up the steps, bursting into the marbled, silent foyer, seeking help – something – what?

The attendant's heart lifted to see her again. Too late for tea, he did not feel in the pink. Indeed, he felt extremely in the blue. And then in she came, looking even wilder than before. Distraught you could say. Negativism blossomed.

'Telephone?' she implored him breathlessly. 'I must use a telephone.'

He remembered a glorious moment several years ago when he had been a ticket collector at St Pancras. A man had come rushing up demanding to know when the next train for Sheffield departed. He, in full pride of his powers, had turned in jubilation, perhaps his finest hour, and said, 'It's just gone mate. It's just bleeding gone.'

And now Magnificent Opportunity to let this current Negativism bear fruit.

'Out of order,' he said happily. 'Out of *Order*.'

And was rewarded, this time around, with a cry somewhere between temper and tears. Which was solace for the lost tea, and a considerable improvement on last time when the bloke had punched him on the nose.

Tabitha turned away. She drooped. She shuffled. She wondered what her life had all been about. You are no oil painting, he had once said. Well – sure – she remembered the luscious Isabella, oil painting and cold as yesterday. Her shoulders straightened. *Sure*, she was no oil painting – she was living, breathing, scented flesh. And that was the price you paid for being alive, not fixed in some gilded frame all primped and winsome, stuck for ever at youthful beauty's age. 'Be Buggered to *That*,' she muttered defiantly, moving more resolutely, shoulders square. 'I have done no wrong. Nothing at all. Nonsense.'

Behind her, picking up speed as she did, came her shadow. He did not like what he saw, which was akin to a renewal of confidence. But perhaps it was false? He bloody well hoped so, the dance she'd led him.

With each step towards the revolving doors and the freedom of the world, she felt better. All a silly mistake. All her overworked mind. All perfectly understandable, since she was more than ready to retire. The mind plays tricks, she counselled herself, the brain gets silly. Chloe was fine. The salon was fine. The world of beauty was fine, fine, fine.

Chloe was even educating herself – all those books, all that insight, all the sympathetic understanding it would bring. Nothing wrong at all. How silly of her to think it. After all, they were giving women what they wanted, weren't they? If they had wanted what those nasty graffiti-bound lesbians had implied they did – they would go elsewhere.

No, *no* … Tabitha's Beauty Parlour still had a role for women. And a good one. Their last great Bastion against the dilution of their feminity; to be beautiful, their unique role along with having babies. Had they not given up enough, without giving up the Joy of that?

He was in trouble. He knew it. He could see by the shadow she cast on the marble walls that her chin was up, her nose towards the air and she definitely had a look, suddenly, of being sane. Damn. *Bugger*. And ginger nuts too.

Near the doorway to the world outside and the clear blue of a summer sky at evening, she paused. Buses had begun to move again, taxis gleaming as they sped along, and hurrying people showed signs of smiling, faces bathed in the low golden sunlight. Near the door there was one very large painting hanging alone. Not, she saw thankfully, a portrait.

She paused to look.

The artist in residence had chosen this, the card said, as the key painting in his selection. Very important. A new departure in the use of paint – its thinness so daring – the hint of canvas beneath so audacious – the composition so perfect. She stared at it, seeing what he meant.

Behind her, her shadow stared too. Very valuable picture this. He waited. He would see her off the premises completely, just to be sure she didn't do something all of a sudden, and him miss it. Once a woman had written 'Bingo' in lipstick on one of the pillars of the outside portico, and no one had noticed it until they went home. He wouldn't let *that* happen again. She stepped forwards, and so did he. She stared. She *saw*.

Titian's painting of a *Pieta*. Great, dignified, honourable art. Christ brought down from the cross, the slack paint expressing the life gone out of Him. Held on each side, tenderly, sorrowfully, by two deeply grieving women, both the Marys. The Magdalen's face was wet with tears, the eyes wide and full of pain, beauty in agony, and fittingly so, for she was young.

But it was to Mary the Mother that Tabitha turned. Depicted here should be a woman in the deepest grief humanly possible, more wretched than any who have not suffered the loss of a child can know, and as Tabitha stared she saw the painter had understood, had reached the heart of the mother's ultimate darkness. Mary the devastated mother could not fail to move an observer with the agony in her face.

And yet – Tabitha did a quick calculation on her fingers. This woman must have been in her late forties, perhaps early fifties when her son was crucified, yet the Madonna of those earlier paintings, the bright-eyed, round-cheeked girl of the Annunciation and New Motherhood, had scarcely been allowed to change physically.

One thing, thought Tabitha sourly, to portray the new mother of God as full of beauty and light and perfection – but this woman, this old woman who had suffered so much – that *she* should be shown as still young, still lovely even in her grief – that was, she said loudly, 'Sheer Bloody Travesty.'

And then she began to sing. Even more loudly.

Keep young and beautiful
It's your duty to be beautiful
Keep young and beautiful
If you want to be loved.

She thought of Chloe and the women whom she had consigned to her. Three women, caught in the Beautician's snare, anchored to her couch, while she, Tabitha, moved aside, considering herself of no value now the light was unkind. She smacked fist into palm, stamped her foot, saw red where once the light had been calm and white, and with the might of madness threw her handbag hard and strong at the offending image.

But it was a futile gesture. She knew that. She was already far, far too late. Even had she caught a bus, flagged down a taxi, ridden the tube, she was far, far too late for Chloe.

Oh Joy! thought the attendant. Oh Joy, Oh *Joy!* She must *surely* have dented it at least.

22

Chloe sat in front of her mirror, waiting for Gemma.

She was musing over what got into print nowadays, having discovered quite a long piece of writing in *Great Authors Salute the Ladies* which had read very much like Chloe's own attempts at school composition. Not a full stop or a comma in sight, but there was no teacher standing at the front of the class with a nasty smile on her mouth, reading it out at a breathless gallop so that the whole of 5D laughed their horrible heads off.

All there was, was a bit at the beginning saying that the man who wrote it was considered to be one of the finest modern writers, and – a bit bloody stupid in Chloe's opinion – one of the finest users of the English Language – and he was Irish! Well, that sounded a bit Irish to her, frankly. Anyway, she thought she would read it to Gemma at some point because it seemed quite suitable, and Gemma would be impressed.

Gemma. Poor old thing. Gemma, she thought, stretching her mouth wide as a clown's, would be easy. Gemma, she thought, outlining her lips with Cha-Cha Crimson, was basically about Mouth. Gemma, she thought, pouting now to brush in the colour, needed to have the emphasis taken away from what Chloe could recognize perfectly well as her victim's eyes. Right away from the eyes and concentrated on those potentially sexy lips. Everybody had *some* good feature or other, she supposed. That was Number Three's. Such lips, if emphasized and displayed, would not stumble over saying Yes, *Yes*.

She blotted her own mouth and smiled at her reflection, slipping the piece of tissue between the relevant pages of the book. She was really getting into all this now. She could never go back to being merely an assistant again.

Gemma met Jim on the doorstep as she was leaving for the beauty parlour. She was holding up the lipstick like some kind of crucifix, and found his hunted, shifty look as he focused on it deeply irritating. Whereupon she looked into the hall mirror, did a quick whip round the oral region, and turned back with a provocative smile, a very *red* provocative smile. She put her head on one side, a hand on one hip, half closed her eyes Monroe-style and said 'Mmm?' And when he remained speechless and staring, she had a sudden rush of pure wickedness, as one with mouth so coloured might, and leaned towards him, pouting.

'Do you think it's a bit too red?' she asked.

'No,' he said.

And off she skipped.

Chloe, leaning up against the reception desk, held up a lipstick and said, 'I wonder when they first thought of this – '

And then wished she hadn't because, as always happened with old people, Betty knew and Betty was going to *tell her.*

'Certainly the Egyptians, who were the masters of artifice, knew its value. They made theirs out of henna and cochineal – makes quite a good colour I believe. At any rate it lasts: some of the mummies still had red lips when the tombs were opened – everything else withered and dead and the lips bright red. Rather a nice touch, putting on make-up for the last journey to the gods.'

'Of course, in our culture its not the same,' she paused to make a pencil note in the margin of her notepad. 'For instance, they made up Marilyn Monroe with such a vivid scarlet mouth that the priest refused to bury her, said she wouldn't be let in to see God looking like a harlot. They had to clean her up and start again. They finished her off with baby pink. Or so I read.'

'Cochineal,' said Chloe, buffering her Cha-Cha nails, 'what's that?'

'Ground-up beetle, dear,' said Betty.

Chloe put the buffer down again. 'Filthy buggers,' she said.

'Don't say buggers, dear,' said Betty mildly. 'And needs must when the devil drives. Red lips have always been seductive. *Femme fatale. Homme fatal.* Men used to wear it too. Certainly the Egyptians did.'

'Foreigners!' said Chloe. But she was thoughtful.

Irritatingly, Betty continued. '*Femme fatale.* The Painted Lady. The Wicked Lady. Remember Margaret Lockwood?'

'Who?'

'Before your time. Film star. Now *there* was a mouth. Full, red, and shaped like the bows of Agincourt. A devilish mouth. Fatal. Women have always wanted to be the *femme fatale*. I wonder why?'

'Here comes Number Three,' said Chloe thankfully, hurrying to the door.

On the way she winked at the twisted cherub. Her last – and who knows – maybe her best.

*

Gemma had bought herself a Hot Little Number and damn the expense. She knew it was exquisite, and she knew she would feel exquisite wearing it. But little Joseph suits in pearl-grey silk do not come cheap. She told the bank manager it was money needed for an operation – which it is, she thought, in a manner of speaking. It had cost so much she felt faint afterwards, but you could not go half measures in a venture such as this. A man with half a château, an MG and a taste for good living can soon spot if it's Marks and Spencer, or The Biz. You could convince yourself of anything once you had done it.

'Very nice,' said Chloe, who personally thought it could be cut an inch lower, and an inch higher all round.

'What about my body?' said Gemma doubtfully, feeling the pneumatic depths of her midriff, squidging bits of herself up in her fingers.

'It'll do,' said Chloe, who was not here to flatter. 'And the mouth will take his eyes off everything else.' She sounded very positive.

Gemma told her about the incident with Jim.

Chloe took it very seriously. 'It is always good,' she said, 'to try things out where you can. I'll bet he's got the hots for it now and *she's* getting the benefit.'

'Ah well,' said Gemma, 'she's welcome. *I certainly* don't want him.' And she told Chloe of her bargain with God.

'Always good to take fate by the balls,' said Chloe.

Gemma decided that this frankness in such a setting was no bad thing. Times change, she decided. And so must she.

Chloe would show the way. Lipstick was the feature for Gemma, there was no doubt about it. A large red, willing mouth would say Yes, I Will.

You did not open the bidding with your worst card, after all, said Chloe, thinking of Otto. 'Take it or leave it,' she had said to him, right at the beginning, and he had. Taken it. Oh yes, that was what you did. She was in control there, too. You eased the way, soothed the masculine doubts, played the game of Will She, Won't She, Stay – made yourself more special than any of the others. Power. Real Power. Very Pleasing Power. But first – as she had said – You Have To Hook Him.

Last week, when Gemma actually pronounced the words 'Marriage' and 'Babies', Chloe nearly vomited on the spot. And she quickly shoved a hand over her client's mouth whether the watchful Tabitha could see it or not. For she had been shocked beyond all reason. If ever a woman required an Initial Consultation, Number Three had.

You don't say *that*.

You don't give a hint that you are anything but a fun girl.

Fun in a château? Easy.

Fun in an MG? No problem.

Fun in the bedroom. CERTAINLY.

But not – I want to tie you down, want to pin you down, want to hold you down with weddings and homemaking and staying in for the telly on a Saturday night.

Leave it out, as Chloe remarked. What you say is – Me? Want that? You have to be joking.

Smile at it, laugh at it, say it through scornful lips, big fat red lips. A red lipstick, if loud enough, if bright enough, if applied thickly enough, will say all this and more.

That was when Chloe saw that Gemma's eyes *were* victim's eyes. For she had forgotten both the tune and the words of How To Be Predatory.

'Red lipstick,' said Chloe firmly.

'I have one,' said Gemma. 'I will bring it.'

And now, Good Girl, she had.

Gemma handed over Evening Crimson to Chloe who opened it and sniffed it.

'But next time, buy one from here,' she said. Deciding to take another run at the verbal hill, she gestured to the display of lipsticks on the trolley: 'I think you should definitely purchase all your future requirements from our wide range of beauty products available.'

'Why?' asked Gemma.

So much, thought Chloe, for the verbal runs. There was really no answer to that, except her commission. Nobody ever said 'Why?' to Tabitha. Well – just wait. When *she* was in charge she would make it a condition of treatment that you had to buy the stuff from her. Like champagne in nightclubs.

Perhaps, thought Gemma, Evening Crimson would be a talisman. Despite being sceptical (apart from touching wood, never picking up a dropped glove, declining to walk under ladders) Gemma thought that it might bring her luck. Something had to.

Chloe then trotted out her little piece about 'it's what lovers desire and what husbands fear' – to her client's perplexity.

'Well what,' Gemma asked, 'do you do about that? I mean, if you start off being the hottest thing since Mata Hari –'

'Martha Who?'

'Er – Madonna?'

'Got you.'

'If you start off like that, and then you want to transmogrify ...'

'I'd keep that to yourself if I was you.'

'What?'

'That last bit. I don't think you'd get very far suggesting *that*. Well, not unless he was a bit that way inclined himself.'

Gemma frowned.

'Don't do that, either,' said Chloe.

'What way inclined?'

'You know – dressing up in women's clothes sort of thing.'

'Jesus,' said Gemma, 'it never occurred to me he might like *that*.' Perhaps it was more of the New Wave. A stylistic thing? Like multi-coloured and flavoured condoms in her own heyday? The little beautician seemed to know everything.

'Well, he might go for it,' said Chloe with sympathetic brightness, thinking that you wouldn't think it to look at her. 'They often like you to take a bit of a lead. You could test it out later on. You know, slip into a pair of Y-fronts – say it's a bit of a joke – that sort of thing. He might really go for it.' She sounded doubtful.

'I hope not,' said Gemma fervently. Suddenly she felt quite weak, talisman lipstick or not. 'I don't think I could.'

'Could what?'

'Go for transvestism.'

Chloe shrugged with irritation. 'Well, one minute you say you want to and the next you don't. You should have a clear point of view about things like that. He could get very confused.'

'I never said I liked it – '

'You did. You said it after you mentioned that Martha something.' Gemma laughed.

It was true, even unmade-up, her mouth was delightful. 'Mata Hari,' she laughed, 'was a beautiful woman spy who got her way by using sex.' And she laughed more. Chloe felt quite cheesed off.

'Oh yeah?' she said, with less than her customary decorum. 'What's the joke?'

'And I said *transmogrify* – not transvestism. It just means to change your shape.'

It was on the tip of Chloe's pert little tongue to say Gemma could certainly benefit from Transwhatevering in the bum department, but she stopped herself. This was Number Three and she wanted it to be really good. But she did not like to look thick. It weakened her hold. So she reached for her book, opened it, and removed the blotted tissue which had left, in a neat little O, a very slight imprint of her lips. It reminded Chloe to check on something.

'By the way – Jo-Jo's lipstick story. The one I said to use as an ice-breaker ... '

Gemma nodded. 'Word perfect,' she said.

'Good for you,' said Chloe. 'He'll love it to death. Everyone I tell thinks it's great. They love all that.'

No need to ask who *They* were, since Chloe was clearly not talking about Argentinian peasants.

'*They* want,' she said,'what *They* think *They* can handle, and never can ... ' She pushed at the side of her nose. 'What lovers *love* ... ' she pushed again ' ... and what husbands fear. Remember that.'

Then she began to read:

'Or shall I wear a red yes and how he kissed me under the Moorish wall and I thought well as well him as another and then I asked him with my eyes to ask again yes and then he asked me would I yes to say yes my mountain flower and first I put my arms around him yes and drew him down to me so he could feel my breasts all perfume yes and his heart was going like mad and yes I said yes I will Yes.'

Then she closed the book, leaned across towards Gemma, tapped its cover with her finger and said, 'And that's supposed to be fucking art. Can't even put in a full stop. But you get the drift?'

'Oh yes,' said Gemma lying back on the couch, 'I get the drift.'

As Chloe switched on the steamer and prepared to dim the lights she said, 'Remember now – avoid the truth at all costs. You can tell whopping great lies out of a shiny red mouth and they just slip out without being noticed.'

'Lies?' said Gemma dreamily.

'Fibs then,' said Chloe.

'Cautiousness?' said Gemma, happier with the word.

While her client steamed the dirt of the world away, Chloe wandered around the salon touching the pink walls, eyeing the chandelier, running distasteful fingers over the fluted shells. Then she clicked her fingers, wiggled her bottom and did a little dance step or two. With Otto behind her, so to speak, there'd be no problem. She wandered back to the reception desk and the scribbling Betty.

'What did the salon you trained in look like then?' she asked loudly. 'Like this?'

'Pardon?' said Betty.

'I Said What Did Your Training Salon Look Like?'

'Bauhaus!' barked Betty.

Chloe jumped. 'No need to be rude about it,' she said. 'I only wondered.'

*

She had done her best. And she had to admit that of them all, Number Three was by far the most promising.

Chloe had succeeded in emphasizing lips which could be controlled in what they said, and diminishing eyes which could not.

'You'll do,' she said cheerfully, tucking down the neckline of the pearl-grey silk a little more. 'Now chin up. Smile. And stick out those tits.'

'What?' said Betty, since they were standing nearby.

Chloe raised her voice. 'I said pucker those lips.'

So Gemma did both as she went over to Betty to pay. Betty took the money, peered long and hard at Gemma's finished face, and said to Chloe without smiling: 'Very nicely done, dear. The Film Star look.' And closed down the till for the night.

She watched Gemma leave, saw the spring in her step, the roll in her hips, and she said to Chloe as the door was finally bolted, 'Sad you know, but none of those screen goddesses, not *one*, ended up happy ever after.'

'Who cares,' said Chloe, shrugging. 'You can cash up now. I'm all finished.'

23

As soon as her taxi turned the corner and the Beauty Parlour was out of sight, Margery realized that she had forgotten a rug. Oh well, Reginald would just have to sit on her skirts, wouldn't he?

She said as much to the taxi driver, but he was far too involved radio contacting his base to make conversation. His ears had gone very red, she noticed, and you could tell he was upset. She, of course, felt wonderfully calm and happy. A Beauty Parlour did that for you.

Willingly as a Christian *en route* for the lions, the taxi driver helped her carry the things from the road, through a small coppice, over a field, down a short rutted lane and into another field, next to the honey farm. Bees buzzed about them as they walked, single file, carrying the bags and boxes. The day was hot. The Beautician had been right though – in all this heat it was very refreshing to be knickerless – much cooler. She'd just have to be *very careful* where she sat.

The lovely young Chloe had told her how you got taxi drivers to help: you paid them only when they had completed the service you required. He therefore followed her as pack mule because he could do nothing else. As would Reginald Postgate in due course.

The taxi driver was glad that the only observers of this deeply humiliating scene were dumb animals: a field of extremely silly-looking sheep; numerous voles, mice, and hedgerow riff-raff who very sensibly hid; wise bees who knew that nothing in human terms could compete with the strangeness of their apiary theatricals and kept away; skulking wasps, assorted insects and one small human who was supposed to be on a three-hour cross-country with his class, and who pointed out to his best friend Wilkins that he could see no reason for not cheating, given that his ambition was to become rich enough to own a sodding car, and who therefore stayed behind a tree with a can of Fanta while his plebeian classmates ran past. The small boy stared at the sight (uncommon in Hinkley

Wood), and wondered what a woman, at least as old as his mother, was doing dressed up like Goldilocks, with her face painted to match, and carrying what appeared to be a teddy bear's picnic into the woods.

The taxi driver, fearing the bees and wasps and feeling not a little waspish himself, said sarcastically, 'Rug? Sure you wouldn't like me to run back and fetch one for you?'

It occurred to him to wonder, as he waited for her to pay, how she would get back. Conscience fluttered around him, nearly settled, then flew off to join the bees. Let her work that out for herself. Nutters.

It did occur to him that Beadle might be About with his secret camera, but she was too serious about it all, and too barmy-looking by half. All the same, he did not swear once, just in case, so that if Beadle *was* about he wouldn't suffer the humiliation of being beeped every few seconds during the showing of his exploits on telly.

He was disappointed, when he left, that no one leaped out of the bushes. For a moment he thought a skulking small boy might be part of a plot, but he made no move. At any rate, the *woman* couldn't be Beadle; both her hands were the same. He shrugged. Pity really.

After he had gone came the loving ritual.

She spread out the circular white tablecloth, embroidered with honeybees, and smoothed it lovingly over the grass. Upon this she set the honey sandwiches, the honey-glazed ham (sliced thinly and elegantly), the little individual brown rolls of bread, the butter still ice-hard from its coolbag, the sweet little amber tomatoes which she scattered on the white linen as if they were jewels, the hydromel, still fizzing slightly but smelling delicious, honeyed cakes of fond memory – how it all began, she would say – pretty pots of almond and appleblossom honey, all fitting into the circular snowiness of the tablecloth (circular for sweet food): the whole thing looked like a feast for the gods.

She was delighted, and spread out her pretty skirts so they were not creased, folded her hands in her lap, and waited. She sat very still, only shifting occasionally from the strange discomfort of sitting on the grass without benefit of underwear. The heat of the day was fierce. It was a little after four. He should be here soon – traffic was bad on Fridays.

She knew he would come. Her map had been absolutely accurate;

he would find the place. Nothing would pass her lips until he arrived. She felt a little trickle of moisture run down her face, but she sat on imperviously, skirts spread, hands dutifully folded, waiting, waiting.

The boy, watching from the undergrowth, took bets with himself on how long she would stay like that, so still, even when the bees came buzzing about her and then the wasps, chasing off the bumblers and setting themselves up for a good feast on the picnic. He waited until his growling stomach told him it was time to leave – he was thirsty, he was tired, above all he was aware that not many yards away was a feast of tuck. He crept out. Perhaps the woman was asleep? He could maybe just edge his way forwards and reach out from behind her?

Margery heard. She turned, the light of hope in her eyes, a welcome about her lips – he had come, he had come – she screwed up her eyes against the sun – he had *not* come.

'Hallo,' said the boy.

'Go away,' she said fiercely, for she had seen the look of hope in his eyes too, and this feast was not for the likes of him.

And he didn't want any, either, for as he drew closer, what had seemed so delicious was repulsive.

The butter had melted to oil, the ham was curled and dry, its brown-edged line of fat white and glistening in the sun, the honey sandwiches cockled upwards revealing the glaze of sweetness below, now dotted with happy insects and crawling, delight-dazed wasps, the tomatoes had lost their sheen, the tablecloth its sparkle, ants fed in determined relays, beetles crawled, and Margery – as if woken suddenly – began to itch.

The boy looked at her face and then he was glad to escape, glad to leave all this, whatever it meant, for she was frightening. There were brown streaks running down from her lashes, smears and smudges where she had brushed investigating insects away, her eyes were swollen and puffy, with lids that were patchy brown and one cheek glowed russet, the other dirty white. She was scratching somewhere beneath her skirt, scratching and scratching, rhymically without sign of relief. And he didn't like her expression much either – it was scary and odd.

'Yah!' he said suddenly, 'Yah!' and then he got up and ran for dear life.

Margery, jerked back into the world again by the boy's yell, ceased to scratch and reached across the tablecloth for one of the bottles, the hydromel, for she was thirsty. She drank some and felt better for it. A pity to waste all this food. She broke some of the bread rolls, which were crisp by now, opened one of the special pots of honey, spread it thickly and began to eat. She drank more. She ate more. She cried a little when she began devouring the honey cakes, because that was how it all began. Those beautiful new teeth he had created for her, those beautiful appointments when it was only him and her and the honey world. She ate on.

As she opened the second pot of honey she heard his voice telling her that he had done his best, that they should last her lifetime, that she could eat all the honey cakes she wanted if she cleaned her teeth. 'Do that,' he said, 'and you will stay away from the dentist's chair a good long while.'

And then the voice, *his* voice, ceased, the tape rewound itself, went back and repeated, 'Clean them very carefully ... stay away from the dentist's chair ... clean them very carefully ... stay away a good long while.'

So she went on eating and eating, digging her fingers into the honey pots, licking them clean, washing it all down with ambrosial drink. It shouldn't, she counselled herself, as she settled back on the grass in the evening sun, it shouldn't take long for the sweetness to get to work. It would probably begin right away.

She had almost forgotten the Makeover. It was so long ago and so lovely. She felt so attractive with her frock as well.

'It should last the day if you are careful,' Chloe had said when she left the salon. Well, she had been careful, hadn't she? She touched her face. It seemed all right – a little sticky here and there, but not too bad. How he would have loved it. She knew perfectly well what had happened – the first Mrs Postgate had stopped him in some way. Margery would have to deal with that. Meanwhile, meanwhile – perhaps she would just lie here for a while, warmed by the sun, and have a little sleep before setting off home. How? Well, well, she thought, yawning, cross that bridge when I come to it.

The boy brought his father to see. Parents never believed you, but this time they had to, because there she was.

'Poor thing,' said his father, and he touched Margery's arm gently. She woke. She had a slight headache, but nothing too bad.

'I need a taxi,' she said, when the boy's father enquired if there was anything he could do.

'Tall order round here,' smiled the man.

'Well, I shall just have to walk.'

Not so much to carry now. She began clearing up the debris, singing 'Honey-pie … You are driving me crazy …' Suddenly she yearned for him, so much that she felt she was melting somewhere in the region of where her knickers ought to be. Mrs Postgate! Old Queen!

Already she could feel the voracious sugar in the crevices of her teeth.

The man said, 'Perhaps I could drive you to a taxi rank?'

'That,' said Margery, staggering a little so that the boy giggled and the man held her arm to steady her, 'would be very kind.'

'Wait here,' said the man, and he went to collect his car.

But no taxi would take her. Not a drunken middle-aged woman who must be living rough and whom they would probably be lumbered with.

So the man took her.

He asked her for her address and she gave it to him, crystal clear, very firm. It was not, however, an address in Kingston upon Thames, but an address in a rather grander area of London. It was a shame to waste the Makeover that pretty girl at the salon had achieved. She wanted Reginald to see it, at least, before she washed it away. And besides, she was quite looking forward to confronting Mrs Reginald Postgate, vile woman, and would prefer to do so now while she was dressed for it, and while her face was done so nicely.

She knew the address. Had even visited the street in secret. The man said, 'Where now?' and she pointed, a smile on her lips; how kind he was.

Somehow the Old Queen had found out. Or he had been stricken with conscience (how like him *that* would be) and felt he could not seek the blossom of happiness after all. The girl at the Beautician's had said it *might* happen. She said that men were notoriously difficult to wrench away from their homes and families but that There Were Ways.

'Like what?' Margery had asked.

'Little love letter, or confirmation of a hotel. Something tucked in a pocket so that when Number One finds it, the balloon goes up.' And she had smiled, and winked, as she checked Margery's rouge for symmetry.

'Nearly there now,' said the driver.

'Very kind indeed,' murmured Margery. '*Doesn't* the heat make you tired?' And she gave a little belch which the driver ignored, while the boy in the back giggled ostentatiously.

Margery sat up, smoothed her ruffles which were now sadly limp, the full skirt creased and stained, and wished she had a handkerchief to mop her face. She would have asked the driver for the duster she saw tucked in his side pocket, but he was frowning with concentration. Ah well, she decided, needs must, and she took the hem of her frock in her fingers and brought it to her face. The driver, no longer concentrating, turned to ask where exactly she needed to be dropped, focused on his strange female passenger apparently playing peek-a-boo above the edge of her frock, revealing her curvaceous and completely naked torso below, and braked so sharply that the picnic items were hurled about.

'That was good, Dad,' said his son from the back.

A remark too ambiguous for comfort.

She left all her unloaded stuff by the side of the road, watched the car drive off with a confused expression on her bedraggled face, shrugged – for what was such unpleasant changeability in all this happiness – and walked the rest of the way up the road. It was not far, and now that the evening was well on it was cooler. Nice neighbourhood. Large houses. She could be happy here. She gave her hair one more pat, smoothed her frock one more time, and entered the gate, walking firmly up the path.

Lobelias, she noticed, as she waited for the door to open, and pink verbena – lots of hanging baskets and well-tended tubs. She rang the bell again. That was what the woman spent her time doing, instead of spending it with a lovely husband like Reginald who needed care and attention. Well, she had come to give him that all right. A bee buzzed nearby; out for a last nip of nectar before closing time, he smelled her sticky face and settled near her mouth. She left it there and girded her naked loins.

Mrs Reginald Postgate, who had been preparing barbecue dips by removing lids from Marks and Spencer cartons, and who hoped Reginald would answer the door, was stirred into life at the nightmarish sight of Margery, smiling with her mouth, glaring with her eyes. A bee attached to her lips as she opened them and said she had come to claim Reginald for her own.

We Are In Love.

Something like this *would* happen on the night of the Practice Barbecue.

'I think you've got the wrong house,' said Mrs Reginald Postgate, as indeed, she might be forgiven for saying.

'I think not,' said Margery.

And the bee, dazed by the sun, dull-witted by the lateness of the hour, and seeing a haven, crawled into her mouth as she spoke.

'This is number eight,' said Mrs Reginald Postgate irritably, 'and there is only my husband in.' She could have added, At The Moment, and become even more ratty. Soon the guests would arrive.

'I need your husband,' said Margery, attempting to pick the bee from her mouth as she spoke.

'There is an emergency number,' said Mrs Reginald Postgate firmly. 'Use it.' And she barred the way.

And then Margery screamed. A scream of pain. A scream not usually associated with the leafy byways of this part of London, and one which brought several neighbours rushing to their doors in shuddering excitement.

Mrs Reginald Postgate looked embarrassed and perplexed. She tried to give a round-robin look to the assembled opened doors intimating that she knew nothing of this woman.

Margery opened her mouth and the dying bee, sting spent, crawled out.

From behind her Mrs Reginald Postgate heard her husband call, 'What the *hell* was that? The chicken wings are burning.'

From in front of her she heard a voice belonging to a navy and white sprigged frock, requiring much fancy bridgework, sing out, 'Yoo-hoo, here we are then. Where's Reggie?' Followed by a half-plate in voile with hat-trim to match saying, 'Well, hallo at last. *What* a nice evening.'

'Do you know,' hissed Margery through her swollen mouth, 'what the Queen Bee does when she's had it? She Buggers Off! Go on – Bugger Off then ... '

And she ducked and wove her way round the astounded Mrs Reginald Postgate and into the hall, from whence she was heard to call 'Reginald!' Followed by his testy response of 'What *now*?'

'Where the bee sucks there suck I,' sang the horrible voice, receding into the garden.

'Honey-pie!' it called. 'Honey, honey-pie ... '

Mrs Reginald Postgate yearned for a quiet sit-down and a leaf through a catalogue. Reginald Postgate was decidedly cross anyway, given that the barbecue, as barbecues will, was being what he termed femininely fickle.

She followed the horrible voice out into the garden. Behind her, following eagerly, came the navy and white sprig, the printed voile and a selection of Jaeger and Country Casuals. All just in time to see Margery, smile broader than Lewis Carroll's feline, complexion as if it had been left out in the rain, lift her skirt high and say delightedly 'Peek-a-boo, Reginald. Peek-a-boo!'

24

Caroline drank off two fingers of whisky. It was not a very sensible thing to do, expecially since the little trainee back at the Beauty Parlour had said she should watch her shattered capillaries, but then, Caroline was well past being sensible. She peered into the mirror – especially with these plum-coloured lips and siren-dark eyes. How very glad she was that she had not abandoned this plan. More glad than she could say, *now*. Because she had just learned that – if all went well – Rita was putting herself up as the Photographic Society's *Caterer*. Rita and Bernie were going into *partnership!*

Since learning of this cosy little scheme she had meekly submitted to being kept out of the kitchen by Rita (looking devastating in a short black frock, very high red heels and a winsome little white pinny tied round her teeny little waist) and to being given the minion-like task of polishing the glasses while Bernie was upstairs changing. At least that meant that he, too, was kept out of the kitchen and away from the temptation of tasting anything.

'Where's Bernie?' said Rita. 'I need his help.'

'Changing,' said Caroline, so smugly that Rita banged the door.

But he came down too soon.

Whistling and pleased with himself because he had made love all afternoon, because he was going to become *Chairman* of the Photographic Society, and because he had a whole new outfit of clothes, he descended the stairs.

The only slight distraction was that his own dear, soft Caroline was looking rather – well – dangerous came to mind – but what did that matter? The two women in his life were both friendly at last, and resigned to each other's existence. Life was good. He would be Chairman, Rita would help him, and Caroline would always be there to fill in the places between.

He smoothed the new tie against his new shirt and whistled some more, putting his hands in the pockets of his chinos. Lovely clothes – the sort of thing he would never dare wear in the old days. Wearing them now certainly boosted his confidence. It had taken him no time at all to change.

He stopped whistling at the foot of the stairs and smiled as he saw Caroline polishing away at the glasses. He advanced, spreading his shoulders in relaxed relief to hear his ex-wife busying herself in the kitchen.

Indeed, he might well have quoted 'God's in his heaven, all's right with the world' as he strolled across the room towards his lover and put his arms around her waist. He might well have felt so optimistic, despite the strange sparkle in Caroline's eyes, and he might well have continued to feel optimistic, had not Caroline looked at her watch and then said sharply, 'You can't wear *those* clothes. Go and change at once.'

This was very confusing. Last week she liked them. And now here she was, flapping the tea-towel, pursing her vampire lips, and telling him to Go And Change At Once as if he'd come down wearing a frock. He had never, in all his wildest dreams, aspired to actually *understanding* women, but he had thought in this instance he was dancing on thick ice. Apparently not.

'But you like these clothes,' he said, bewildered.

'Keep your voice down,' said Caroline.

Another odd thing to say.

'You said you liked them,' he whispered, immediately getting into humouring mode.

Caroline seemed to implode. 'Well – I *don't.*'

'Why not?' The question was one of genuine interest.

She thought. Rapidly. 'Because the shirt doesn't match the trousers,' she said positively, and folded her arms, looking not unlike a slightly less confident version of Morticia Munster.

'Well *you* said they did.'

'When?'

'When you bought them,' he said huffily.

Oh fuck.

Caroline peered. She had not, in truth, noticed what he was wearing, in her desire to keep him out of the way. 'Ah,' she said, waiting for inspiration. And 'Ah' again. 'Must be the light.'

'That's all right then,' he said with relief. He had backed away a little, for truth was this new look of Caroline's was best viewed from a distance.

'No, it's not,' she said positively.

'Why?'

'You might spill food on them.'

'I'll use a serviette,' he began, and then rebelled. Bloody cheek. 'I don't spill food, as you put it. I'm a very clean eater.'

Caroline had a sudden riveting vision of Bernie taking a big mouthful of the ceviche, followed by an even more riveting vision of his spitting it out.

'Not always,' she said, and then several thousand years of deep-rooted feminine sensibility came to her rescue again. She slunk over to him, put her hand on his shoulder, gazed into his eyes, her own so disturbingly wanton with their belladonna lids, and said 'Please.'

So off he went, and when Rita put her little head round the door for the second time and said, 'Where *is* Bernie?' Caroline said, 'Still changing.'

Rita wrinkled her brow, perplexed at this new sartorial side to him. 'They'll be here in a minute.'

'Yes, I know,' said Caroline happily. 'How's the food?'

'Fine,' said Rita, with just the faintest touch of arrogance.

'Anything I can do?'

'Yes,' said Rita. 'You can open the bottles of red to let them breathe.'

She should not, reflected Caroline as she tipped a tiny little dribble of TCP into each of the bottles, have sounded quite so arrogant when she said that. She began to understand why people went on bumping off victim after victim – you could get hooked on the power of it all.

She was still digesting the whisky when Bernie came back down the stairs. He was no longer whistling and the spring had gone out of his step. He wore an old denim shirt and his jeans. He looked defiant.

'Lovely,' said Caroline, scarcely noticing.

Rita peered round the kitchen door. 'Where have you been?' she said to Bernie. And looking him up and down said, too wifely for comfort, 'Haven't you changed *yet*?'

'Yes I sodding well have!' he snapped. And he gave her a look that suggested he had further to say on the matter if she did.

Rita jumped, fluttered, blinked. But before she could get into her distressed kitten pose, the doorbell rang.

Saved by the bell, thought Caroline, swaying just a little as she went to open the door.

You Are What You Look. Later, putting up a remonstrative hand with nails like inky talons, Caroline said loudly and firmly to Rita, enunciating very carefully so that their guests should make no mistake, '*You* cooked the meal. *You* did it all. It is only fair that I should do the running around and serving of it. *Sit!*'

And so firm was her intent that Rita did as she was told.

Caroline began to serve each course.

Taking the hidden portion of ceviche from the back of the fridge, she gave it to Bernie, who therefore ate with relish. Caroline, knowing she had to go through with this or perish on the battlefield, ate hers with gusto. Knowing what the horrible taste was helped, as, indeed, did the whisky. Rita looked at them each in turn, picking at her plate, hope in her eyes.

She must be praying she's got the only bad bit, thought Caroline happily.

Bernie had spent many a lyrical moment explaining how brilliant Rita's cookery was, and what an asset she would be to the Photographic Society. He licked his lips – the ceviche was delicious – now they would *know*. He paused to give Rita a grateful look, and she looked back at him with a question he did not altogether understand.

Caroline was eating away, going 'Yum Yum' a little too loudly, which was slightly embarrassing, and the Current Incumbent and his wife were poking their food around on their plates as if it were infectious. Perhaps they did not like fish? He was about to enquire when Caroline said, 'It certainly tastes of the sea,' very gaily, and proceeded to refill their glasses with Saumur.

She had not trifled with the white wine because Bernie drank only white. And anyway, one should not gild the lily. The amenable Current Incumbent and his amenable wife drank with relief and hoped they could fill up on the next course. Whatever that raw fish had tasted of, it was certainly not the *sea* ...

Bernie expounded his views of the role of the new Chairman, were he lucky enough to be elected. With Rita firing so brilliantly on all her culinary guns he thought there was little question of that. So did the Current Incumbent, but for a very different reason. Smiling, Caroline stood up to clear away. Well, she was behaving too. Though there was a little too much rattling of cutlery and businesslike clucking.

'Mmm,' she said, 'the neighbourhood cats are in for a treat.'

'You hate the neighbourhood cats,' said Bernie, discomfited to see how much the guests had left.

'I know,' said Caroline, even more gaily, and tripped off to the kitchen. Nothing could stop her now.

'Will you pour the red wine Rita?' she called over her shoulder, 'while I get these delicious-looking pheasants dished up?' She gave the Current Incumbent and his wife a broad smile, with an unmistakeable hint of sympathy. 'Apparently,' she said 'this wine is from one of the top small vineyards in France. Rita's friend gets it. Bung Ho!'

The guests relaxed a little. *Pheasant*. That was more like it.

A frowning Rita whispered, 'I'll come and help now. I think I'd better.'

And Caroline hissed back, 'No, no – you stay here and help Bernie along.'

Which was indisputably reasonable.

'Go shooting often, Bernie?' asked the Current Incumbent politely.

'No,' said Bernie.

'But he'd like to, wouldn't you?' said Rita.

'You should come and stay with us sometime. Have a go.'

Bernie said, 'I'd like that very much.'

Rita beamed. 'Bernie always was good at things,' she said vaguely.

Caroline heard it all as she set down the used plates in the kitchen, and wanted to vomit. But she remembered the washing-up liquid and instantly felt better. Fairy Liquid was particularly thick and rich. Much as one might want one's men. Only Caroline wanted Bernie, who was neither.

She consigned the rejected ceviche to the bottom of the rubbish bin.

Next the pheasant. The Current Incumbent went so far as to rub his hands. Bernie had promised him a veritable feast. He hoped it improved.

His wife was asking Rita about châteaux and suppliers and Rita was expounding confidently. 'Smell,' Caroline heard her command.

She would have given her eye teeth to see the woman's face as she took a good sniff from her glass.

Hubble, bubble, she thought, taking in the plates.

Rita took a good dig at the stuffing piled on hers and placed some in her mouth. She immediately went bright scarlet, and nearly gagged.

I have lived for this moment, thought Caroline. For this moment, I Have Lived.

Conversation was now non-existent. The wine, château-bottled as it was, did not flow. Bernie noticed how little his guests and Rita had eaten. Again. Though Caroline had tucked in, bless her. He waited politely to see if they wished to finish what was on their plates. They did not. Funny people, he thought, and looked at Rita. Her eyes were very, very bright. He knew that look – teary-wearies not far away.

'Well, wasn't that just delish?' he said bravely.

Response to this was minimal.

Bernie looked across at Caroline. In the candlelight she looked more and more dangerous. He did not know whether to be excited or afraid. Excited, he hoped, and picked up the bottle of red wine.

'More drink,' he said heartily. And he, who normally only drank white wine, poured some red into his own glass before Caroline could stop him. But even as he raised the poisoned chalice, she put out her hand with its dangerous dark nails and – if not exactly dashing it from his lips – she took it from him with a little tug saying, 'No, no, Bernie. *Pudding* wine.'

Which was undoctored, despite the temptation.

The Current Incumbent's wife said she would stick to bottled water.

'Good job I bought some,' said Caroline, giving Rita the benefit of her sumptuous smiling lips.

'Bernie,' said Rita, 'I must talk to you.' She gave a little jerk of her head in the direction of the kitchen. 'Alone.'

Too late, thought Caroline, for it was all in the bin.

Rita opened the lid, from which wafted a pungent aroma of Forest Pine. She put her perplexed head on one side, as if thinking, and said to herself 'Was it all right? Was it?'

'I must say though,' said Caroline, as she cut at the tart carefully, and Rita held out each plate, 'the wine tasted a bit off.'

'I know,' said Rita miserably.

'But then – it might be because it was so *special* and of course *I* am not used to special wines.'

Rita did not look convinced. The canary, noted the vamp with glee, was definitely moulting.

'At least this tart is OK,' she said flatly.

That's what you think, said Caroline to herself, for she had cut a sliver of Bernie's unadulterated portion for Rita to try.

As she sat at the table and watched the guests toying with their dessert, and at the Current Incumbent who, having found some palatable alcohol in the muscat, was knocking it back, she thought it was the most successful dinner party she had ever not given. To hide behind a mask helped – couldn't have done it otherwise.

Bernie had finished his tart. Caroline managed to continue talking despite getting very little response. He rather resented her competence. Especially since little Rita – usually so vivacious – was silent, pale and definitely weepy eyed. Indeed, the teary-wearies had finally overtaken her, and she had fled to the bathroom. Caroline, looking quite nonplussed, suggested coffee.

'And this time *I'll* make it,' she said, as if it were part of an ongoing text.

The Current Incumbent's wife said, 'Oh *good*.'

Bernie was bemused. He looked up at Caroline. Her eyes looked mysterious, dark and deep; her mouth curved, enlarged by the shiny purple (replenished frequently as advised) and he had a sudden cold clutching at his heart. She looked distinctly evil.

'Coffee and then we must go,' said their male guest firmly.

Rita returned, damp and ruffled and pink about the eyes. Caroline gave her a look of triumph and glided into the kitchen, a smile of victory about her mouth.

While the water heated she added the rejected almond tart to the rest of the leavings and loaded up the dishwasher. No evidence remains, she told herself as she carried the tray back in. No one will ever know. I am safe. She set the coffee upon the table and could not resist saying to the wan-faced Rita, 'Like to taste it?' Rita fled bathroomwards once more.

Bernie stared after her, feeling agonized. What *was* the matter? From the upstairs bathroom he could hear the faint sound of Rita's sobbing. The others, now quite cheerful at their imminent departure, could not. He was puzzled by their guests' behaviour – perhaps they were vegetarians? Poor Rita. So much effort, so little response. And all for him. Caroline did not seem to be sympathetic either, so where had this sisterhood thing gone?

He excused himself from his guests and ran up the stairs two at a time. He heard what might have been a pair of little fists pounding the bathroom walls, and what might have been some kind of incantation regarding Caroline, but it probably wasn't, because when he got to the top of the stairs and called out, it ceased.

Gently, he knocked at the door and waited a short while. 'Let me in darling,' he said, mouth pressed up against the panel. She opened the door slowly, looking downwards with pink puffy eyes, little shoulders shaking, dabbing at the tip of her nose. She smelled of something sweet and flowery as she laid her hot damp cheek against his chest and put her arms around him very tightly. 'Don't leave me,' she whispered. 'Please don't leave me ever again.' And he, who thought there was something not quite right about the statement, but who was in no mood for analysis, held her to him, kissed the top of her little fair head, and said that he never would.

Together they descended the stairs and entered the living-room, standing close to each other, framed in the doorway.

The Current Incumbent and his wife rose from the table. 'Thank you so much,' he said, barely touching Bernie's fingertips, 'for a simply delicious evening.' His voice was even fainter than his touch.

It should have been the crowning joy. It should have made Caroline sing as they turned at the front door to give her one final look of conspiratorial sympathy. But she stood there, in the hallway, showing no such happiness. Instead, in the sharp hall light, she looked as an actress might look coming down from the stage to face the ordinariness of life, lit only by a forty-watt bulb. There was none of the vamp left.

Just to be sure she looked at Rita, who moved fractionally closer to Bernie, and put her head on one side, birdlike, delightful, with a little smile, not unlike Caroline's earlier smirk of victory, lighting up her round little face and playing about her shiny, newly lipsticked beak.

25

Gemma took a very deep breath on the steps of the brasserie and remembered the beautician's orders. She pouted so proudly, and stuck out her chest so magnificently, that she might have been modelling the little Joseph suit instead of merely wearing it on a date. Chloe had been absolutely right. Every male head turned as she walked in, and she remembered the little trainee's words – yes I said yes I will Yes – and never mind anything else.

Pouting and smiling was tricky. Nevertheless she managed both, and sustained both, even when the Denim and the Levis stood up and she saw the unmistakeable glint of a medallion around his neck. What, after all, was a medallion? Didn't *have* to mean he liked Match of the Day and James Last meets Richard Clayderman. Besides, when you were a woman of a certain age, broke and lonely, you could be accommodating about such things. Think Château, she thought, and she did.

Above the gleaming disc was the well-used face – not what you'd call *handsome* exactly, but with a nice head of hair. Not bald at all. Better than nothing. She was quite philosophical. Frankly, with a château and an MGB he could wear a gold-plated dustbin lid around his neck and be called *Wayne*. He did not look much of a prat – hardly at all – and the fifty-one years were fairly approximate. Besides, she had said she was in her late thirties – it was all a matter of *cautiousness* as she and the beautician had agreed. She lowered her eyes quickly. He certainly must not read those.

'Hi,' she said, also finding speaking and pouting a bit of a problem. And she slid into the bench seat beside him.

He looked appreciative. She licked her lips, made a little moue, and said she was sorry if she was the teeniest bit late. He liked that, she could tell. His chest went out a couple of inches. She could play the demure little lady if she chose, she suddenly discovered.

Moue. Moue. Tell me all about yourself. And she sipped her aperitif as expertly as a tart giving French.

She pouted as she listened to him, hanging on to his every word, leaning forwards to express eagerness, crossing legs to establish a few inches of thigh. 'What else? What else?' ran through her head as she supposedly listened. Oh yes, smile, smile a lot. Bright red gooey mouth for smiling with. She did so. Touch, touch a lot. They like that. *They* do. She did so, patting his arm as he made a little joke, tapping the back of his hand to agree with something he said, shifting a little nearer so that the silk rustled and inched a little further up her leg.

Do not be too clever. Do not say things like, In General I Support The Chaos Theory – or – Interesting Man, Balzac. Say things – when you are not smiling and looking agreeable – say things like, Oh Really? – or – I Never Knew That. And remember to nod.

You have to be joking, thinks Gemma.

But she is not.

Where did intellectual equality get you? A packet of wine gums and a Saturday night in. That's where.

She says 'Oh Really? I Never Knew That.' Repeatedly. And she nods like billy-o when he says, 'I Nailed My Colours To The University of Life.'

She couldn't believe it. The more you played the role, the more it worked. Was it so simple? Why was it so simple? What had she spent all those years being a bright young thing for, if all she needed was a bit of lipstick and a lowered IQ? You really just hung on to his every word, intimated he was someone you could look up to (keeping yourself a little lower than him to suit deed to words) and in general gave the impression that you were shy but arousable, and once aroused *very* dangerous.

The red mouth said that. The red mouth said a lot of things. She heard it. The red mouth said Do Go On, Fascinating: and *especially* said it when she was at her most bored. The more bored she felt, the more she said *Fascinating*. Any minute now he'd think she was ESN, the way she appeared to have an intellectual orgasm over the efficiency of French toll roads.

She drifted off. She thought, no wonder men and women found life ever after hard – it was usually based on an erroneous start position. After all, here she was all attention as he grappled with the difficulties of route planning, kilometres, ferry times, and there he was thinking that this was just the sort of thing she wanted to know. But hey presto, two years on and if he tried it she'd be saying, 'Who fucking well *cares* if Cherbourg could fit in an extra sailing – did you collect the dry cleaning?'

But this little game should be child's play. She was a woman. Women were good at it. Not a lot had changed in a few thousand years. Ancient Hittite woman undoubtedly sat in much the same position in which Gemma sat now and flashed a juicy smile at the Ancient Hittite man she was after, while he engaged her in debate regarding the benefits of mud over stone for the *bit hilani*, and how he'd rather like to spend more time in the Lebanon sniffing cedar if he could get away for a few days. Quite what Ancient Hittite man and Ancient Hittite woman then went on to argue about after the first two years Gemma was unsure – what might the Ancient Hittite equivalent of dry cleaning be?

Did you pluck those grasses like I asked you?

Why can't we have a *brick* kiln like everybody else?

She opted for I Dug Up The Roots Last Time – a cry that must be beyond time or culture. She began to feel the part. She began to feel pretty and silly and feminine, and from the way he was looking at her, he was beginning to agree. Poor man, she thought rather fondly, it wasn't – really – fair.

She stroked the silk, licked her lips, and thought the investment had certainly been worthwhile. He admired the suit, and he admired her in it. Easy. Never mind that it really belonged to the bank manager.

She went on listening, accommodating. Mustn't forget that she had Chloe's friend's lipstick story to tell him if the conversation lagged. Didn't seem any sign of that for the moment though. He was going great guns over his entrée.

Keeping her red lips slightly parted, she let her mind dwell on such important matters as whether her Rafaello bikini from six years ago was still stylish enough for draping around the Château's sun-loungers, and whether she could do anything to stop her stomach draping itself around them too.

She needed a pee and would have to be careful since she had said she knew the place well. Wouldn't do to be tripping over the dust-bins at the back. A silly lie, really. Imagine bringing a moron from Crawley here and telling him that peapod soup was a mere five pounds a bowl? Goodbye to all that.

All the same, she needed a pee. She recrossed her legs. She would have to hang on until the waiter came and then hope by standing up he would immediately point her in the right direction.

He had been speaking. She exchanged the grimness for bright cheer.

'You smile a lot,' he said. Not *altogether* delightedly.

She swallowed, thinking If Only You Knew …

Out loud she said, 'That's because you are hugely entertaining.'

He smiled. Looked questioning.

She prayed he wouldn't ask, because her mind had drifted a bit. Something about his MG, she thought vaguely.

'Have a moule?' she offered.

He declined.

'Go on with what you were saying,' she said. 'It's fascinating.' She gave a girlish giggle. 'Really amusing.' She gave a wicked pout and tapped his hand. 'Go – on – ' she urged playfully, 'Do.'

He looked puzzled.

He stared for a moment. Then he said slowly, 'You find my having a near miss on the N155 amusing?'

Fuck.

'No no – the bit before that.'

What *was* the bit before that?

'Foreign purchase rules or local cheeses?' he asked, slightly irritatedly.

She knew what to do.

She leaned forwards.

She traced the vein on his hand.

She opened those big red lips in a wide inviting smile.

She shrugged.

And she said, 'I just like the way you talk.'

She widened the smile even further.

'That's all.'

And from then on she *concentrated*.

He really was rather nice. Just – well – not quite fully illuminated – one or two of the lights hadn't been switched on. And not very demanding at all. In fact, now she came to think of it, he hadn't exactly asked her much about herself at all. She had a cheering thought. He might not be demanding in bed either. She wasn't exactly consumed with lust for him and the thought of attempting pyrotechnics with a medallion flapping in your face was ... She played with the stem of her glass provocatively, and felt a fleeting regret that he didn't have a bit more brain about him.

But what was she saying? Not very demanding? Couldn't this be viewed as positive? Hadn't she had all those demanding men? Hadn't she been worn out by all that keeping up? Why did she want a male partner to be cleverer, brighter, more intellectually demanding than her? Why shouldn't she have the edge this time?

One very good reason.

Back to the little beautician, Chloe, whose argument was growing more convincing by the minute. Chloe said, as she formed the top bow of Gemma's naked lip, that *Real Men* ...

Define this, said Gemma.

The little beautician did.

Real Men, she opined, were those interested in balls. First their own, and then anything ball-like made of rubber, leather or wood. Well, such Real Men would run a mile at too much cleverness. But you can be funny once, she said. Which was when she told her the Jo-Jo story. The kind of story, thought Gemma, which sorted out the ewes from the shepherdesses. She hoped she'd get the chance to tell it. It was too good to waste.

'Use it wisely,' said Chloe. Just like a fairy godmother granting wishes.

So far he had talked so much, she hadn't had the chance.

But this was certainly a Real Man all right, hacking his way through a galantine of rabbit and grouse, the backs of his hands strong and suntanned, gold ring on his little finger, careless manner of chewing – and though clearly advanced from his Tabloid swigging rivals he was certainly not that mythological male creature who reputedly admired the female mind over female matter. Hard bloody job this, needing to be both attractive *and* good company, without being threateningly bright or asleep.

'I am beginning to like you very much,' he said. He meant it. She could tell.

So I should think, she mused, the way I've been carrying on.

'You are?' she said.

'Yup.'

She pouted and puckered some more.

Think unneedy.

Marriage.

Security.

Affection.

Companionship.

Don't think.

Dangerous to have such words brimming near those juicy lips of hers. She buried them quickly and nodded agreement that yes, indeed, Loire wines were the finest of all: Sancerre (she fluttered her eyelashes), Reuilly (and looked down, remembering Chloe's recommendation to go easy on the eyes), Pouilly-sur-Loire (big, wide, welcoming grin), Chinon (a lick of her lips), Vouvray (ooh), Cabernet d'Anjou (aah).

Already, she was sure, she could love this man.

Gemma, she said to herself, Do You Love This Man?

And Gemma said, 'Yup.'

Megan was in luck.

Jim was quite, quite safe.

'Oh really?' says Gemma brightly, cursing herself for having momentarily lost it again, praying he hadn't just said his granny died. 'Do go on.'

'No *wonder* that corner of France was adopted by so many kings and courtiers. Do you know that it has *more than one hundred and twenty châteaux*?'

Gemma implies with gesture and expression that if she could, she would be swooning at the very suggestion. Her mouth lusting on his every word.

'Yup. Each more grand and beautiful than the next, lying beside the banks of the area's meandering waterways, their turrets and pinnacles reflected in the lakes.'

Something of the old Gemma rises. It twinkles briefly in her eyes. She says, 'You sound as if you could write a guidebook for the place.'

He looks pleased.

She knows perfectly well that that *is* from the guidebook about the place.

He takes her hand. He looks enamoured, serious, convinced.

'You say all the right things. You look all the right way. You aren't too serious about life. I thought you might be the right one.'

Serious about life?

180

Me?

Gemma shrugs again as if Life was a mere bagatelle. 'I'm all for fun. Life in the fast lane. I'm like your MG really.'

'Classy bodywork,' he says, with as much pride as if he were Oscar Wilde at his peak.

She has not rehearsed the MG, and hopes she will not be called upon to know more than that it has bucket seats and wire wheels and is British Racing Green. He doesn't seem the sort of chap who would want his girlfriend to understand the finer points of piston slap, otherwise she would have read it up. Like she read up the Loire, thus knowing he has swallowed the *Blue Guide* whole.

They eat on.

Eventually she gets to the loo safely without appearing to be unfamiliar with its whereabouts. She does this by observing other women, and when she is sure they are not going for a quick look in the kitchens or slipping out the back way because they Just Can't Stand Any More Of It, she takes the same route.

She notices how all these women return with smoothed hair, refreshed faces, the animator's paint. The loo provides quite a relief in more ways than one. Here she is herself again. She leans towards her reflection and applies more glossy redness to her faded smile. She looks in the mirror, and exaggeratedly mouths, Sublime to the Ridiculous. Which is satisfying for some reason.

If the woman who appears beside her in the mirror thinks her odd, she doesn't show it. How can she, when she is frowning and concentrating on the twist of an eyebrow, the shine of a cheekbone, the position of the curl?

Back at the table she mentions finance, forgetting for a moment that she should not expose her knowledge.

His eyes cloud.

She says brightly, 'But I Know Nothing.' And immediately adds, 'My beautician told me a funny story. Want to hear it? It's a bit *risqué*.'

His eyes light up. She crosses her fingers and hopes he is broadminded, remembering Megan and Jim's reaction. She begins.

'Jo-Jo's friend Mike has two married friends, Pam and Eric, who are getting divorced. They are not getting divorced amicably. In fact, Pam and Eric have had to be separated by the police on several occasions. Over the weeks Jo-Jo's friend Mike has oscillated as a listening ear. One night Eric, one night Pam. Sometimes it could be acutely boring. But not on this particular night ... '

She checks. Is he listening? He is. But he is not *concentrating*. She smiles to herself. He will be in a moment. Carry on ...

'Eric apparently has a girlfriend. Pam, though not wanting her husband, is nevertheless not happy about this. She has been away for a week and when she returns, she rings up Mike, in some perturbation, and arranges to meet him in the Dog and Duck. Where, over a bottle or three, and having railed to Mike about the Other Woman, Pam becomes extremely tired and emotional. She can scarcely speak.

'Nevertheless, she suddenly stands up, climbs on to a table, and declares to the world, as assembled in the Dog and Duck, that the *one* thing she can never forgive Eric's fucking fancy woman – *ever* – is that when she, Pam, came home from Lanzarote, – and here she, Pam, nearly fell off the table with acute emotion – when she, Pam, returned to her home – she found that his fancy woman had left – and she stabs the air at each subsequent word – had left *Her Lipstick On My Vibrator.*'

Gemma stops. She looks at him. His face registers astonished speculation.

Perhaps Jim's response was unusual? For a moment she thinks she has gone too far. Then his expression changes – to slight confusion – but overriding *lust*. She breathes a sigh of relief. Thank you, Chloe, she thinks, *thank you*.

*

The meal is over.

Duck with Peas at his suggestion.

Duck is his favourite.

He pronounces *Canard* with the d.

Very good, she says.

Very greasy, she thinks.

And hopes she isn't sick.

It has been Very Hard Work but she knows that she has won.

'Will you come to France with me soon?' he says, fondling her hand.

No pudding, then? she thinks, disappointed.

'Will you?'

Gooey and gummy, of course she will. Was ever woman won

thus? Indeed she was. Was ever man seduced thus? Indeed, indeed he was.

Her heart, which should feel elated, feels dry.

Now they are outside, on the pavement, leaning up against his car. She has put a little scent in her cleavage which the warmth of the night brings out. And she has put as much energy into that mouth of hers as she possibly can. Up to him now, to consider its coloured mobility and dream of where the redness might be smeared and lost later on his skin. So she knew. And she waited, the pulse between them, for confirmation.

'Aren't you going to ask me back?' He made a sort of scuffling with his nose in her hair, She blinked, right into his medallion, and was surprised to find she had made a mistake. He wanted to go to *her* place. Damn. She had confidently *and* pointedly told Megan that the flat was theirs for the night.

Megan or Jim, and sometimes both, snored. They ate from cartons which would be in the kitchen. Megan might well have washed some of Jim's socks and underpants and they would be drying in the bathroom along with Megan's mammoth bloomers. None of that went with erogenous promise.

Oh bums. Now he was nuzzling the nape of her neck, and his chin rasped slightly, tickling her very pleasantly. She could get up a head of steam, she was sure, if only they could keep the thread alive.

'I really like you,' he said. 'So come on. How about asking me back for coffee?'

It was on the tip of her tongue to be a real Bimbo and say, 'But we've just *had* coffee.'

Instead she said, 'My mother's staying.' As fibs go, not bad.

He stopped nuzzling immediately.

She put up a hand and touched him on the cheek.

'Mothers!' she said brightly. And then she tickled his chin.

He was beginning to look twitchy.

Oh well – in for a penny, in for a demi-château. 'You could ask *me* back she said.

'Ah,' he said. 'Um.' And then, 'Oh.'

She got quite wheedling. Perhaps he hadn't done the washing-up? Perhaps *his* underpants were festooned around the place. She would just have to reassure him, that was all. She brightened her smile, widened her gleaming lips. 'It can't be *that* far,' she said encouragingly. 'And I really don't mind.' She moved closer. She planted a kiss with moist parted lips upon his cheek. She breathed rather than spoke. 'Really I don't.'

He jumped as if scalded.

He looked hunted.

'Ah,' he said again.

'Don't tell me,' she laughed, 'that you've got a mother there too …'

'Um. Oh.' He shook his head. Suddenly he looked as if his medallion was too small for him. His eyes bulged slightly, and he had changed colour. She decided to ignore the unattractiveness for the Greater Good.

'Not a mother exactly,' he said. And then, as if yielding to a greater force nudging him from on high, he added, 'Actually, a *wife*.'

Sod the Greater Good.

A *wife*?

A fucking WIFE?

She looked at him anew.

He was positively gross.

Her mouth reverted to normal with extraordinary facility. Indeed it went, immediately, rather thin. 'You never said,' she accused.

'You never asked,' he said indignantly.

Truth was never honest. *Never.*

She had been quite prepared for anything. Mother, father, any amount of siblings – even, perhaps, she thought wildly, a goat or two – but *not* – most definitely *not*, a wife. How much of a wife? she wanted to ask. I mean, big? little? some of the time? all of the time?

'Children?' she asked.

He nodded and had what was in her opinion the serious temerity to look proud. 'Two. Boy and a girl. Six and ten.'

Six and ten? Hardly poised on the threshold of life.

She waited.

Would he actually say his wife didn't understand him?

No. What he actually said was, 'We haven't been happy for some time. Ever since our son was born. No sex.'

'Separate bedrooms?' Had her voice gone up a few octaves?

He looked shifty. 'Er.'

OK, she thought, try this. 'When are you moving in with me?'

He looked even more unattractive.

She shook her head pityingly. 'Why did you do it?' She was as close to tears as a woman can get without spillage. Why did *I* do it? she thought. And her friendly *alter ego* stepped in to remind her that they were not here to discuss that.

'I *want* to leave. I just need some kind of fulcrum, that's all.'

Some kind of fulcrum?

Sounded like a gynaecological implement.

'I got a lot of replies, you know,' he said defensively. 'And I chose you top of the pile.'

She licked her lips. A moment ago that would have given her silly female heart quite a lift. Now she wanted to cry.

He went on, 'You are so game. So uncomplicated. So well stabilized –'

Christ, she thought, now he thinks I'm a bloody boat.

'Up for a bit of fun. Thoroughly independent. Free.' He leaned forwards. He lowered his eyes and then his voice. 'You have the *sexiest* lips,' he said, and added with winsome regret, 'My wife never wears make-up.'

'Poor woman,' said Gemma, and meant it.

Then she moved towards him, raised her face and gave him the kiss of her life, and very probably his too. She took his breath away completely, and most of hers. She moved her lips in a rubbing motion, pressed them deep into his flesh, licked and sucked and smacked her chops until he looked liked a dying man haemorrhaging. And then she walked away to her car, slowly, aware that the Joseph silk clung to her in wonderful erotic counterpoint. Over her shoulder she called, 'You'll just have to go for number two on the pile now, won't you? Bye.'

*

Back in the flat she wondered how long she had sat in the dark. At least a couple of hours, maybe more. She had been wakened by a noise coming from the bathroom. She stood up, went to the door, looked down the passage and saw Jim padding – naked – out of the bathroom towards the kitchen. From the opened door of Megan's bedroom came the sound, so familiar, of her flat-mate's gentle snores. Mirror, Mirror On The Wall …

In the reflected light from the kitchen she peered at her face. Smeary and pinkish from the residual lipstick. She took the sleeve of the Joseph jacket and rubbed it all over her mouth and cheeks, removing what she could. The pearl-grey silk looked violated and for some reason that satisfied her. Then she removed the lipstick from her bag, very carefully reapplied it to her mouth, smiled once into the mirror, turned its face to the wall, and took a slow sashaying walk towards the kitchen. Once inside, she pushed the door closed behind her very softly, smiled up at Jim, then pouted as she let her eyes move slowly down his body towards his already half-aroused penis. 'Kiss Kiss,' she said. 'Kiss Kiss.'

26

By the time Tabitha left the stolid marble frontage of the gallery the summer's night was well advanced. The air was still warm despite the lateness of the hour, and the city was in a gentler frame of mind, less crowded, more peaceful. Tabitha wished she could say the same of herself.

As she made her way home she wondered why she had done it. The handbag had damaged nothing, bouncing off the opulent frame like a badly-aimed penalty. The image remained unmarked, exactly as its creator painted it. Grieving Woman: Ageless: Beautiful to Behold. Titian or not, Tabitha wished she had made a hole right through that lovely face. She had said as much as she was hauled off to see the Superintendent. 'Travesty,' she repeated to her captor as he marched beside her holding out her handbag like a mace, smiling ecstatically and unaware that it looked, to the dwindling evening visitors, as if the gallery was holding a very silly Art Event.

'Yes, well' he had said proudly. 'Yes, well – I'm not very fond of it myself – seen better on the railings outside – but you still can't go around chucking missiles. Public property, and worth a packet.'

'Wish I'd *really* damaged it,' she said fervently.

'So do I,' he echoed, with equal fervour. 'I could have sold my story to the *Sun*.'

And then, from the Superintendent she had been taken to the very Head of the Museum Himself. It could have been God for all she cared.

'We will have to wait until the Restorer can be located. It depends on his verdict,' he said loftily. 'Charges may be pressed.'

'You can press anything you like,' said Tabitha wearily. 'Only hurry, because I have to get back to my salon.'

She had then turned to the stony-faced Museum Director, raising her chin as if scenting prey. Her eyes glittered. 'Meanwhile, can *you* tell me why Giorgione chose to paint an ageing *woman*, and not an ageing man?'

She did not pause for answer. She advanced. The attendant, standing close, moved with her, perhaps hoping she would pounce and attack. And she did, indeed, bring up her finger and poke the Museum Director rather hard in the ribs. He gave a little grunt, still dignified, and the attendant looked quite pleased.

'I'll tell you why,' she continued. 'He did it because he was painting a tragedy as well as a morality. And it just wouldn't be the same if he had painted an old man. If he had painted an old *man* it would have been a picture about mortality … Whither the soul? … The Big Issue.'

Poke, poke, she went.

'But paint an old woman and it's about the death, not of the soul, but of boring old *Beauty*. And until we redress that disparity, Sunshine, all the arts in the world are false. *All* based on untruth.'

The stony-faced Museum Director was rather amused. Perhaps no one had ever called him Sunshine before.

'Giorgione?' he asked, puzzled. 'The Gender Issue? But I am planning a show by Mandelstam – you know Mandelstam?'

She shook her head.

'A modern master who has captured the gap between the idea and the object rather well, using gold-plated hosepipes. No gender issue there, surely?'

Tabitha bit back a rather rude comment. She could see he was congratulating himself, and wondering what on earth Giorgione had to do with an Ageing Woman?

'Hosepipes!' Tabitha was disgusted.

'Don't bring your scissors, will you?' said the Museum Director, and it was impossible to tell whether or not he was joking.

A restorer had been summoned. 'No real damage?' he was asked.

The restorer, who had been wrested from a Camden Town dinner party, shook his head, peeved. Apparently he was missing the bream, which they never used to get in Pinner.

'Nothing,' he said. 'Even the frame is unmarked. Built to last.'

The Museum Director looked relieved, side-stepped Tabitha's finger, and pursed his thin little lips.

Charges need not necessarily be pressed.

No harm done.

'No?' said Tabitha. She had raised her immaculate eyebrow as superciliously as possible. It quite often put Chloe in her place. 'No?' she had demanded, taking a step forwards. '*None?*' She leaned towards him, hands on hips. 'You'd be surprised.'

The pink-with-pleasure attendant had been eager. 'There *may* be,' he said. 'Shall I go and have another look?'

'Oh, fuck off,' said Tabitha, which seemed a satisfactory arrangement.

The Museum Director gave a hint of a smile. The restorer and the attendant were dismissed. The hint of a smile turned to the glimmer of a twinkle. 'No harm done,' he pronounced firmly. 'Charges will not be pressed.' He took her jutting elbow and escorted her to the museum exit.

No. No charges pressed. No damage done.

And he stood to watch her running down the steps, out into the darkening summer's night. When she turned once, mid-flight, she saw that he was smiling appreciatively at her legs.

She had hailed a cab. 'As fast as you can,' she urged.

With the streets being almost empty the journey was short. Big Ben rang a sonorous single chime as they circled Parliament Square and she knew she was far too late. Too late to do anything. Futile, futility. For the first time her heart sank at the sight of the salon.

The swathed satin curtains perfectly puffed.

The overnight light giving a faint rosy glow of promise.

The golden door-handle gleaming, inviting.

Her salon. Tabitha's Beauty Parlour. Her very own creation. As Chloe was her very own creation. Both so beautiful, weren't they?

She let herself in. The air was sweet, the scent seductive. She closed her eyes and drew in a fragrant breath. With the door shut behind her the world was banished again – no traffic, no loud mouths, no barking of dogs or calling for alms.

Empty.

Betty had gone.

Chloe had gone.

The three clients had gone.

A pile of books sat neatly on the table surrounded by the fan of magazines. Smiling cover-girls, perfect creatures, not a blemish to hide.

Monstrous perfections.

Too late.

Tabitha stood there, panting, scanning.

No one.

Could have been the Beauty Parlour on the *Marie Celeste*.

Except that Betty had left a note.

'Chloe did very well. Clients happy. Roman women depilated by using the blood of a wild she-goat mixed with sea-palm and powdered viper or she-goat's gall. Hare's blood was used to stop the hair growing again. Certainly would on the hares, Chloe said. Interesting girl ... '

We learn from history that we learn nothing from history.

Betty had trained her.

She had trained Chloe.

The long tradition stretching back thousands of years. *Secrets of the Boudoir, Woman to Woman* – Betty's Great Work, her text, created to Illuminate the Efficacious Virtues Inherent in the Perpetuity of These Secrets (it said in the foreword).

Solidarity of Sisterhood?

Wisdoms of Womanhood?

All mythology. All myth.

She leaned on her elbows and stared at the profane little cherub.

Well *quite*, she said to the thickly scented air.

She had always supposed it was a positive thing: that the very skin she worked on responded to the creams and oils and lotions; and that the minds and hearts which that skin held together responded in kind and softened too. Softened for the Positive. Softened to make pliable. Softened to temper the steel of the world.

Wrong, Tabitha, she told herself. Wrong.

She slumped down on to the couch and passed a tired hand across her forehead. She felt faint and pushed her head between her knees. She might be sick. Perhaps it was the powdered viper and she-goat's gall? She could do with a nice hot cup of jasmine tea. Damn it. She could do with a nice stiff whisky. She looked up. And why *she*-goat? she asked the Venetian chandelier indignantly. Surely that was keeping the Boudoir within the Sisterhood a bit too rigidly. Why not *he*-goat since that was the gender supposed to *like* all this smoothness?

She looked down at her own legs and stroked them – they would be just about ready for a waxing when she went to Spain. It was too late to have any regrets about passing the salon on to Chloe. For

Tabitha, bringing her head up slowly to see if the faintness had passed, understood that she herself had been supremely arrogant.

Suddenly supremely arrogant.

There she was, considering herself so sensitive and caring towards her women with her sweet, calming voice. Training Chloe's voice to be less like a cracked tin bell found in the gutter and more like her own, lulling them. Lulling them; teaching Chloe to lull them. *Lull. Lull.* Correcting Chloe in matters of taste, creating a soft and secret dream world that had nothing to do with Out There.

Make-up for your:

First Job.

First Date.

First Fuck.

First Fuck-Up.

And *Wedding Make-up.*

For God's sake, *Wedding* Make-up.

Why?

If he didn't like you the way you were, naturally, at *that* point, you hadn't a snowball's chance in hell with all the rest.

She scratched her head. Do *you* know why? she asked the eau-de-Nil carpet, because I'm sure I don't.

She suddenly remembered seeing the young rabbits in the market, stretched out lazily on the fat knees of the stall-women who stroked them lovingly.To keep the meat sweet, they whispered through their blackened teeth. *Calmar Calmar*, stroking, stroking with their strong, coarse hands until a buyer came along and those same hands *snapped* their little necks.

Best when they are young and tender, the women would wink with their wall eyes and wrinkled lids. Who wants them when they are old and tough? They knew what they were talking about. They'd seen it all.

Tabitha looked up. She was beginning to hate the pale green of the carpet and to feel ill again. She tried to imagine the activity taking place here today without her. Three women, stroke them, *Calmar Calmar.*

Snap, snap, snap.

What, she wondered, *was* happening to them now? Best not think.

Chloe with her little dream trolley.

Betty with her Grand Old Story.

Cosmetics, cosmetic, from the Greek *kosmetikos*, to adorn.

Adornment equals Useless Beauty. Ephemeral, like women's strength – all gone into the curl of a lash, the curve of a painted smile.

She gazed at the cupid. Vanity, lust, folly and foolishness. And she had the nerve to blame *Bronzino*?

It was quite a shock to the system.

So, for that matter, was the whisky.

*

Chloe lay along the black leather couch and let him manoeuvre her into the required position. She ran a fingertip along the line of his hairy back, avoiding running it down and round to where hung his great fur sack of a belly. Not that she minded. Men did not have to mind if their bank balances matched their underhang, but he was a little self-conscious regarding its girth.

She and he were in perfect accord about it and pretended it did not exist, even when it got in the way during some of the more complicated positionings. Chloe shifted to accommodate something slightly more unusual that he was in the process of choreographing. He watched a lot of movies; studied a lot of books.

She thought about the salon. Well, she'd studied a lot of books too, and at the end of the day, what did they tell her? No more than what she half knew: that Beauty was a business just like everything else – always had been, always would be – and that people were prepared to pay a lot of money for it, both to *offer it, and to own* it. Like Otto. She looked at him, his face in fleshy folds of concentration. Pathetic. She smiled.

Lift arms above head and stretch, cross ankles, keep the smile, half close eyes (certain ecstasy), wait. Smile the question, smile his answer. Let him take her crossed ankles in his huge hairy hands and swing her upwards so that she dangled from his grip, powerless, her buttocks bumping against his great belly which, of course, was not there to bump against.

Now what? she wondered idly. What does he intend to do now he has me hung up like a piece of game? Put my head in a paper bag? She nearly laughed out loud, but clenched her jaw and buttocks against it. This was no laughing matter.

Reaching behind her she gave his joystick a tweak. That was *probably* all right. She was never quite sure how much to participate in these shennanigans of his. Tweak, tweak – that seemed acceptable. Even at full thrust it lived in the shadow of the belly above, and it was a bit of a prawn – but then – she tweaked it again and made little bubbling noises of pleasure with her mouth – it scarcely needed to be any bigger with six noughts to play around with. There was nothing like telling someone a lie often enough for them to believe it, and to see the disproof and *still* believe it. Ooh you are so *big* she would say, and grunt a bit. So very *big*.

He believed.

That was all that mattered.

She pretended, in return for his pretending the money for the business was a loan. And so she had done very well. She knew that and she was utterly, utterly happy. I give it to him, she repeated to herself as she hung there. I give it to him.

Soon he would let her down, and then she would twine her legs in a very interesting cat's cradle around and about his girth. I give it to them too, she thought, for something interesting to dwell on while all this was going on, and she remembered each of those three women and how *wet* they were before she got to them.

Wet as water, as her granny would say.

Puerile, puerile – she was cultivating words, good words like that, so that one day she would be as good as Tabitha, with never a fucking this or bugger that if she dropped something. 'Oh how *puerile*' Tabitha said of a nutter who popped his head round the door and gave them the finger the other day. Oh How Puerile sounded so much better than Chloe's immediate response. The man had looked quite upset at Tabitha's comment – words could obviously be powerful. As well as money. She looked up at Otto. Concentrating, he looked like a schoolboy playing with cars – but he had power; he had *money*. She wriggled a little in the hopes he'd get on with it. *Money*, she thought. He has the money. Men have the money. *Egyptians* ... Now there was a thought.

She closed her eyes. She had done very well really. She tweaked at his cock again, heard him grunt, swung herself a little in an ecstatic manner even though the blood was rushing to her head (good for the circulation). Yes, she had done very well.

Only the day before yesterday she had sat round the table in her mum's kitchen, listening to her elder sister Viv telling her Gran that you could make a very economical curry out of a tin of pilchards, a tin of tomatoes, an onion and some curry powder. Hah! Very nice I'm sure, she thought, but not for *me*. Oh no – for her it would be *king prawns* at the very least. Which reminded her.

She tickled his scrotum.

He liked that.

She was a beautician after all, and knew a lot about pleasing people with her hands. Just the male was different, that was all. If she went on hanging here for much longer she'd vomit. Better finish him off quick. You could always get the better of them in the end.

She twisted her head round and opened her mouth, making a noise of ecstasy from the back of her throat. You beautiful, beautiful man, she said firmly, over and over and over again.

*

Tabitha retired to bed early and lay awake all night. The whisky – and something else. What? She knew. She was thinking again of the three women who had passed through Chloe's sharp little claws. What had happened to them? Why did she get that panic in the gallery yesterday as she looked at the beauties of the past? After all, women took their own destinies in their own hands – what difference did it make if they had a makeover first? She threshed about looking for a cool place on the pillow, closed her eyes, and hoped for oblivion. Those three women. The *Thumbs Up*?

Something was troubling her – something so close she could not see it. She opened her eyes. What? She snuggled down and closed her eyes again. And just as she was drifting off into the soft, downy world of forgetfulness, she heard:

Ping! Ping! Ping!

To which her panicking heart responded:

Boom! Boom! Boom!

She sat up again, feeling sick. And it was nothing to do with gall of goat. For she who had dispensed beauty, controlled beauty, realized, quite suddenly, that she, too, had been its dupe.

Chloe!

Consider *Chloe*.

She was beautiful beyond her clients' wildest dreams. She looked the part. She was truly a walking advertisement. Beautiful. *Beautiful* and – *Disastrous*.

All those terrible mistakes – the Baker, the Pargiter, the O'Rourke –

even that poor woman whose stockings got stuck to her toenails. And *others* – *lots of others*. Why – really – Chloe had been *Appalling*. And she had got away with it –

Because

She

Was

Beautiful.

Oh!

Chloe was *Appallingly Disastrous*. And why was she still there? Because Tabitha was seduced by her *looks*. If she had been Brenda, she wouldn't have kept the job – probably wouldn't even have *got* the job. Wendy Woods all over again. Shame on me, she thought, shame, shame on me. A purveyor of the Arts deceived by them. Thus would the world continue to seek the Beautician's Couch, because it cut you a swathe through life, put you at the front of the queue, got you there quickly, safely, and in very good time. To be beautiful was to have a First Class Ticket.

The only question, really, was To Where?

She knew now what had been troubling her. She knew what she had to do.

She rose, dressed, and walked in the primrose light of morning towards the salon. Saturday, her busiest day. She rang each of the clients on her books and cancelled them. And then, with a shaking hand that had nothing to do with last night's whisky, she turned back the pages of the appointments book, found the three telephone numbers, and began to dial.

She had to know. She had to.

But really,

she already

did.

The pink cards were blank.

To Chloe, the Dawn.

27

Margery had been practising with cheap make-up. Somehow it never looked as good as it did after the Beauty Parlour, but when she asked the little beautician for help, the little beautician said not if she couldn't afford it. Fair enough. Reginald wouldn't do her teeth again, either, not until she had saved up. That was why the make-up was cheap. She was saving.

Reginald was only being noble when he became angry, she knew that. Mrs Postgate had called the police, not him. The Old Queen Bee would just have to go. She fluffed up her hair, put a very cross expression on her face, and tapped at the window.

'Buzz Off!' she mouthed, when Mrs Reginald Postgate pulled aside the lounge curtains, which were still persimmon and peach because of all this time-consuming honey mania flying about. It made Mrs Reginald Postgate very upset – both the unfinished colour scheme and the madwoman.

'Mine,' she mouthed back at the disgusting creature, 'mine, mine, mine.'

Mrs Reginald Postgate became very distressed as she followed the baleful gaze towards the nests of tables, the suite, the silver carriage clock with the chimes that said London Bridge Is Falling Down and all the other nice things she had accrued.

'Mine,' she mouthed again. And pulled the curtains. Margery smiled with teeth that were already yellowing from lack of a good brushing. 'Don't bet on it,' she mouthed back.

Mrs Postgate winced. Reginald would just have to cope, that was all. Otherwise *she* would have a nervous breakdown. She felt one was quite close already and, after all, she had never had one before. She picked up the telephone.

'HallomynamesKarenhowmayIhelpyew?'

Mrs Reginald Postgate very nearly said Bygivingmemyhusbandrightaway – but stopped herself. 'Put me through to my husband,' she said.

'Outallday,' said Karen. 'TennismatchinBrighton.'

Mrs Reginald Postgate put down the telephone and began to giggle. It really was quite mad, and hysterically funny. She lay on the couch and began shredding the Bentalls catalogue. He loves me, he loves me not, she repeated. OutalldayinBrighton. And the silver carriage clock went –

Ping, Ping, Ping.

Margery was giggling too. It was no use the Old Queen pulling those curtains and thinking she would go away. How unintelligent of her. There was a back entrance to the house, with a little potting shed just below the wall – quite easy to drop on to. She knew, because she had reconnoitred. And not a policeman in sight this time. She tucked the gingham ruffles into her knickers (it was a bit too cool nowadays to go without them) and began to creep along the wall. You had to be one jump ahead in this game. As the little beautician said.

*

Caroline had looked perfectly normal when he went round the next day, and felt perfectly normal when she put her arms around him and apologized.

She had even made him a cup of tea and tried to laugh about it all. Just a silly joke, she said, just a whim – she had meant no harm, only tampered a little, nothing genuinely poisonous.

For a moment, *just* for a moment, he nearly joined in the humour. But then he remembered Rita, and it was impossible. She was very upset. Very, *very* upset. And frankly he had had enough. He'd been up all night calming her – camomile tea, foot massage – he had even washed down the paintwork on the stairs which was covered in multi-coloured streaks from Caroline's alarming outburst. Smeared and rubbed there – disgusting – *disgusting*. Rita was right: she was probably unbalanced. Anyone who would do such a thing, anyone who would even *think* of such a thing must be unbalanced.

And besides, what was there to laugh about? Was it amusing that he and Rita were both shattered? Well, she was, certainly. Believe me, he wanted to say, when Rita's shattered *nobody* laughs. Not unless they want their heads examined. And here was Caroline, arms round

197

his neck, saying see the funny side. Saying she got carried away in a Beauty Parlour. *Beauty Parlour?* He had never seen anything less beautiful in his life.

'I could sue you,' Rita had said. 'You ugly great tart.'

'Aah,' said Caroline, in a voice that had Bernie believing the best, 'was he a Little Bit Pansy Then? Aah.'

And that was when it really started.

It was very hard to equate either the sweet little thing his wife had been a moment before, or the sobbing apologizer who had held fast to the newel post. Caroline suddenly seemed to discover an ability to pack a startlingly accurate punch and – even more surprising – Rita showed herself to be what might be called Wiry but Powerful. Bernie remembered thinking, as the shrieking women toppled on to him, how accurate the sound-effect of smacking a cabbage was.

He finally separated them at a particularly dramatic point, over the completely mystifying, 'Go to the gym did you?' from Caroline, which incensed his wife so much that she returned fire inaccurately and fell clinging to her opponent's neck instead. Having pulled them apart they both looked out from faces much besmeared, and said together, as if rehearsed:

'Bernie. Bernie I *love* you.'

You could have fooled me, he thought. You could have fooled me.

And now here was Caroline, draped all around *his* neck, wanting to be nice – which made it hardest of all.

He stepped back and held out her key. And he said, 'Could I have mine back please?'

He felt a little resentful that she did not plead with him, simply doing as she was bid and then opening the front door.

He went back down the path feeling low in spirits. It had been easier than he thought, yet harder. And he pondered during the walk home about last night. Was there any more puzzling sight than a woman whose face had once been feminine and who seconds later, and seemingly effortlessly, with the shedding of tears, had the face of a nightmare?

Yes there is, he answered himself:

TWO women with perfectly immaculate faces which then descended into hell.

In which case, he thought, as he turned into his gate, it was a case of Better The Devil You Know.

He used Caroline's key, and felt a momentary twist in his heart as it turned in the lock. No going back now. No going back ever again. He stepped into the hall. He could hear little Rita busy in the kitchen. Comforting.

So much sweeter than Caroline; so much more vulnerable; so much more *feminine*. He tucked the key out of sight in a drawer. Wouldn't be needed again. 'I'm home,' he called.

*

Caroline read the label on the bottle of moisturizer carefully. It said: 'Used Daily It Protects And Cherishes.' Mere propaganda, important to any offensive. She dropped it into the rubbish bin and slammed the lid.

Watchful Venus gave a little sigh, and then a chuckle. She reached out and rubbed her finger under Mars' stubbly chin. 'Just goes to show,' she said, amused, 'there are never any winners when *you* are involved.'

And he – smiling too, sleepy for once, said through his yawns, 'Nor you, my love, nor *you*.'

*

Well, you didn't feel better and you didn't feel worse. You had just done it, that was all. Done it standing up in a pair of heels with your back against the fridge, your Joseph pulled up round your fanny and an urgency about it that gave him no time to consider the morality of the event.

First time she had ever heard him say Yes. Half asleep and looking for the fizzy water, and there it was. All over before he could quite believe it and shooed back into bed, where Megan lay peaceful as she would never be peaceful again, for Jim was an honest man. Gemma didn't care – she had made her pact with God and been passed on to the Devil who had obliged her by providing the circumstances.

'Why?' he had asked afterwards, and not unreasonably.

'Why not?' she shrugged. 'Now – *shoo*.'

Gemma had got out early this morning to avoid the confrontation. For confrontation there would be. Jim was not many things, in Gemma's opinion, but he was certainly honest. To Megan's inevitable waking question of, 'Jim dear, what are you doing with lipstick all over your face?' he would come back with an honest answer. And Gemma really could not cope with the rotating ordure that would follow. Anyway, it was best being out and about – she'd done a good morning's work, surprisingly, and her conscience was reasonably quiescent. Megan would move out, of course. But she'd find someone else.

If she thought about Megan, the sap of sympathetic human kindness seemed to have dried up. Somehow when she thought of anybody just at the moment, the sap of sympathetic human kindness seemed to have dried up. It did not help that her half-leg and bikini was growing back rather itchily and she thought she had a touch of folliculitis in her crutch – folliculitis in the crutch being a great determiner of the strength of one's Sympathetic Human Kindness.

If someone were to make the smallest transgression with her now she had a feeling she would either bark or bite. She pulled up at the lights in Battersea's Restaurant Mile. Perhaps she was hungry? It was more or less lunchtime.

She drummed her fingers on the wheel. Funnily enough, she thought idly, as she waited for the lights to change; funnily enough, she thought, as she gazed at the teeming pavements awash with humans; funnily enough, I thought that you only saw His Face In Every Crowd when you *loved* the bugger – not when you were *enraged* and contemplating doing a pit bull terrier on him.

Yet apparently this was not so, for looking across the street, whom should she imagine she saw but M. Le Fulcrum of last night. Even down to the glint of that ghastly medallion. And next to him a woman who looked not unlike herself, but minus the sumptuous mouth.

Mind playing tricks? She blinked, tried again. Bared her teeth. Growling imminent. Shook her head. Silly old me. Scratched her upper thigh and regretted it because all the other cousins and aunties of the Big Itch suddenly wanted attention too. Gritted her teeth, still bared, and looked again. Nope, it *was* him. It was him, and it was him with a *her*. Number Two on his list, no doubt, about to be put through the whole sordid, high-expectation process – a man with a Château and an MG, what more could a lonely woman want? Not one who required a Fulcrum, that's for sure.

She did not look like a lonely woman, Number Two On The List. She looked very together, well-groomed and perfectly at ease. Not quite so dashing as Gemma, perhaps, but not bad – not bad at all. Poor woman. Gemma's gorge rose. From the depths rose a pit bull and a Rottweiler to merge into one canine hellhound – a Cerberus whom no amount of cake seasoned with poppies and honey could quell.

The British Telecom van-driver behind her had his view of women drivers reinforced when she slewed the car into the kerb and parked it on white zig-zag lines at an interesting angle. With a last thorough scratch that had the entire family demanding more, she exited stage right, streaked through honking traffic, and fetched up at the door of the restaurant they had entered. An Oyster Bar. For some reason this made her even more wild, so that when she entered and spotted them sitting calmly together, poised, as it were, for a feast, her hand shot out, finger pointed with accusing zeal like a Conan Doyle sleuth:

'Ah-ha – It *is You!*'

Well, it was an interesting colour, no doubt about it, and not unlike the oysters on the next table – drained you might say. Whey-faced, oyster-eyed, such descriptive phrases came to mind as she stood there, finger never wavering, staring from his face, stark with terror, to Number Two's face, stark with incomprehension. She looked at least as old as Gemma – a fleeting thought, but a gratifying one. She approached the table, changing from Fury to dulcet-toned sweetie-pie. She slid into the chair opposite them, and the waiter, who had been hovering, ceased to feel anxious and asked if they would care to order.

'Not yet,' said Gemma, never taking her eyes off M. Le Fulcrum. 'We may not be staying very long.'

M. Le Fulcrum looked even paler. Gemma found this interesting since she would have said, on a racing certainty, it was impossible.

'Please don't have a heart attack yet – not until I have finished.' She smiled even more sweetly and then turned to the woman.

'This man,' she said, 'is looking for a Fulcrum. That is what he requires you to be.' She paused. The woman said nothing, simply looked astonished. It was possible, thought Gemma cruelly, that she did not know what a fulcrum was. 'Fulcrum,' said Gemma evenly. 'Something to push against in order to break free.'

He covered his face with his hands and made a small groaning noise. The woman looked at him, startled.

'He may well groan,' said Gemma. 'This man, I have to tell you, is a married man. I expect you answered the advertisement in *The Times*? Man with Château seeks lovely lady to share it with? That one? I did too. As did a good many other women, I gather. I was number one on the list of applicants for the position. We had a very jolly dinner together last night.'

She reached out a hand and removed his from his face. He had his eyes screwed up very tight. 'Didn't we, darling?' He replaced his hand. 'Before he told me that he was – surprise, surprise – A Married Man. But all he needed was a Fulcrum. Someone to get him out of his beastly old marriage to a woman he despised and children he cared little for, someone like me who was single, attractive, willing ... '

She pinched his earlobe very hard. 'Only I wasn't – alas, alack – now was I?' And she pinched considerably harder. It says much for his mental agony that whereas someone else might have needed peeling off the ceiling at such a painful physical assault on such a tender organ, M. Le Fulcrum did not flinch.

The woman, on the other hand, did. Stark incomprehension changed to rage. And a depth of rage, Gemma was interested to note, that was considerably more striking than she would have believed in one of such quiet style and new acquaintance. Truly, if Gemma had thought *she* was a desperate female, this one was much, much worse.

The woman said, 'Tell me what the advertisement said again.'

Gemma did so.

'He had a lot of replies?'

Gemma concurred. 'Feel flattered,' she added, 'that you were number two on the list. He got a sackload.'

'A sackload?'

The woman turned and looked at him. 'Graham Prothero,' she said, 'remove your hands at once.'

There was something distinctly proprietorial about the way she said it. And, more to the point, there was something distinctly obedient about the way he responded.

Gemma had an inkling that this might not be their first date.

Gemma had an inkling, considerably worse, which she refused to dwell on further.

She had no need.

'Oh my God,' said Graham Prothero.

Graham Prothero? thought Gemma idly. Better or worse than Keith?

'Oh my God,' repeated Graham Prothero.

Interested diners stopped eating to watch.

Woman Number Two said, 'I'm not sure He can help at this point, Graham.'

And she got up, moved to their neighbours' table, asked if they were enjoying the show, picked up two very large full oyster shells from a dish, returned and tipped both of them over Graham Prothero's head. Then she picked up her bag and marched out with not so much as a backward glance.

Gemma smiled, knowing that she had saved the woman.

Graham Prothero dripped. He turned towards Gemma with a ghastly smile upon his face.

'You gave me no time to introduce you,' he said witheringly, 'but you have just met my wife.'

28

'The keys,' said Tabitha, 'are yours.'

She put them down, rattle rattle, on top of the reception desk. Out came Chloe's hand like a painted claw. Chloe had plans. Big plans. Plans that she would not reveal to the current owner. Not until she had signed on the dotted, official, which would be soon. Very big plans. Otto was delighted. And Chloe just knew it was whacky enough to work.

But Mum's the word.

For now, she must stay very civil. She must appear quite cool, quite calm. Not even hint that Tabitha looked, especially today, well past her sell-by date. Do not rock the boat which will soon be hers to rock.

Meanwhile, she must service the woman who was still her employer – the woman who needed (Chloe eyed her critically) eyebrows tidied, face deep-cleansed, complexion enlivened with a quick knock-up of fuller's earth, magnesium and rose-water (when Tabitha had gone Chloe would no longer mix her own – time-consuming – she'd buy them in bulk), a good pore treatment, *much* needed, manual cleansing, vapour, herbal or ozone steaming, vacuum and manual massage, setting mask and corrective toning.

That'd sort her out, deal with those open pores, relax her so the lines showed less. And get those hairs off her legs.

She'd neglected herself lately. She must not, she must not, she must not.

Chloe repeated it like a mantra under her breath. *That* was why women went wonky – neglect. Look after yourself and you'd be all right. Look at Joan Collins. Compare her with Mum. Mum had legs and feet where you couldn't make out where the leg stopped and the ankle began – all sort of bluey and mauve.

Sometimes, when she'd had a drop, Mum'd lift one of these up and say, 'Pretty colours, eh? And they'd all have a good laugh, especially Gran, who would then lift hers up too – skinny in comparison and not quite so colourful, but the same idea all right, as if a kid had come along and done some blurry finger painting with the blue/pink palette. Chloe never wore blue or pink or mauve – bad colours – reeking of decay and old slippers. NOT FOR HER. Neglect was a very bad thing and unnecessary. Look at Joan Collins. Look.

Behind her, in the softly-lit mirror, Tabitha observed herself. She could see no reason to relinquish her role – no lines, wrinkles, bags, pouches, thin dryness or dullness of eye. In that pink-tinged light she looked completely smoothed out, beautiful. But in her gaze – oh in her gaze – what light of knowledge shone. Ancient wisdoms, she thought. Anciently wise.

The pocket of her pristine eau-de-Nil overall felt immeasurably lighter by the handing on of its contents and – did she mistake it? – as Chloe clutched them up did not her hand have a sudden look of age? Not quite the rosy paw of flower-petal girlhood? Tabitha shivered. She could feel Chloe eyeing her as if she were inert flesh waiting for the cleaver. Treatment Day. All arranged. Before Spanish lift-off.

Snap, snap, snap.

She remembered. You're No Oil Painting. She smiled. A compliment now.

She looks at Chloe. Chloe who laughed. Chloe who shrugged as Tabitha relayed to her the outcome of her three telephone conversations: madness, exile, revenge.

'So?' she had said. 'Plenty more fish in the sea.'

You cannot paint cosmetics on the heart.

Now Tabitha waits for her own Makeover. Her first and last at Chloe's hands. The girl winks. 'I know a joke about Joan Collins,' she says, young green shoot. 'It's a good one. Want to hear it?'

Tabitha waits, listens.

'What?' says Chloe smiling, beautiful, 'is the similarity between Joan Collins and a parakeet's cage?'

Tabitha shivers. Already the girl approaches, her hands outstretched to pinch her flesh and feel its shortcomings.

'Give up?' she smiles to soothe and comfort, so that the body may go gently on its journey.

'Need a clue?'

Tabitha's face is pulled tight into a permanent smile, as if she were a rabbit, held up by long silken ears.

'Have a guess.'

Tabitha watches, turning away from the soft pink light to see how Chloe prepares her bed for her with its soft pink towels.

'Give up?'

She nods.

Chloe laughs. 'The similarity between Joan Collins and a parakeet's cage is that …'

She turns on the huge, raking arc light that will shine down upon Tabitha, prone, and reveal that nothing can be hidden, that all roads lead to and from the Beautician's Couch.

' … they've both had a cockatoo in them.'

Ha Ha.

'Get it?'

*

Chloe smiled through the glass at Jo-Jo and nodded for her to Switch On. She then folded her arms across the uncompromising *décolleté* of her gold-trimmed overall and looked up at the sign with satisfaction. 'Isn't it,' she said, '*great*? Now that *is* Beauty for you.'

Myopic beside her, Betty blinked. If the lettering was blurry the colouring was sharp and clear – a very hot pink indeed – she peered closer – a mouth by the look of it – and above that a pair of startling electric-blue eyes with deep black fringes, one of which – she blinked again and – yes – it blinked back – or rather it winked back – one startling blue eye slowly closing while the pink mouth seemed to part its lips and smile.

Chloe took a long drag on her cigarette and as she inhaled, the carcinogens and dehydraters within the tobacco began their work, accelerating the ageing process of her skin. She found it very enjoyable. She really was going to live for ever.

'The thing is,' said Chloe, 'that you have to catch the passing trade.'

'I think,' said Betty weakly, 'that you will do that all right …'

'Because,' said Chloe, 'you can't rely on customers coming back. None of my Makeovers came back. *Not one*. After everything I did for them. And none of them was exactly an oil painting when they came in, as you know.'

206

'Nor when they left,' muttered Betty to herself.

'Pardon?' said Chloe.

Betty shook her head.

Chloe looked back at the salon with pride. The name CHLOE'S PLACE blazed forth. 'Well?' she said, 'how's that for tricks? What do you think?'

Betty stepped back, nervously clutching her manuscript to her ancient bosom. 'How does it do that?' she said wonderingly.

'Neon,' said Chloe proudly. She walked towards the window and posed, hand on hip. 'Do you see how my overall matches the pink?'

Betty could scarcely miss it.

'Yes dear,' she said, 'but what does it *say*?'

'It says – UNISEX' said Chloe. 'Don't see why the men shouldn't have a Bit of the Boudoir too.'

Betty stepped back even further, opened her mouth, was about to say 'No, never – you will destroy the mysteries, you must never let them in, never, never … ' when Chloe advanced, the light of true evangelism in her beautiful, clear, blue-white eyes. She raised a finger, wagging it at no one in particular, and spoke warningly, 'Yup,' she said, 'why not? I'm all for equality.' The finger wagged harder. 'But nothing puerile. Strictly proper. I've told the girls – no quick handjobs on the side. Not those sort of tricks. Oh no. Well, at least, not on the *premises* like. You agree with me, don't you?'

But the question was rhetorical, for Betty had fainted clean away.

And the Eye went –

Wink, wink, wink.

29

Well, it was very nice around the pool, Tabitha decided. Not too hot, nice breeze in off the sea, no sand to get in your sangria – talking of which – she raised a lazy finger – she needed another one. The waiter smiled, acknowledged, was gone. Tabitha smiled back. A full, stretched, show-every-line smile. Why not – the brightness was like an arc lamp anyway – no point in pretending.

She ran a finger down the line of her shin-bone. Shocking, for she could feel the hairs. She ran the same finger over her knee and up towards her bikini line. Shocking, for she could feel the fluff. On she traced it, past her most private swelling towards her neck, negotiating the naked channel between her unharnessed breasts, then gently, in circular motion feeling her way around jaw-line, cheeks, eye sockets, nose bridge and forehead – a greaseless journey that told her what only a Beautician's fingertips could say.

Her body was growing as it chose, her eyebrows were untidy, she had not anointed her skin with costly unguents – myrrh, frankincense, odours of the tomb – just a bit of Ambre Solaire to keep the cancer out. And drinking alcohol in the noonday swelter with no thought for capillaries or geranium oil. She smiled comfortably to herself.

No more shall she *souffrir pour être belle* – she had said as much to the advancing Chloe.

She said, '*NE faut PAS souffrir pour être belle*, Chloe,' and Chloe, still waiting for her to laugh at the Joan Collins joke, said 'Yew wot?'

Well *quite*.

'It is puerile,' she replied.

Chloe looked confused, then hopeful, then enlightened. And went on to tell her the Jo-Jo lipstick story.

'No more!' Tabitha held up her hand. Begone and do your worst.'

So Chloe left her alone. As one who is mad is left alone.

Not the new green shoot upon the bough after all – merely Maureen, dew of the sea, brackish and undrinkable, soon to be reclaimed by the heartless ocean. Plenty more fish, Chloe – plenty more fish. Your time, my lovely, will come too.

She sat up, shading her eyes to look at the sea beyond the hotel gardens. It looked very beautiful in the sunlight. And the boats on the horizon moved towards the shore elegant as a fleet of swans. She would wander down there later and greet them as they landed. They might even offer her a sail some day. She was open to the experience. Perhaps she would sail home again, show her face exactly as it was. But not yet. Not with Chloe in charge …

A shadow fell across her. A cold glass was placed in her out-stretched hand, the hand which had a most noticeable change of age about its fingerjoints. So be it. She smiled up. Above her a dazzling row of white teeth smiled back down. Just a Spanish waiter. But she did not look away. Neither, for that matter, did he.

Vanitas Vanitatum, she thought, and she twirled her drink so that the ice moved delicately. Cheers, Brenda, she said, raising the glass high. Cheers Bren, wherever you are. This one's to you.

And the ice in her glass clinked like the glass of the salon chandelier –

Clink, clink, clink.